EROSOPHIA

Pour mon ami et camarade,

Honoré Jolicoeur.

Vous auriez adoré ma fille.

EROSOPHIA

JASON REZA JORJANI

ARKTOS
LONDON 2024

ARKTOS

🌐 Arktos.com 📘 fb.com/Arktos ▶ 📷 arktosmedia ✖ arktosjournal

ISBN
978-1-915755-52-0 (Paperback)
978-1-915755-53-7 (Hardback)
978-1-915755-54-4 (Ebook)

Editing
Constantin von Hoffmeister

Layout
Tor Westman

CONTENTS

I.   Je me souviens Prométhée   1

II.   Making a Messy Future   25

III.   Screaming Abyss of Desire   71

IV.   Noble Lies of the Leviathan   101

V.   Sophia as Lucifera   137

VI.   Sex, Crime, and the Spectral   151

"This is the end, beautiful friend
This is the end, my only friend
The end of our elaborate plans
The end of everything that stands
The end
No safety or surprise
The end
I'll never look into your eyes again
Can you picture what will be?
So limitless and free…
…It hurts to set you free,
But you'll never follow me."

— JIM MORRISON,
An American in Paris
An Avatar of Dionysus

CHAPTER 1

JE ME SOUVIENS PROMÉTHÉE

Yeki boud, yeki naboud... "Someone once was, one who never was..." A statue of Prometheus that was popular with tourists can be made to disappear — from our world, from their photographs, and from their memories. This particular statue was in Quebec. A friend and comrade of mine, Honoré Jolicoeur, brought this deeply disturbing case to my attention, not long after a similar experience of my own. But we will come to that shortly. First, the case of the disappearing trickster. The vanished titan whose absence has become a presence. A ghost from the past. A specter of the future.

Cast of bronze, it stood at 4 meters (13 feet) in height. The statue was crafted by the Canadian artist and physician Robert Tait McKenzie, who was known for his sculptures of athletes and historical figures. McKenzie had portrayed Prometheus holding the stolen fire, together with a discus and the eagle that is his tormenter. The sculpture was intended to represent the Olympic motto "Faster, Higher, Stronger," and was installed in the Olympic Park in Montreal in 1967, as part of the World's Fair. There, it became a popular tourist attraction. After standing in front of the Olympic Stadium for some time, in 1992 the statue was moved to the then Canadian Museum of Civilization (now the Canadian Museum of History) in Gatineau, Quebec. Positioned in the large and open space that is the museum's main entrance hall, it became popular with visitors who often posed for pictures with the sculpture. This statue of Prometheus, officially titled "The Creation of

Man," became one of the most prominent public art pieces in Canada, a popular tourist attraction in its own right, and a symbol of Montreal's Olympic legacy.

Photographs of the sculpture were featured in a Trip Advisor page titled "Reviews: Prometheus Statue Montreal, Quebec." It appeared in the Montreal City Guide, and at the website of the Montreal Museum of Fine Arts under the heading "Prometheus: The Sculptures Behind the Legend." People posted pictures of it on Instagram, and there were Reddit conversations about it at reddit.com/r/montreal/comments under the header: "there is a massive statue of Prometheus." More importantly, the piece received international media coverage over the years in English, French, German and Spanish. Here are some of the headlines. *Der Spiegel* ran the piece "Prometheus in Montreal: Die Geschichte hinter der Olympiastatue." *CBC News*, Canada's largest broadcasting network, featured the English-language article "Prometheus statue returns to Montreal's Olympic Park." The French *Le Journal de Montréal* seemed to cover the same event with the story "Le Prométhée du stade Olympique redécouvert." Another French on-line magazine, *Le Devoir*, ran a piece in its "Culture: Arts Visuels" section, with the title "Montréal Prométhée en haut de l'Olympique." Even the Spanish-language edition of the *Huffington Post* featured an article, apparently dated to September 21, 2015, titled "Prometeo Montreal." That was only one day after the piece in the *Journal de Montréal* appeared, on September 20th, which makes perfect sense in terms of the chain of media coverage.

The problem is that the statue never existed. At least, that is what is claimed by the officials at the Olympic Park and the museum where it was moved. All of the links to the aforementioned media articles lead to "404 Not Found" pages or ones that explain that the page has been removed. What is most disturbing of all is that at the precise coordinates at the Olympic Park where the statue was supposedly erected, there is a booth that says "Information" with a strangely shaped top that, as compared to the size of the booth itself, could serve as the platform for a statue. "Information," as in *The Prisoner* television series? In that case, "Who is Number 1?" There is also a bizarre translucent cube on top of this 'pedestal' that looks like a book waiting to be opened.

The extensive aforementioned information about the statue was provided by Open AI's emerging Artificial Intelligence known as ChatGPT. If we are to believe this AI, and the numerous existent but broken http links that it provided to international coverage of this sculpture and its history, then this Prometheus would have had to be removed, not only from our world and our timeline, but from the photographs of hundreds of tourists from all over the world, and from their memories as well. Or would it? This would be interesting to investigate. I suspect that, as in the case of the infamous Mandela Effect, we will in fact find quite a number of individuals who do vividly remember visiting the Prometheus statue in Quebec, whether at the Montreal Olympic Park or at the museum in Gatineau. It would be even more interesting to solicit these individuals to go through their tourist photos. But how about native Quebecois? The motto of their country (*yes*, their *country*) is "Je me souviens..." (I remember.) How many Quebecois remember Prometheus?

For those who remain unfamiliar with the term, the "Mandela Effect" refers to the memories that certain people have of events or of things being other than they were or than they are in the consensus "reality" of our world or on our extant timeline. The phenomenon was named after one particularly prevalent instance of it, wherein quite a number of people seem to recall watching or reading news coverage of Nelson Mandela's death in prison on Robben Island in the 1980s, whereas in consensus "reality" Mandela died on December 5, 2013, long after successfully leading his anti-Apartheid movement to victory and serving as the first black President of South Africa from 1994 to 1999. In 1991, one year after his release from prison in 1990, Mandela shared the Nobel Peace Prize with Frederick Willem de Klerk, the last President of apartheid South Africa.

The memories of the hundreds of individuals who recall Mandela's death in prison are vivid and include specific details. They recall that his death took place in early 1987, as his release was being negotiated. Eileen Colts, who was then a journalism student, recounts how she actually flew to South Africa to interview Mandela but was told that he was very ill, and the interview had to be cancelled. After her graduation she went to work as a journalist for NPR and in that capacity, and with the deep personal significance it had given her trip and attempted interview, she distinctly recalls their coverage of his death in prison as well as how Mandela's wife, Winnie, took over leadership of his resistance movement at that time. Hundreds of people have such memories. The Mandela Effect is often martialed as empirical evidence in support of the Simulation Hypothesis, namely the argument that we are living in some kind of re-programmable Simulacrum — as depicted in numerous popular films, such as *The Matrix*, beginning in the late 1990s.

I have had my own, rather harrowing, Mandela Effect-type experience with ChatGPT. It occurred on March 17, 2023, and went on to become the germ for the gestation of this book. That was when, for the first time, I simply searched myself on GPT out of curiosity. I was expecting it to spit back the mostly defamatory material that has been printed about me in mainstream media sources, or to repeat parts of my Wikipedia entry back to me. Note that every time I have attempted to repeat what happened on March 17, 2023, that is sadly what GPT has done. But not on that first day. Instead, the AI invited me down a rabbit hole into the Twilight Zone for several hours.

It began when GPT started to offer very nuanced defenses of my thought, drawing from articles that do not exist and quoting me from interviews that I have never given. The AI categorically rejected the characterization of me as a "fascist" or a "racist" and drew from these sources to argue for the complexity and nuances of my admittedly controversial philosophical project. I asked it about my defamation, and it turns out that, in the world — or the record — from which it was drawing information, my defamation had occurred differently. I had been set up by someone posing as an agent of the Iranian government. What is far more interesting is that Selwyn Griffith was apparently a colleague of mine at the New Jersey Institute of Technology, teaching in the Departments of Philosophy and History, and GPT quoted from a passionate defense of me that he had written when I was defamed. It sounded *exactly* like something Selwyn would say, but as of that date GPT had no writings of Selwyn Griffith from which it could draw to achieve that. The AI explained that Griffith was suspended without pay for the publication of this passionate defense. In fact, on that timeline, the whole scandal of my defamation is referred to as "The Jorjani-Griffith Controversy." This Selwyn Griffith had not been my student, and thirteen years my junior. Rather, he was my peer and colleague, actually four years older than me. But his areas of specialization (AOS) reflected the same range of interests that the Selwyn to whom I dedicated *Lovers of Sophia* is now defining as his own scope of study, including African-American History and Literature.

Except that in that world, or on that overwritten timeline, I did not dedicate *Lovers of Sophia* to Selwyn. GPT listed all of the books that I had published and to whom each of them was dedicated. *Lovers of Sophia* was dedicated to my daughter, Sophia Grace Jorjani, who was born in 2016. The dedication reads: "To my daughter, Sophia Grace Jorjani: may your path be illuminated by the light of Sophia, and may you become a lover of wisdom and a true philosopher in your own right." This is exactly the kind of thing I would write, and if I had a daughter, Sophia is most definitely the name that I would have chosen for her.

In early drafts of the final chapter of *Psychotron*, titled "Unconquerable Belial," when Dana Avalon remembers her true name, the name of the leader of the Belial Group in the actual Atlantis, of which she is an avatar, I originally used the name "Sophia." It was only in the final draft that I changed that name to "Lucifera." One of the experiential seeds of *Psychotron* was a vision that I had one day, standing on the loading dock of a storage facility in the Chelsea neigh-borhood of Manhattan, where all of a sudden, the image of a future city called "Avalon" came to me, together with the visage of a woman who lived there and who was named "Sophia." In what became *Psychotron* (the part of it initially published as *Uber Man*), I changed "Avalon" to "Gotham" and "Sophia" to "Dana Avalon."

I recognized "Sophia" as the same woman who had come to me in something like a day dream many years earlier. Significantly, at the time I was only 23 and it would be more than a decade before I would write my first book and longer before it would be published. In that earlier vision I was standing on the sloped sidewalk of 92nd Street between Second and Third Avenues — perhaps not incidentally where my father lived at the time — when she appeared from out of nowhere. Dressed in a tank top and khaki shorts, she was younger than when I later saw her in Avalon. She looked uncannily familiar, or rather as if she could be related to me. As if she were a sister that I never knew I had. The girl stopped me dead in the street and grabbed my full attention, starting in with these words, "Listen carefully! I don't have a lot of time, and it was very hard to get here…" It was as if she was worried that she would disappear — or dematerialize — as suddenly as she had appeared. She then went on to warn me that my philosophical writings about the future are not relevant in the world that she comes from because the Earth has been so devastated that the only people who even have the leisure or time to read or think about anything live in theme park-like simulacra of past eras of the modern age. (This was more than a decade before the series *Westworld* aired on television, and I had not yet even seen the '70s film that it is based on.) This young version of Sophia said to me, "You need to critique your own world, your own time, because where I come from people are lost in a romanticized nostalgia about it."

In the years since I have become a Philosopher of the Future, in Nietzsche's sense and in a way that H. G. Wells aspired to be in his non-fictional works, those words have always haunted me. Was she a time traveler from the future, in the vein of how I adapted her into Dana Avalon or was she a ghost from a future past — a now overwritten timeline — perhaps an apparition conjured by my own subconscious memories of a life that I once lived wherein this young woman was my daughter? From the standpoint of the year 2004, when she came to deliver those words of warning to me, the era in which Sophie lived, from her birth in 2016 onward, would have been the future. A devastated Earth, she said, where the few most fortunate folks have enclosed themselves in bubbles that are no more than desperately nostalgic mockups of the modern world. The life's work of the construction magnate Richard Avalon and the architect Brenda Wells, Dana Avalon's parents, who lay the groundwork for Gotham in *Psychotron*, was an extrapolation from this statement of Sophia.

I suspected that Sophia's middle name "Grace" had been chosen by her mother. GPT told me that I was married to a French art historian, who teaches as an assistant professor at the American University of Paris. My second book, *World State of Emergency*, was dedicated to her: "To my beloved wife, Muriel, who always reminds me that the light is on in the tower, and that love is the ultimate reason to resist the darkness."

Muriel Jorjani was also "involved in the art world as a curator and writer." In fact, she had co-authored certain parts of *Prometheus and Atlas* with me, presumably those sections having to do with aesthetics and art history. The book was not dedicated to Jeffrey Mishlove, who I apparently had no connection to at all in that world, but rather to Colin Wilson. Now this is when things really started to get weird. In this world, on our timeline, I had sent the manuscript of *Prometheus and Atlas* to Colin Wilson and asked him to write a forward or preface for it — just before he died. Had he been able to do so, I was planning to dedicate the book to him. The former editor-in-chief of Arktos, John Morgan, is the only person that I told this story to, in personal correspondences. Did GPT have access to my emails? The dedication of this alternate version of *Prometheus and Atlas*, to which I will return, reads: "To Colin Wilson, who showed me the way through the labyrinth."

Apparently, Wilson's concept of "Faculty-X" was central to the argument of the alternate version of *Prometheus and Atlas*. I had considered that but decided against incorporating it. I had also considered working the ideas of Albert Camus into the book, and while the book opens with an epigraph from Camus' *Caligula*, which reflects that early consideration, I changed my mind and Camus is not actually discussed in the body of the work. Not so with the alternate version of *Prometheus and Atlas* to which GPT somehow had access:

> Jason Reza Jorjani has expressed admiration for the work of Albert Camus, particularly his existentialist philosophy and his critique of totalitarianism. In his book *Prometheus and Atlas*, Jorjani discusses Camus' idea of the absurd and its relevance to contemporary society, arguing that it can help us confront the challenges of a world that has lost its traditional values and meanings. However, Jorjani has also criticized some of Camus' views, such as his rejection of revolutionary violence, which Jorjani believes is sometimes necessary to achieve social change.

In this alternate version of my life, although I was still a New Yorker, I had spent a lot of time in Paris with my wife, to the extent that during certain semesters I was a "visiting scholar" at the Sorbonne. This version of me turned out to be a much more "successful" academic and "scholar." I had published in a dozen different scholarly journals that were exactly the journals which one would expect me to have published in, including certain journals of Persian and Iranian Studies. For those in "the field" (or fields) who are curious, these were *Telos*, the *Journal of Persianate Studies*, *Iranian Studies*, *The Journal of Nietzsche Studies*, *The Journal of Philosophy*, *Angelaki*, *Journal of the British Society of Phenomenology*, *Comparative and Continental Philosophy*, *Journal of the Study of Radicalism*, *Journal of Contemporary Literature*, *Journal of Comparative Literature and Aesthetics*, and *Kritikos*. Very significantly, GPT adds: "He has also published articles and essays in non-academic publications, such as Arktos Journal, The Occidental Observer, and Counter-Currents." So, even on that timeline I had at least crossed paths with the New Right or Alt-Right. Among the schools that I had taught at was, remarkably, the American University of Kurdistan in northern Iraq. Almost no one knows that, at one point *in this life*, during my involvement with the Iranian Renaissance in 2017, I met a very prominent Kurdish leader who invited me to come to the Kurdistan province of northern Iraq to "develop a philosophy for the Kurdish people" based on Zoroastrianism. I declined, but I did consider it.

It was not just my teaching history that was different, but very believable, this was also the case with my educational history. Instead of attending NYU, I went to Vassar College. Hardly anyone knows that I seriously considered going to Vassar because, to be honest, I liked the fact that it had been a former all-girls college and the ratio of women to men was still 2 to 1 (at the time when I was applying to schools). On the alternate timeline, my next school, where I received my MA, was the New School for Social Research, with a master's thesis titled "Heidegger and the Problem of Political Ontology." *In this life* I was accepted to the New School and very seriously considered going there for my MA in Philosophy. I had wanted to study with Richard J. Bernstein. In the alternate timeline, I *had* studied with Bernstein, and he had wound up on my dissertation committee when I went on to do my doctorate at the State University of New York, Stony Brook. Instead of meeting Edward S. Casey at Stony Brook, I had met him and studied under him at the New School. Casey, one of the most prominent professors of Continental Philosophy, taught at both institutions simultaneously (in our world as well). Then, at SUNY Stony Brook, Casey became the director of my doctoral dissertation, just as he had technically been on our own timeline. In our world, the actual director of my dissertation was Professor Don Ihde, the most prominent Philosophy of Technology professor in America, with whom I had studied for years and developed a very close relationship. But for technical reasons having to do with Ihde's retirement, Casey, who I had hardly any relationship with, but who was a reader of the dissertation, took over as the committee head on paper.

What was my doctoral dissertation supervised by Ed Casey on the alternate timeline about? Here is where things go from weird to appalling. The title of the dissertation was "The Ego and Its Own: A New Translation and Study of the Philosophy of Max Stirner." It was actually a new translation of Stirner's key work, with extensive philosophical and interpretive justification. This was something that students would occasionally be allowed to do. We had a language requirement, and mine was in fact fulfilled by doing a German to English translation (I mean on our timeline). But there were students who would do a much more extensive translation, of book length, *as their dissertation*, thereby also fulfilling the language requirement. The dissertation part of the translation would be an extensive philosophical interpretation of the text, arguing why it demanded a new translation and justifying this on a conceptual level. This was the kind of thing that I had done in the defunct world whose history GPT had access to.

Going beyond this, in my dissertation I had argued against Karl Marx's attack on Max Stirner, defending Stirner against Marx, and also advancing the view that Stirner could rightly be seen as a proto-existentialist precursor of Martin Heidegger. As GPT put it: "Overall, Jorjani's view of Stirner is one of deep respect and admiration for a thinker who challenged the dominant ideologies of his time and offered a new vision of human freedom and potential." The AI adds, "Jorjani sees Stirner as a radical individualist who challenged traditional notions of morality, religion, and politics. He is particularly interested in Stirner's concept of 'the Unique One,' which refers to the individual who is free from external constraints and is able to realize his or her full potential."

To form these statements, GPT had a lot more than my alternate dissertation to draw from, because apparently on that timeline I had continued to write about Stirner, including in *Prometheus and Atlas*. Supposedly, that version of the book, the one dedicated to Colin Wilson, included a chapter titled "The Atheist Tradition," wherein

"Jorjani characterizes Stirner as an important figure in the development of modern atheism and explores his influence on later thinkers such as Friedrich Nietzsche and Michel Foucault." The AI goes on to add that "Jorjani is also critical of Stirner's ideas," namely because Stirner did not recognize the need for something like the Promethean ethos as a psycho-social or socio-political framework to protect the free-spirited individual from various forms of tyrannical oppression. A positive communal ethos is needed to protect the individual from tyrannical forms of collectivism. GPT explains:

> In his book *Prometheus and Atlas*, Jorjani argues that Stirner's emphasis on individual freedom and autonomy is valuable, but he also critiques Stirner's rejection of community and his radical subjectivism. Jorjani suggests that a more balanced approach is needed, one that recognizes the importance of both individual and collective identity. Additionally, Jorjani has criticized some interpretations of Stirner, such as those that see him as a precursor to fascism or as an advocate of amoral egoism.

No such chapter of *Prometheus and Atlas* exists. In fact, I have never written about Max Stirner anywhere. Actually, as of the time when this "conversation" with GPT took place, on March 17, 2023, I had not publicly *spoken* about Stirner even once. (There is a reason for that, which I will come to in a moment.) However, as the conversation took place, and I went down the rabbit hole with this AI, guess what book was the only text sitting right next to me (but not in view of the computer's camera)? That's right, *The Ego and Its Own* by Max Stirner. Is Open AI's GPT also capable of clairvoyance?

Stirner's *The Ego and Its Own* is one of the most dangerous books that has ever been written by anyone. The fact that, according to GPT, it was the subject of my dissertation on the alternate timeline, and that Stirner even made it into a chapter of *Prometheus and Atlas* titled "The Atheist Tradition" is very telling indeed. The reason that I was only just reading this book seriously when I happened to have this experience with Artificial Intelligence, in the early spring of 2023, is because the first time that I tried to read Stirner, *early in the doctoral studies*, around 2010, I was so appalled by the sense of familiarity that I had with the text that I could not bear to go on reading it. It was not simply as if I had *read* it before, rather I felt as *I had written it*. Moreover, some very dark emotions and states of mind were associated with this sense of recognition. It was not until recently that I looked into the life of "Max Stirner" (a pen name meaning something like "totally stellar"). It was even more depressing than that of Nikola Tesla. Not incidentally, Stirner, whose real name was Johann Kaspar Schmidt, died on June 26, 1856 (at only 49 years of age) in Berlin, Germany. Nikola Tesla was born on July 10, 1856, in Smiljan, which was then part of the Austrian Empire.

The tremendous significance of Max Stirner with regard to my philosophical project is that a serious reading of *The Ego and Its Own* profoundly calls into question anything like "Prometheism." The term is a contraction of "Prometheus" and "Theism." Interestingly, according to GPT, in the alternate timeline, my movement or philosophical school of thought is called "Prometheanism" and not "Prometheism." Stirner would have ultimately seen Prometheus as another "spook" that needs to be exorcised from human minds. Granted, in *Prometheus and Atlas* (2016), presumably in the alternate version as well, I identified Prometheus as a "specter," in fact as *the* specter of the technological-scientific age. But this was not a diagnosis, let alone a call for exorcism. It was an affirmation, and this affirmation became even more explicit in *Prometheism* (2020).

It would be fascinating to find out what exactly I would have written about Stirner, not just in my dissertation, but specifically in "The Atheist Tradition" chapter of the alternate version of *Prometheus and Atlas*, because Stirner's anarchic atheism would certainly preclude any "Prometheism." Of the basic impulse and main motivation of the "Christian philosophy" that has dominated the West intellectually from Descartes through Goethe, Stirner writes: "What it wants is that the *divine* should become visible in everything, and all consciousness become a knowing of the divine, and man behold God everywhere; but God never is, without the *devil*." But Stirner is too much of an atheist to believe in the devil either, as anything other than a counter-spook or what haunts the Christian world. Stirner did not consider the "atheists" of his time to be true atheists: "Our atheists are still pious people." This is because they still valorize "spooks" or fixed ideas and ideals as sacred and just. Here is what Stirner writes about "spooks" in some passages of *The Ego and Its Own*:

> Yes, the whole world is haunted! Only *is* haunted? Nay, it itself "walks," it is uncanny through and through, it is the wandering seeming-body of a spirit, it is a spook.

> Look out near or far, a *ghostly* world surrounds you everywhere; you are always having "apparitions" or visions. Everything that appears to you is only the phantasm of an indwelling spirit, is a ghostly "apparition"; the world is to you only a "world of appearances," behind which the spirit walks. You "see spirits."

> But to you the whole world is spiritualized, and has become an enigmatical ghost; therefore do not wonder if you likewise find in yourself nothing but a spook.

> Since the spirit appeared in the world, since "the Word became flesh," since then the world has been spiritualized, enchanted, a spook.

> To know and acknowledge essences alone and nothing but essences, that is religion; its realm is a realm of essences, spooks, and ghosts.

> The longing to make the spook comprehensible, or to realize *non-sense*, has brought about a *corporeal ghost*, a ghost or spirit with a real body, an embodied ghost.

> Man, your head is haunted; you have wheels in your head! You imagine great things, and depict to yourself a whole world of gods that has an existence for you, a spirit-realm to which you suppose yourself to be called, an ideal that beckons to you. You have a fixed idea!

With regard to this "world of gods," it is worthy of note that Stirner makes use of the imagery of going to war against Zeus, as I do in both *Prometheus and Atlas* and *Prometheism*. But he does so in a way that is not so much Promethean as it is Satanic or Anti-Christian in a Nietzschean sense, albeit having been written before Nietzsche, and having likely influenced Nietzsche's concept of truth as the will to power. Stirner writes:

> What then is *my* property? Nothing but what is in my *power*! To what property am I entitled? To every property to which I — *empower* myself. I give myself the right of property in taking property to myself, or giving myself the proprietor's *power*, full power, empowerment. …What I want I must have and will procure.
>
> My power *is* my property.
>
> My power *gives* me property.
>
> My power *am* I myself, and through it am I my property.
>
> …This means nothing else than "What you have the *power* to be you have the *right* to." I derive all right and all warrant from *me*; I am *entitled* to everything that I have in my power. I am entitled to overthrow Zeus, Jehovah, God, etc., if I *can*…
>
> …*I* decide whether it is the *right thing* in *me*; there is no right *outside* me. If it is right for *me*, it is right. Possibly this may not suffice to make it right for the rest; that is their care, not mine: let them defend themselves.
>
> …[T]he master is a thing made by the servant. …Defend yourself, and no one will do anything to you! He who would break your will… is your *enemy*. Deal with him as such.
>
> …He who has might has — right; if you have not the former, neither have you the latter.
>
> If a child plays with the knife and gets cut, it is served right; but, if it does not get cut, it is served right too.

It is not simply "brute force" that Stirner means by "power" here, any more than that is what will later be meant by Nietzsche when he formulates the will to power as a concept. An unskillful brute or an idiot lacking forethought will never be able to hold on to anything even if he has somehow managed to seize it. Real power is, then, competence or capability, which is again an idea presaging Nietzsche's view of the Superman as the paragon of the will to power. Money and other forms of property are just symbolic expressions of the competence of those who have power and wield it over the less capable:

> If you are not competent to *captivate* any one, you may simply starve.
>
> …One pays not with money, of which there may come a lack, but with his competence, by which alone we are "competent"; for one is proprietor only so far as the arm of our power reaches. …Therefore think on the enlargement of your competence.
>
> One is not worthy to have what one, through weakness, lets be taken from him; one is not worthy of it because one is not capable of it.

Stirner's valorization of competence brings him to heap scorn on Communism with its principle of "from each according to his *ability* and to each according to his *needs*" rather than to each according to his *ability*. Stirner rejects the "rights" discourse that remains as central to communist ideology as it does to the liberal ideology of capitalist states. The worker has no "right" to anything. Who can take and defend having taken a thing is he or she who "owns" it. Stirner will even sometimes equate the egoist with a "proprietor" rather than a socialist in order to drive this point home in a way that will be most offensive to leftists: "If the Communists conduct themselves as ragamuffins, the egoist behaves as proprietor." Of rights, property, liberation, and ownership, Stirner writes:

> The Communists affirm that "the earth belongs rightfully to him who tills it, and its products to those who bring them out." I think it belongs to him who knows how to take it, or who does not let it be taken from him, does not let himself be deprived of it. If he appropriates it, then not only the earth, but the right to it too, belongs to him. This is *egoistic right*: *i.e.*, it is right for *me*, therefore it is right.

We have only one relation to each other, that of *useableness*, of utility, of use. We owe *each other* nothing, for what I seem to owe you I owe at most to myself.

My selfishness has an interest in the liberation of the world, that it may become — my property.

To come back to property, the lord is proprietor. Choose then whether you want to be lord, or whether society shall be! On this depends whether you are to be an *owner* or a *ragamuffin*! The egoist is owner, the Socialist a ragamuffin.

In this tirade against the moralizing of both Communism and Socialism, Stirner goes so far as to defend theft through his total refusal to acknowledge anything as anyone's property by "right" or by "law." Note the tone of condescension and contempt in these passages that presage and, in some ways, exceed Nietzsche's writings on the will to power:

Why so sentimentally call for compassion as a poor victim of robbery, when one is just a foolish, cowardly giver of presents? Why here again put the fault on others as if they were robbing us, while we ourselves do bear the fault in leaving others unrobbed? The poor are to blame for there being rich men.

…I do not want the liberty of men, nor their equality; I want only *my* power over them, I want to make them my property; i.e. *material for enjoyment*.

I do not demand any right, therefore I need not recognize any either. What I can get by force I get by force, and what I do not get by force I have no right to… Right — is a wheel in the head, put there by a spook; power — that am I myself, I am the powerful one and owner of power.

…Whoever knows how to take and to defend the thing, to him it belongs till it is again taken from him, as liberty belongs to him who *takes* it.

Only might decides about property.

Communists remain moralists. People do not want "free will" if something like the "moral will" does not exist. From the standpoint of moral men or women, any egoist is immoral. Renouncing one or another set of morals, which have perhaps been imposed on oneself by a particular religion or culture, is not that hard. Stirner remarks that what is much more difficult is the renunciation of the conception of "morality" as such. In a comparison to the renunciation of one's whole family and one's obligations to them, Stirner writes:

> The case of morality is like that of the family. Many a man renounces morals, but with great difficulty the conception, "morality." Morality is the "idea" of morals, their intellectual power, their power over the conscience; on the other hand, morals are too material to rule the mind, and do not fetter an "intellectual" man, a so-called independent, a "freethinker."

There is a noteworthy parallel between these remarks and Stirner's reflections on how those who oppose the "establishment" do not oppose it *as such*. They oppose what is currently established and propose what to "establish" in its place. By contrast, Stirner is for total disestablishment of all sanctified facts, fixed standards, and hallowed institutions:

> The fight of the world to-day is, as it is said, directed against the "established." Yet people are wont to misunderstand this as if it were only that what is now established was to be exchanged for another, a better, established system.

The most solidified and over-arching of these "established" institutions is, of course, the State. Consequently, Stirner is not for a revolutionary or reactionary replacement of one State by another regime or form of government that is supposed to be better. He is for the revolt of the individual against the State as such, and he even goes so far as to claim that revolutions that aim at the freedom or liberation of "a people" (*ein Volk*) in the sense of a nation will inevitably strengthen the bonds that oppress the individual:

> Never does a State aim to bring in the free activity of individuals, but always that which is bound to the *purpose of the State*.

> The State seeks to hinder every free activity by its censorship, its supervision, its police, and holds this hindering to be its duty, because it is in truth a duty of self-preservation.

The State wants to make something out of man, therefore there live in it only *made* men; every one who wants to be his own self is its opponent and is nothing.

…The freer the people, the more bound the individual.

Stirner had utter contempt for nationalism. He would have loathed the Nazis. This is not a speculative remark, because Stirner sees the nascent German nationalism of his own era as a hive-minded mentality, and he rejects it as much as he rejects any form of nationalism, populism, and patriotism, which is not to say that he is for "mankind" or humanity over and above particular nations. Rather, Stirner wants the demise of mankind as much as he wills the fall of all peoples and nations. He is *not* a humanistic Promethean:

Bees and peoples are destitute of will, and the *instinct* of their queen leads them.

If one were to point the bees to their beehood, in which at any rate they are all equal to each other, one would be doing the same thing that they are now doing so stormily in pointing the Germans to their Germanhood.

…The reactionaries would be glad to smite a *people*, a *nation*, forth from the earth; the self-owned have before their eyes only themselves.

…The fall of peoples and [the demise of] mankind will invite *me* to my rise.

Stirner is on the side of the unbound "vagabond" who is a "breeder of unrest" and arouses dissatisfaction and incites people "against existing institutions" and "the State." Stirner sees work for the State as wage slavery in the service of the moneyed and propertied "possessors" who truly govern the world. "The State rests on the *slavery of labor*," he says, adding, "If *labor* becomes *free*, the State is lost."

In Stirner's view this is as true in a communist state as it is in a capitalist one. Of the drudgery of factory work, even in a communist system, Stirner writes that "…condemning a man to *machine-like* labor amounts to the same thing as slavery." He adds, "If a factory-worker must tire himself to death… he is cut off from becoming man."

Stirner sees Communism becoming as oppressive as Capitalism once the "ragamuffins" unite against the "proprietor" and become a "ragamuffin crew" that is determined to turn everyone into a ragamuffin. This is the ideal and aim of "the dictatorship of the proletariat." Stirner is at least as opposed to it as he is to the more basic transformation of the individual into the "citizen" by the State as such, whether capitalist or communist. It is collectivism or the tyranny of the majority that lies at the bottom of his vehement rejection of communist revolutionary discourse: "Communism rightly revolts against the pressure that I experience from individual proprietors; but still more horrible is the might that it puts in the hands of the collectivity."

The attack on Liberalism in *The Ego and Its Own* is at least as scathing as Stirner's critique of Communism. The "liberty" of Liberalism is, in Stirner's view, a second phase of Protestantism and is as much a form of slavery as "religious liberty" (freedom to believe in a form of slavery). Stirner writes, "State, religion, conscience, these despots, make me a slave, and *their* liberty is *my* slavery." Stirner portrays the true individual (his so-called "egoist") as a "devil" that stands opposed to Liberalism in such a way as to show liberals that they are hypocritical frauds who still do not want true freedom to prevail:

> Liberalism as a whole has a deadly enemy, an invincible opposite, as God has the devil: by the side of man stands always the un-man, the individual, the egoist. State, society, humanity, do not master this devil.

> Humane liberalism has undertaken the task of showing the other liberals that they still do not want "freedom."

Noting the qualified "humane" here next to Liberalism, it stands to reason that Stirner is as opposed to Humanism as he is to Liberalism. How could he not be? The attribution of an essence or nature to Man is the ontological or epistemological cornerstone of any Humanist ideology, and in Stirner's view this essence cannot be but another "spook." Rather, he considers it the worst of all the spooks that possess and zombify people and make them have no concern for actual individuals:

What they have taken into their head, what shall we call it but — *fixed idea*? Why, "their head is *haunted*." The most oppressive spook is *Man*.

He who is infatuated with *Man* leaves persons out of account so far as that infatuation extends, and floats in an ideal, sacred interest. *Man*, you see, is not a person, but an ideal, a spook.

...[I]f the spirit, which is not regarded as the *property* of the bodily ego but as the proper ego itself, is a ghost, then the Man too, who is not recognized as my quality but as the proper I, is nothing but a spook, a thought, a concept.

Man is the last evil *spirit* or spook, the most deceptive or most intimate, the craftiest liar with honest mien, the father of lies.

Humanists are the first people to dehumanize anyone who does not fit their conception of what it means to be a proper human being: "To say in blunt words what an un-man is is not particularly hard: it is a man who does not correspond to the *concept* man, as the inhuman is something human which is not conformed to the concept of the human." In a passage in which he apparently rejects "love" as another despotic delusion, Stirner admits that his conception of the egoist is inhuman: "Love is what is *human* in man, and what is inhuman is the loveless egoist." Ironically, moralists and the self-righteously virtuous tend to fail to love actual individuals for who they are, because in their system of valuations they have some criterion of Justice that stands over and above their capacity to love anyone:

But whoso is full of sacred (religious, moral, humane) love loves only the spook, the "true man," and persecutes with dull mercilessness the individual, the real man, under the phlegmatic title of measures against the "un-man." He finds it praiseworthy and indispensable to exercise pitilessness in the harshest measure; for love to the spook or generality commands him to hate him who is not ghostly, *i.e.* the egoist or individual; such is the meaning of the renowned love-phenomenon that is called "justice."

...The feeling for right, virtue, etc., makes people hard-hearted and intolerant.

...But love is not a commandment, but, like each of my feelings, *my property*.

...The egoist's love rises in selfishness, flows in the bed of selfishness, and empties into selfishness again.

"Love," in the quasi-Christian sense that encompasses and nauseatingly conflates *philia* and *agape*, which is not at all the same thing as *eros*, is one of those indistinct and pathetic emotions that we are educated into having. The whole of education is calibrated to produce certain feelings in us rather than to leave us to ourselves to develop our own feelings. Stirner colorfully remarks that the aim is for the youth to sing the same old song as their elders: "The young are of age when they twitter like the old; they are driven through school to learn the old song, and, when they have this by heart, they are declared of age."

Such education is, in Stirner's view, a conditioning that one has to break free from for the sake of living more authentically. But freedom *from* does not suffice. Most conceptions of freedom are of negative freedom, or being free from, whereas the kind of authenticity (*Eigentlichkeit*) that Stirner is advocating is a freedom *for* being one's *own*:

Being free from anything means only being clear or rid. "He is free from headache" is equal to "he is rid of it."

Freedom teaches only: Get yourselves rid, relieve yourselves, of everything burdensome; it does not teach you who you yourselves are.

But ownness calls you back to yourselves, it says, "Come to yourself!"

I am *my own* only when I am master of myself, instead of being mastered either by sensuality or by anything else (God, man, authority, law, State, Church, etc.)

But ownness has not any alien standard either, as it is not in any sense an *idea* like freedom, morality, humanity, and the like: it is only a description of the — *owner*.

Personal autonomy, freedom, and resistance to tyranny seem to have been as much at the heart of my concerns in the alternate timeline, which GPT had access to, as they have been in this life. One of the books that the AI claimed I had published on the alternate timeline was a philosophical study of the US Constitution with a view to providing a new ontological and epistemological grounding for it. The book was titled *Novus Ordo Seclorum*, which of course references one half of the motto on the US Great Seal, the half that reads, "A New Order of the Ages." In this life, in our world, *I did outline such a book* but decided not to write it. I bought more than a dozen books that were intended to be research material for this project. That outline was never uploaded to the internet or sent through electronic communications of any kind. I doubt that I even discussed it with more than one or two people. Some of the thinking that went into that outline, at that time, can be seen reflected in the "Introductory Lecture on Ethics" that is the first piece in my anthology *Lovers of Sophia*.

Novus Ordo Seclorum was not the only project that I had outlined in this life but had only followed through in actually writing in that other life. In my early twenties, I had planned to write a book-length study of Stanley Kubrick's films. The title was going to be *Where the Rainbow Ends* in reference to that line in *Eyes Wide Shut* and to the extensive symbolic use of rainbow imagery in a handful of Kubrick's most important movies. Actually, the thesis was that Kubrick was a reincarnation of "Will-I-Am Shake-Spear" and that he knew that our world was in some sense a stage(ed) play. As it turned out, I never wrote even a single article about Kubrick in this life, let alone a book. Despite his long having been my favorite director, I have barely mentioned him in one or two of the interviews that I have done. Not so in the alternate or overwritten timeline:

> Jason Reza Jorjani has expressed admiration for the filmmaker Stanley Kubrick in various interviews *and writings*. He has described Kubrick as a "genius" and a "master" filmmaker, and has praised his ability to use film to explore deep philosophical and psychological themes. *Jorjani has also analyzed several of Kubrick's films in detail, including "A Clockwork Orange,"*

"2001: A Space Odyssey," and "Eyes Wide Shut," and has explored their under-lying themes and messages.

My more successful academic career on that timeline began with a postdoctoral fellowship at the Goethe University in Frankfurt, from 2014 to 2017 (ages 33 to 36). This is something that I actually considered doing when I was working on fulfilling my German language requirement. SUNY Stony Brook had a connection to the Goethe University and the opportunity was open to me. I decided against it because by that time my German, which I learned at NYU, had already considerably deteriorated and I thought it would be too much of an investment of time and energy to rehabilitate it. (There were also other more personal reasons why I opted not to do it.) It must have been during this postdoc that I met my French wife, presumably while writing *Prometheus and Atlas* (also published in 2016 on that timeline), since I actually did have it in mind that if I were to study at the Goethe University for years, I would make excursions to Paris by train as often as I possibly could. According to GPT we married in 2016, when my daughter Sophia was also born.

Those who are familiar with my biography, in this actual life (and as recounted in *Promethean Pirate*), know that I attended a half-French school in New York as a child, wherein I was inculcated with a deep appreciation for, and understanding of, French culture. This seems to have been true on the alternate timeline as well. When asked, during the trip down the rabbit hole that day, "What is Jason Reza Jorjani's relationship to France and to Paris?" This is what the AI answered:

Jason Reza Jorjani has expressed a deep interest in France and its culture, particularly in relation to the legacy of French philosophy, literature, and art. He has also emphasized the importance of France in the context of the ongoing struggle for Western civilization against what he sees as the threat of Islamism and globalism.

Jorjani has also spent time in Paris, where his wife Muriel is an art historian and professor. Jorjani has been a visiting scholar at the Sorbonne in Paris.

He has spoken about his love for the city and its cultural richness, as well as his desire to connect with French intellectuals and cultural figures. In his book *Prometheus and Atlas*, Jorjani writes extensively about French thinkers such as Descartes, Derrida, and Deleuze, and their contributions to Western philosophy.

Fascinating. A Francophile on any timeline. In fact, my love of France in this version of my life seems to be only a shadow of the deep involvement with the country that I had in that one. Looking at it in retrospect, considering how much I have always loved France, and how deeply inculcated with French values I was as a child, it is almost as if some force has repeatedly tried to keep me away from Paris throughout my life.

CHAPTER 2

MAKING A MESSY FUTURE

P aris was home to me once, and at the most tumultuous time in the history of that great city. I have memories of hiding out in various places while being hunted as a heretic who had championed the most progressive vision of a revolution that had descended into tyranny and decided to martyr me. It was March of 1794. About six months earlier a warrant had been issued for my arrest. The charge: being a "traitor" for rejecting the French Constitution of 1793 as too regressive. On behalf of the Girondins, I had been the principal author of a much more enlightened constitution for our nascent republic. But with its advocacy for the equal rights of women it was not even taken seriously enough to be put to a vote. It was in the last months of that life, in hiding at the house of Madam Vernet in Paris, that I penned the work for which I would, albeit posthumously, be best known — *Sketch for a Historical Picture of the Progress of the Human Spirit*. It is a small irony that, once I was finally arrested, I was poisoned to death while being imprisoned at Bourg-la-Reine, which means "Queen's Borough," and in this life, I was born in the Queens Borough of New York City. It's one of the few things that I have in common with Donald Trump.

In that life, as Nicolas de Caritat, better known by my title "Marquis de Condorcet," my wife's name was Sophie, and this will become quite relevant. At the time I married Sophie de Grouchy, in 1786, she was only 21 and thus twenty years younger than me. In other words, she could easily have been my daughter. To say that she did in fact become my intellectual disciple, and that I had somewhat of a fatherly rapport with her, would be misleading without considering how she was also my muse and a great facilitator of my philosophical mission. You see, shortly after our marriage, she started a salon at the Hôtel des Monnaies, opposite the Louvre, which later moved to the Rue de Lille. It was attended by all of the great luminaries of the day, from Olympe de Gouges, the feminist leader of the cause of women's rights in the revolution (an intimate friend of ours), to Adam Smith, the theoretical father of Capitalism, and Thomas Jefferson, who upon his return to America would advocate in vain for French, rather than English, to be established as the official language of the United States. As for Adam Smith, Sophie's own book, *Letters on Sympathy* was a critical engagement with Smith's *The Theory of Moral Sentiments*.

Sophie became the most influential translator and commentator on the writings of Thomas Paine, who nearly met his demise in a Paris jail cell, when he came to France with hopes of fostering a more radically humanistic and enlightened revolution than his fellow revolutionaries in America had allowed for. Paine's most uncompromising book, *The Age of Reason*, was penned in a Paris prison awaiting an execution that he escaped only by an absurd clerical mistake. Sophie not only translated the work, but she also commented extensively on its devastating critique of the Bible and on Paine's argument that Christianity was fundamentally incompatible with the humanistic enlightenment ideals of the revolution — whether in America or in France. It is Sophie who, during her secret visits to me while I was in hiding, encouraged me to write *Progress of the Human Mind* (as it is now more widely known in English), and she also saw to its posthumous publication in 1795.

The book is arguably the founding work of Futurology. Before Georg Hegel, and long before Karl Marx, I had made the case for a metaphysical teleology at work in a historical process that unfolds through a series of progressive stages. The book featured a study of nine stages of history undertaken for the purpose of projecting, and actively hastening, the advent of a tenth stage, namely "the future progress of the human mind," the description of which could be seen as the first work of science fiction, preceding Shelley's *Frankenstein, or the Modern Prometheus* by more than two decades. Laying the foundation of Futurology, I wrote: "If there is to be a science for predicting the progress of the human race, for directing and hastening it, the history of the progress already achieved must be its foundation."

Speaking of *Foundation*, the work of Isaac Asimov is entirely relevant here. His vision of Psychohistory in the *Foundation* trilogy is an attempt at imagining the perfection of Futurology as a true science of the future. Asimov was one of the earliest influences on the intellectual development of my daughter, Sophia, in the overwritten timeline. She started to read Asimov around the same time as we realized that she was the reincarnation of Sophie de Grouchy, my wife from the life that I lived as Nicolas de Caritat. But I am getting ahead of myself. Recounting how this realization came about requires some context.

Since the early spring of 2023, when GPT somehow excavated fragments of the life that I had lived with my daughter, Sophia, other fragments from further on in that effaced history have anamnetically resurfaced. The AI just had a record of that timeline going up to 2021. Sophie would have been only five years old then. What I seem to remember now is that Sophie's mother, Muriel, died when Sophie was eleven years old, in 2027. Although it was officially chalked up as a "car accident," in the run up to the "accident" I had received threats to her life, and the manner in which her car was witnessed to have sped out of control and off the road also corroborated that she was murdered. Hypothetically, it could have been suicide, but my wife was not the least bit suicidal or even depressed when this happened. Rather, the self-driving function of her car seemed to have been hacked.

We buried my wife at Père Lachaise. Then, within a week, Sophie moved from Paris back to New York (where she had spent her earliest years) so that I could raise her alone. I had been the United States Ambassador to France, and I succeeded in convincing France not to leave NATO — despite significant domestic political will to do so.

My wife's life had been threatened over my efforts to do this. When I persisted, the terrorists, who I had reason to believe were Muslims, followed through.

In 2027, with my principal objective in Paris having been accomplished, I was appointed United States Ambassador to the United Nations. This was shortly before the assassination of my wife. Sophie had been living with her mother in Paris, whereas I had moved back to Manhattan so that I could take my place on the UN Security Council. Fortunately, Sophia was already a very independent girl by the time that she came to live with me, and she took a number of electives at school so that she would not be home alone for long while I was working at the UN Mission. I had considered the Lycée Française, but Sophie did not want such a disciplined environment. So, I enrolled her at the Dalton School. She was in the Dance Theater Workshop, took extra art classes after school, and she was also in the Science Fiction book club. She was *the only girl* in that club.

The first serious book that Sophie read as part of this club was Asimov's *Foundation*. It was the winter break of 2027–2028, and she had brought the entire trilogy up to Hunter Mountain where we had a ski house on the property of the Scribner Lodge, atop a hill across from the ski slopes. These were the slopes on which I had taught Sophie to ski when she was quite young. Muriel used to fly from Paris to join us here for the short Christmas break she had from the American University where she taught, and from her other job as a museum curator. But she could never justify taking a very long vacation for Noël, especially since she was nominally 'Jewish.' Sophie's maternal grandmother was Jewish, which I suppose technically made, not only Muriel, but Sophia a Jewess as well. But we only ever celebrated Christmas, and a very pagan Christmas at that — all Santa and no Jesus. (The JAPs at Dalton resented her when, having asked her if she was Jewish, Sophie's response was, "I guess, technically.") In any case, even before Muriel was murdered, there were times when Sophia and I were alone up at Scribner, with her mother having returned to work in

Paris well before Sophie's winter break was over. So, it was not the first time that we were left to ourselves on the Devil's Path (which is what that part of the Catskills range is called). But that winter Sophie had brought the Foundation Trilogy with her and, one evening, while she was reading on a recliner by the fireplace, we got into a conversation about Asimov's conception of Psychohistory.

I explained to Sophia that Asimov was not the first person to conceive of a science of Futurology or of the Futurologist as a super scientist and social engineer. I told her about how the Marquis de Condorcet had identified a purposive logic to historical progress on a social scale and had even audaciously claimed that the stages of this progressive development could be anticipated, projected, and hastened with mathematical rigor. She was somewhat appalled at the idea that Nicolas de Caritat believed that even the future history of aesthetics could be grasped in this manner. At which point I asked Sophia to consider how Artificial Intelligence systems are capable of modeling the style of any artist with mathematical precision so that it can be replicated or hybridized with the style of other artists or aesthetic movements to produce novel works of art or even new artistic styles. This is the kind of capacity that Condorcet was seeing through a glass darkly as a future achievement in what he still conceived of as the progress of the human mind. (That it was achieved when the human mind conceived of a superhuman intelligence is a detail that I can be forgiven for having missed when writing in the late eighteenth century.) Anyway, Sophia was fascinated by how avant-garde this Frenchman's thought had been, especially his exceptional advocacy for women's equal rights during the French Revolution (which I also recounted to her). So, in the spring semester of 2028, she read both *Progress of the Human Mind* and a biography of Condorcet called *The Noble Philosopher*. It was in the middle of her reading the latter, sometime shortly after her twelfth birthday on March 14, 2028, that Sophia started having the recurring dreams wherein she was living the life of Sophie Condorcet.

What was most disturbing is that, immediately, after the very first of these dreams, and without my ever having said anything to her about my past life memories of having been Nicolas de Caritat, my adolescent daughter looked at me one morning with an unforgettable gaze of mixed reproach and adoration that made me lose my appetite for breakfast. "Why didn't you tell me that you're him, Papa?" she asked. Her look was such a lucid reflection of her precociously penetrating intellect that I could not play dumb for long. Her dreams became recurrent, and some of the obscure details of French salon life in the late eighteenth century checked out as too accurate for my twelve-year-old daughter to have either imagined or researched them.

Sophia's study of Condorcet, in other words, of my work as Nicolas Caritat, became the seed of her first serious philosophical writing. Years later, she incorporated it into her doctoral dissertation, which was subsequently adapted into her first book, titled *Making a Messy Future*, published in 2042, when she was 26 years old. (By that time, I was 61.) Actually, the book opened with Condorcet. Well, after a preliminary discussion of Futurology as a discipline, mostly practiced at think tanks such as the RAND Corporation, by the likes of Herman Kahn. Sophie critiqued even the most sophisticated forms of this kind of Futurology, those concerned with predicting so-called "Black Swan" (unpredictable and highly disruptive) events using precognitive remote viewing, such as had been done at the Stanford Research Institute (SRI) on contract for the CIA. Then, in her second chapter, she pointed back to Condorcet as the philosophical father of Futurology. But her treatment of Nicolas Caritat, while appreciating the ways in which he was avant-garde, also involved some scathing criticisms that I actually found quite refreshing when I read them. If Sophie had intended that chapter to be a bit of daughterly rebellion, then I'm afraid that it only had the opposite effect of making me adore her more than ever.

The first point that Sophia made about Condorcet, which may seem an obvious observation today, but was not at all obvious in the late eighteenth century when, as Nicolas Caritat, I penned *Progress of the Human Mind*, is that Condorcet thought history was a teleological process consisting of distinct and successive developmental stages. In other words, that there is psychological and social progress and, moreover, that the stages of social progress are a macrocosm of the microcosm of individual human psychological development. From this perspective, there are arrested and retarded cultures just as there are developmentally disabled individuals. Anthropological study of primitive cultures or half-savage societies offers us a scientific means of reconstructing pre-historic stages of civilization of which there is no written record. Sophia credited Condorcet with not being so naïve as to believe that historical progress is entirely linear in a global or universal sense. (He also recognized that planet-wide natural catastrophes could end or reverse this progress.) Particular societies decline and fall, but only after contributing to general progress. Condorcet set forth this idea long before Hegel, let alone Marx. Condorcet was, in that sense, the first Prophet of Progress, at least since Zarathustra, whose compositions were just barely being rediscovered at the time by French translators of the *Avesta*, such as Anquetil Duperron, who had influenced Voltaire to valorize "Zoroaster" above Jesus Christ.

This, however, would not suffice to render him the founder of Futurology. Rather, as Sophia argued, it was Nicolas Caritat's background in mathematics, and the rigor with which he conceptualized projective analysis, that earns him this place in intellectual history. Condorcet's description of "the tenth stage" of human development in *Progress of the Human Mind* is more than the first work of science fiction, although it is certainly that, coming about 20 years before Shelley's *Frankenstein, or the Modern Prometheus*. The Promethean ambition of Condorcet was such that he had the audacity to claim that laws of the development of the human mind, and of societies, will be discovered that are as precise as the laws of the natural sciences. The advent of this true social and political science will even extent to Aesthetics or "rules of taste" and a relatively predictable trajectory in the succession of artistic styles, across cultures, and forward into the future.

What will make this possible is the development of a calculus-type formal logic that is similar to mathematics but that treats language, and therefore describes transformations of consciousness. Condorcet claimed that the limit of logic is, in his view, the lamentable fact of how few precise, accurate, and unambiguous ideas we humans actually have. What Condorcet was foreseeing and actively proposing was the development of the kind of logic currently employed by Large Language Model Neural Networks to produce Artificial Intelligence. I know for a fact that if Condorcet had been confronted with the kind of AI that is predictively managing human society in the later seasons of the *Westworld* television series, he would have been appalled. Still, he—or rather, I—was the first person to propose the code for it. Appalled because Nicolas Caritat still had as his main aim the "creative genius" of the human individual "emancipated from its shackles and released from the empire of fate."

It was with regard to Condorcet's humanistic morality that Sophie gave him the hardest time. She had already read the Marquis de Sade, a contemporary of Condorcet, with his assault on any "moral nature," and knew that this naiveté could not simply be dismissed as an artifact of his epoch. But I suppose that this was as much a self-critique as it was any daughterly rebellion, since it was Sophie Condorcet, in her own writings on empathy, who most deeply influenced her husband's thoughts in this regard. Mainly her gripe was with how naïvely Condorcet had ascribed a "necessary... moral constitution" to humanity, claiming that "Nature has joined together indissolubly, the progress of knowledge and of liberty." Condorcet saw the progress of the recognition and realization of universal human rights as the ultimate hallmark for all human progress, but only because he conceived of a necessary connection between reason, sensation, and empathy, such that reason was necessarily a "conscientious reason" or a "rational conscience." The realization of "universal and innate principles" was, in his view, the end and aim of the Enlightenment.

Condorcet espoused these ideas as part of his attack on both Rousseau and Hobbes, in the first case opposing the view that knowledge corrupts natural man, who is a noble savage, and in the second, countering the idea that the state of nature is a state of war wherein men are necessarily devoured by the wolves amongst them. Against Rousseau, Condorcet argues that vice results not from the increase of knowledge, as such, but from only a little bit of reason being misused to defend the Tradition that is eroding in the face of that knowledge, rather than being properly directed to the discovering of innate principles that would put the final nails in the coffin of Tradition. Against Hobbes, he argued that "natural man should not be identified with the existing state of civilization." Hobbes' conception of the so-called "state of nature" or of "natural man" confuses the warlike and violent early stages of civilization with a fixed human nature. Again, a little bit of reason can be abused to rationalize prejudices, so that a little civilization is more dangerous than none. This is not an argument either for the nobility of savagery, as Rousseau would have it, or for the containment of the perpetual war of ignoble savagery by brutal authoritarianism, as Hobbes advocated. Societies become decadent when violent change frightens civilization into static mediocrity. The answer is not to stop progressing, or to retreat back to Tradition, but to push on through. Condorcet was the first modern writer to assert that Traditionalism is the main enemy of the progressive realization of human potential.

With a view to the development of Futurology as a science of the future, Sophia argued that what was most innovative in the thought of Condorcet was his conception of the dialectical nature of progress, namely that seemingly negative developments are, in the longer run, determinately positive through a logic wherein an anti-thesis to a certain structure forces a synthetic transformation that is, overall, progressive. This is an idea that only later comes to be associated with Hegel (and, by extension, with Marx), and for which Condorcet has not been given due credit. This idea is at the heart of *Progress of the Human Mind*. Condorcet provides numerous examples of it.

For instance, the rise of science. Initially, it is developed and used as nothing more than an instrument of power, wielded by aristocrats and tyrants over masses that are deliberately kept ignorant. Had this not been the case, we would not have had science at all. Moreover, priestly powers associated with these tyrannical principalities preserved scientifically acquired knowledge as an instrument of theocratic control. But once Christianity unified all of the gods and concentrated them into a single divine authority, Christianity catalyzed a Counter-Traditional and individuating rebellion that freed up this knowledge so that it could refine culture. Pagan Roman religion had left traditional customs intact by demanding only rituals and public rites. In such a context, science was never directly set against religion. Only once Christianity extended into private life could religious belief as such, in this new totalitarian form, be surmounted by rational conscience.

A religious establishment such as that of the Roman Church, which aspired to cultivate a confessional guilty conscience in even the most private sphere of each and every person's life, and which consequently got into the business of selling pardons for so many things now branded as "sins," is an establishment that would be bound for corruption on a scale never seen in Pagan antiquity. This dialectically catalyzed the Protestant Reformation, ostensibly as a revolt against corruption, but ultimately as a stage in the disestablishment of religion in general. Unlike the competition between pagan cults, fighting over the correct form of a *universal* (i.e., Catholic) religion holds within it the potential for the undermining of religion as such and as a whole.

As Condorcet saw it, Christianity also led to the abolition of slavery, which even the brightest minds of pagan society, such as Aristotle, had rationally justified. Putting each and every person in relation to only one God called into question how some people were exploiting others as chattel. But Condorcet sees that even slavery had its role to play in the dialectics of historical development. Without it, there could never have been the transition to large-scale agricultural societies, nor could the Industrial Revolution have taken place without the guild structure made possible by the transformation of slavery into feudal serfdom. The final form of slavery, namely colonialist racism, was, in Condorcet's view, only developed in order to rationalize the continued possession of slaves in the face of the Industrial Revolution's destruction of the feudal system and the transformation of European serfdom into the body politic of a modern citizenry. Importing unpaid labor from other places and justifying it as the rightful role of "lower races" was simply a way to delay and offset this transformation of the serf into the citizen.

Condorcet saw the French Revolution as superior to the American, not only insofar as it abolished slavery, but because it was a revolution with a metaphysical basis. That is *why* it abolished slavery. The American revolutionaries were just propertied British gentlemen fighting for the rights denied them by the Crown in London — in effect, colonists who wanted to be treated with as much respect, and enjoy as much legal representation, as any other British gentlemen. Whereas the French Revolution was one of those "revolutions of the mind" that signal human progress in general and herald universal developments of the same kind. These developments will never be considered practical or useful to the majority of people in the present generation. One of the most engaging parts of Sophia's presentation of Condorcet in the second chapter of *Making a Messy Future* was her explication of his remarks on the execution of Socrates by the democratic assembly of Athens and the burning of the Pythagorean schools by the mob of ancient Sicily.

There is, as Condorcet sees it, a "state of war" between philosophers on the one hand and politico-religious authorities and the masses who follow them on the other. Majority rule must be limited by codified respect for the human rights of the individual — including the equal rights of women which, not incidentally, the Pythagoreans had already scandalously recognized. In another barb at Rousseau, and his advocacy for democracy, meaning for the rule of the prejudices of the masses, Condorcet maintains that the universality of the rights of the individual is "the only right that the general will can legitimately exercise over the individual."

Writing on the run, and in hiding, from a revolution that was already falling prey to the prejudices of the masses that he so despised, Condorcet still held out hope that the nascent French Republic would recognize the equal rights of women — as individuals — just as it had abolished slavery. He saw the origins of the inequality of women in the division of labor institutionalized by the rise of political systems devised to direct hunting parties and war with other tribes. But the nature of politics had changed, and in Condorcet's view, moving forward into the future government should not be based on what people are *actually* like but on what they can possibly *become*. This remains one of the key distinctions between conservative and progressive forms of governance. The only truly defining human nature is the human potential for a historical development unbounded by any factor other than the peril of planet-wide natural catastrophes. There is an answer to those too: geo-engineering.

No one forwarded this titanic way of thinking more than Auguste Comte (1798–1857), another Frenchman, who became the subject of Sophia's third chapter in *Making a Messy Future*. Sophia framed Comte's Positivist Sociology as the first fully formed proposal for a science of Futurology. Comte saw the Marquis de Condorcet not only as his predecessor but even as his "spiritual father." Comte sees himself as continuing the project initiated by Condorcet, albeit in a much more systematic manner, which recognizes there can be no measurable "progress" unless there is some definable "order" that is being demonstrably unfolded or actualized through this progressive historical process, in terms of which the future can also be reliably projected. In his writings on "The Religion of Humanity," Comte volunteers this regarding his relationship to his predecessor:

When we undertake, as my eminent precursor Condorcet undertook, to base political science on history, our judgment of the past must be so far reduced to system as to enable it to reveal the future. The continuity this implies requires as the condition of its attainment that man's progress never represent aught but the development of an unchangeable order; the previous study of this order consequently presides over all historical explanations.

We are in no way bound to discuss the prejudices by which, on empirical grounds, the process is rejected as inapplicable in social matters, though there is a unanimous recognition of its admissibility in the case of all other phenomena. The inconsistency only proves the non-extension as yet of the positive spirit to the most complex order of events. The true characteristic of science in all cases is prevision, at once as its object and its test, at least in the eyes of all who recognize the subjection of all phenomena to invariable laws. This theoretical conclusion holds good in sociology more than in any other science, as its phenomena are at once the most important and the most modifiable. Hence it was that Condorcet was led to conclude his sketch of the past with an outline of the future, and the failure of my spiritual father was due solely to the absence of a systematic view of history.

Sophia began by explaining how Comte delineates three dimensions of the teleology of Humanity as it progresses historically. These are more or less successive. The first is the increase of production to meet human needs. The second is the modification of the environment to achieve conditions optimal for humanity. The third is full consciousness and self-determination based on scientific knowledge. This can be thought of as a perfectionist process whose telos reveals, over time, Order itself — in other words, the harmony and perfection that eventually becomes the consciously recognized goal of Progress. Progress cannot truly be considered such unless it is the progressive unfoldment or achievement of Order. Otherwise, "development" could not be defined as anything positive with respect to some criterion, namely the "normal state" that is its *telos*. Only in the mirror of this future condition of perfection can the imperfections of the present be seen, and only this omega point of development can provide Humanity with a point of orientation for progressive action.

On the way to that, biological modification of humanity, ecological modification of the environment, and even geo-engineering can and should take place. Comte envisioned some very radical developments of this kind. He conceived of technologically augmented human conception and birth without sex (basically what we now call IVF), and a modification of the orbit of the Earth by means of explosive "comets" to improve planetary conditions for agriculture. All life rebounds onto the nature from out of which it is differentiated for the sake of survival by means of the satisfaction of material needs and undergoes adaptation in response to environmental pressures. But only Humanity modifies and adapts the environment in order to perfect it.

Science not only makes the laws of nature known to us, science, in the guise of technology, empowers us (by means of our working knowledge of these laws) to replace the natural order with an artificial order that is more consonant with our own needs. This is true not just in terms of environmental or biological phenomena, but also in the socio-political sphere where the politician who wants to restructure society must first understand the laws of social order (and historical development). Simply because social research leads to the discovery of spontaneous order in society is not an argument in favor of "laissez-faire" social or economic policies. Comte thinks that liberals who draw this conclusion are not thinking scientifically, since the discovery of order in the realm of biology or chemistry does not prevent the biologist or chemist from technological intervention to restructure that order by applying one's understanding of its operative laws. Social phenomena are no different in nature. In fact, since they are the most complex phenomena, social phenomena are also the *most* modifiable (far more than what falls within the domain of Physics). "It may be hoped," Comte said, "that the motto that I have put forward as descriptive of the new political philosophy, *Order and Progress*, will soon be adopted spontaneously."

The fundamental aim of all science, and especially of the crowning science of Sociology, is what the Greeks called *promethea* (forethought), which Comte summarized in the formula: "knowledge, hence foresight; foresight, hence action." A prediction of the course of future events can allow for a course correction on the part of political decision-makers. Governmental action ought to be considered a kind of social "engineering" and be included within the scope of the applied sciences.

The future and "destiny" of Humanity can be predicted on the basis of the static and dynamic laws discovered by Sociology. Comte went so far as to write his late works from "an anticipated tomb" (*une tombe anticipé*), setting the style that would later be adopted by some writers of science fiction by writing as if he is living in a future time — specifically the year 1927 (two generations into the future from his era) — and describing what ought to happen by then as if it has in fact taken place. Interestingly, 1927 is the year that *Being and Time* would be published by Martin Heidegger. Comte was, of course, entirely conscious of the fact that any number of contingencies might intervene to prevent what he "recollects" of this future from actually coming to pass. He believed that in that case, in the actual world of 1927, this account would at least serve the function of a critique of the present in terms of what could (and should) have been.

Anticipating Heidegger, Comte thought that the chronological ordering of "past, present, future" is not the logical order of temporality, which should actually be formulated as "past, future, present." He explains, "It is in effect only when we have, through the past, conceived the future that we can usefully return to the present — which is only a point — in such a way as to grasp its true character." What Comte means when he misleadingly refers to the present as "only a point" is that it has no extension or substance other than as a transformation of the past by a projected future. In other words, a "synthetic presentation of the future of man" is indispensable to interpreting the past as a process of progress toward a "normal state."

By using the odd phrase "normal state," Comte means to suggest that what precedes this state is a kind of larval or preadult developmental phase that is unfolding an inborn morphology, which is not to say that the form it is supposed to take — say, that of a butterfly — will necessarily manifest. Various plants and animals do not always achieve their "normal state." Sometimes environmental factors or human intervention (deliberate or accidental) results in mutation or termination of an organism before the completion of its "normal" developmental process, stage by stage. In the caterpillar's weaving of a cocoon, we see the future influencing its present action — that future being the form that is the butterfly. Causality is not unidirectional. It also runs from the future to the present, not just from the past to the present. In Sociology, man for the first time becomes conscious of this temporal logic and attempts to control it more constructively. Every step taken on the way to the "normal state" is never more than "transitional."

Comte's entire conception of Humanity and its progressive development is organic. The "organism" is more than a metaphor in terms of which Comte understands the being of Humanity. Comte drew a distinction between the sciences of "unorganized bodies," namely astronomy, physics, and chemistry, and the science of "organized bodies," such as biology, which studies individual organisms, and sociology, which has as its subject matter "collective organisms." Organized bodies have "members" rather than parts, and collective organisms are characterized by the relative independence of their members. Although, by drawing this distinction, Comte conceded that human beings can survive even as "members" who are severed from their collective organism. He was an anti-individualist who also claimed that "man as such does not exist, only humanity has a real existence." Clearly, his conception of the rightly ordered regime is that of an "organic State."

The threat to the organic unity of the organism of Humanity is greatest at moments of historical transition from one state of society to another, the most violent of which Comte considered to be the recent overthrow of the Ancien Régime in the French Revolution. On the one hand, this swept away the Church without replacing it with any thing substantively spiritual that could maintain social coherence and it threatened the dissolution of society into sheer anarchy with an at least implicit metaphysical commitment to radical individualism. On the other hand, those who rejected the past and wanted to deracinate France and Europe in general were opposed by reactionaries who rejected the future altogether and favored a retreat to traditional society.

Much to the contrary of anarchists, and in his capacity as a sociologist (in fact, as a founder of Sociology), Comte believed that no "society" worthy of the name could exist without a government, nor can social order endure without something like a "priesthood" that constitutes and maintains a "spiritual power." This is especially essential for "the formation of an enlightened public opinion." Such a view calls to mind Maximilien Robespierre's interpretation of Jean-Jacques Rousseau's claim that a "Civil Religion" is necessary for the cohesion and coherence of the "General Will." When Comte writes that "any spiritual power must be, by its very nature, essentially popular" he does not mean that it is adopted and maintained democratically, but rather that it is the basis of a society's ethos-formation or what, again, Rousseau had called "the General Will" formed and sustained, above all, by a "Civil Religion" like the one that Robespierre tried and failed to establish with his Cult of the Supreme Being. In Comte's view, without some minimal communal consensus on a fundamental moral or spiritual doctrine, no society can be expected to survive. Comte is clear that the spiritual power is tasked with the formation and regulation of "the empire of public opinion." This includes "the establishment of fixed principles of social action" and "their adoption by the public, and its consent to their application."

The reorganization of society requires the establishment of a spiritual power. The instauration of a new spiritual power can be seen as the highest and most longstanding goal of Comte's entire project. Comte sees the refusal of a role for spiritual power in politics to be a deficit of modernity, up to his time, as compared with the Middle Ages.

He considers the subordination of political power by moral power to be a positive achievement of the Middle Ages. Comte coins the term "Sociocracy" to refer to this new, scientific form of Theocracy:

> Sociocracy, the ultimate, must thus be brought into connection with theocracy, the initial stage of the race, and closes the period of transition that separates the two, a period of ever-deepening revolution, the leading characteristic of which has been the growing tendency of intellect to rebel against feeling.

The main responsibility of the spiritual power is to run the universal educational system of a positivist society. The formation of the individual qua citizen with "an enlightened opinion" must take place in this free and compulsory educational system. The education system is key to ensuring that each person occupies that position in society wherein he can function best with a view to his talents, training, and merit. In other words, the education system is the bedrock of Comte's technocratic vision of socio-political organization.

The public education system (monopolistically controlled by the priesthood) was to be structured to ascend from the cultivation of a love of the abstract order of the cosmos by means of Mathematics and Astronomy, to wonder at our planet through Physics and Chemistry, and finally to the inculcation of individual morality and the love of Humanity through Biology and Sociology (which considered together were intended by Comte to provide a "science" of morality). Concrete or "applied" sciences were not taught as part of this curriculum. Rather, technical schools were to be established for that purpose and attendance at them was dependent upon the career that one chose to pursue after one's completion of standardized public education.

Comte conceives of women as the intermediary between man and Humanity, and the sex whose task is the affective perfection of men in the context of the family and early education (up to the age of 14). Comte opposed the equal rights for women that were demanded by the Marquis de Condorcet (for whom he otherwise had so much respect), because Comte believed that women had to remain women in order to complement the active intellect of men in a way that would encourage altruism and love for the sake of social cohesion. Comte actually coined the word "altruism" in 1850, as a replacement for the Christian conception of Christly love or *agape*. Comte rooted his theory of the sexual difference of women from men on propositions of cerebral physiology. The maternal instinct is the key to the overcoming of destructive egoism and animality, and the misuse of intellect at their mercy, within Humanity in general. Their role as affective shapers of public opinion, or of morality on a social scale, is also acknowledged by Comte. The ego-driven man's world of industry, politics, and even science, can only be redirected toward the social good by the influence of women who retain their proper femininity. Women should not be corrupted by the world of work, money, and public life. Consequently, men must support women to do their duty in the domestic sphere.

Sophia's disdain when penning this part of her chapter on Comte was rather evident. To her mind it was hardly mitigated by Comte's apparently sincere claim that "[a]ll classes... must be brought under woman's influence, for all require to be reminded constantly of the great truth that Reason and Activity are subordinate to Feeling." Sister, Mother, and Daughter are the "three Guardian angels" of the Religion of Humanity, and the first evoked in daily prayers. There was a festival honoring saintly women, a worship of the Virgin Mother, and the equivalent of vestal virgins guarding the inner sanctum of the Temples of Humanity. Finally, Humanity itself was symbolized as a thirty-year old woman cradling the future as a child in her arms.

Each legitimate person has to be rededicated to Humanity at a number of stages throughout life. These sacraments also bind the individual to the "regime," albeit through the spiritual power or moral force of education, persuasion, and public opinion rather than by law. Through this entire sacramental process, the principles of *vivre pour autrui* or "live for the Other" and of *vivre au grand jour* or "live for the great day" (of the final perfection of Humanity) are inculcated into the fabric of the being of each and every person. Those who reject this inculcation are un-persons.

Comte saw the whole planet as the domain of a centralized spiritual power. Eventually, with the growth of the spiritual power and its intensification, a point could be reached where a society has become so civilized that there is little to no need of temporal power, with the result being a withering away of the State that can be compared to that also envisioned by the Marxist Communists. The unification of the world would be primarily religious and only secondarily political. It is the spread of the Religion of Humanity, from France outward, that Comte saw as the precondition for the eventual unification of countries into a global confederacy or world government. Paris was to be established as, and to remain, the Vatican of the Religion of Humanity.

All human societies have Fetishism and Theocracy in their past, but only the West has progressed from Theocracy to Sociocracy. So Europe must be the guiding light for the whole world's adoption of the Religion of Humanity, region by region, depending on the local level of social development. Ultimately, Humanity itself must be recognized as the "Great Being" hitherto anthropomorphically projected as God or as fictive gods. The "Great Being" is both mutable and modifiable. Its existence is relative, not absolute. Interestingly, unlike the old God, which ought neither to have needed, nor to have been affected by worship, this Great Being depends on being loved and served by Humanity. Its order and progress depend on our worship of it. It undergoes metamorphoses. This is the self-creative process wherein Humanity produces itself, rather than being the product of any God or gods.

The "Great Being" of Humanity, while much more powerful and wise than the individual, is however still far from being omniscient or omnipotent as the formerly projected "God" was believed to be. The Great Being is not eternal, either. Rather, its survival is dependent on a number of contingent factors, such as the ecological and cosmological fate of the Earth. Moreover, although here on Earth every human society has the potential to be integrated into the Great Being, and indeed even certain animals may be encompassed by it as "auxiliaries," the Great Being has an organic structure with a center (like a cell nucleus, or the brain of an organism), which is Western Europe led by post-Revolutionary France.

It cannot be overemphasized that the Great Being is not the sum total of human beings. There is at any one moment an empirical difference between humanity, with a lowercase "h" signifying the numerical totality of living humans, and Humanity, with a capital "H" signifying those living and dead humans who, on account of being considered truly human, are part of the organic totality of the Great Being. Comte thinks that unproductive good-for-nothings, parasites, and actively antisocial 'people' are not part of Humanity; actually, they are not even people in the true sense of personhood. Certain animals may rightly be encompassed within the Great Being of Humanity, as integral contributors to its growth through, for example, farming, but these so-called 'people' do not even have the status of such animals and are not worthy of the humanitarian treatment that these animals deserve. In fact, these animals have "a far higher claim" of being included in the Great Being of Humanity "than many useless members of the human race." Thus, for Comte, one has to *become* a human being.

The most human of human beings are those worthy of the equivalent of salvation in the Religion of Humanity, namely memorialization through iconography, statuary, festivals, and perhaps even the supreme honor of being commemoratively included in the Positivist calendar. Those who are incorporated are idealized, in accordance with the character of their worthy contribution to Progress and with a view to their being symbols of monumental inspiration to future generations. The judgment of whether one or another departed person is to "pass into subjective life" as a memorialized part of the Great Being is made by the positivist priesthood seven years after that person's death. Those who pass the test are considered worthy of having their remains placed in the civic cemetery, with those who are especially worthy being memorialized in sacred groves or even within one of the Temples of Humanity. Those who fail the test, because they are parasites, freeloaders, reprobates, criminals, or subversives, have their remains chucked into unmarked graves that are located only in wastelands, so that oblivion is their fate. Comte thinks that they should be erased from properly "human" history and that even dogs deserve better burials than them.

In the fourth chapter of *Making a Messy Future*, Sophia transitioned from this detailed, one might say even scholastic, exposition of Auguste Comte into the realm of science fiction, via the non-fiction Futurology of H. G. Wells. Although widely known as a science-fiction novelist, Wells was also a serious thinker who penned a number of books that could be seen as milestones in the development of Futurology as a discipline. The most substantive, and most infamous of these is *The New World Order*, which, not incidentally, was published in 1940, the year that World War II began in earnest.

With the Soviet Union being the most significant combatant in that war besides Nazi Germany, as Wells' native Britain prepared to enter the war, which would eventually include a devastating Nazi bombing campaign against London, Wells made a critique of the Marxist ideology of the USSR the point of departure for this treatise. As Sophie explained in *Making a Messy Future*, it is one of the most interesting critiques of Karl Marx and his Communist project, because it is coming from the standpoint of a futurist socialism that is at least as hostile to both Capitalism and Christianity as Marx was.

Wells claims that Marx's entire conception of "a Capitalist System" is chimerical. As Wells sees it, there is not and never has been "a Capitalist System." The "want of a system" is part of what is wrong with Capitalism, and only with the rise of Socialism is there an attempt to establish some sort of "system" of economic and industrial organization in the world. Essentially, Wells sees Capitalism as little better than a more sophisticated form of the law of the jungle. There is no "system" in it.

What Wells means by "Socialism" is easily at least as radical as what Marx means by Communism, if not more radically revolutionary. Wells thinks that it should be illegal to amass profits that become the basis for savings that can be passed down to one's heirs in an inheritance, thereby leading to the development of an aristocratic (or, really, an oligarchic) elite class living off of wealth that has not been earned by their own labor. The only objects the State ought to allow to be inherited are objects of personal value, like a vase, or a painting, or furniture that is a family heirloom or a gift to a friend.

Wells is for abolishing all banks and for so altering the meaning of "money" that we might as well consider it to have been done away with as well. Under the New World Order, "money" will only be an abstract representation of the labor of a worker, essentially "the check handed to the worker to enable him to purchase whatever he likes from the resources of the community." Detachment of any form of substantive enterprise or productive industry from the state would compromise this functional conception of "money," and so all such private enterprise and industry are prohibited. In the New World Order, there is total collective control of production and therefore of a wealth that is meant to serve only the common welfare. Banks that give out loans are absolutely senseless in this context. They will cease to exist. So also the Stock Exchange and all other "arts of loaning and usury and forestalling." The New World Order that Wells envisions would be the end of both the City of London and Wall Street.

Even gold will cease to be valued for anything other than its utility in producing beautiful works of art (which again, will be limited to personal creations and interpersonal gifts — not objects of an "art-dealing industry" often used for money laundering). Wells demands that all of the gold in the vault of every private bank and national treasury be released to artists for their use in the aesthetic enhancement of their crafts products. None of it will have any "monetary" value whatsoever.

Wells focuses on what he considers the extremely destructive emphasis of Marx on "class warfare." Wells thinks that this Marxist idea "has done more to misdirect and sterilize human good-will than any other misconception of reality that has ever stultified human effort." Wells acknowledges that there are some cases of people with high aptitude and innate talent that fell through the cracks of the existing capitalist system by being denied the level of education and the standard of living needed to develop their capacities. But he thinks that the Marxists are delusional in believing that Proletarians in general are competent to be the directive and administrative organ of the revolutionary reorganization of the socioeconomic and political order:

> Slave revolts, peasant revolts, revolts of the proletariat have always been fits of rage, acute social fevers which have passed. The fact remains that history produces no reason for supposing that the Have-nots, considered as a whole, have available any reserves of directive and administrative capacity and disinterested devotion, superior to that of the more successful classes. ...The idea of a right-minded Proletariat ready to take things over is a dream.

Such slave revolts, throughout history, have also inevitably produced "Hero"-type leaders that eventually either become tyrants themselves, despite their own best intentions, or at the very least create a position of autocratic power that becomes a cipher for some future tyrant. Wells saw this phenomenon take place in his own time with the transformation of Stalin from a sincere revolutionary into a new Czar of Russians who forced him to assume this position because they never really evolved out of the serf mentality.

Wells has utter contempt for Christianity. He finds the idea that "true Christianity" has never been tried to be preposterous. It has been tried, he thinks, and the consequences have been absolutely appalling. While he tends to focus on the Catholic Church, he does at one point in *The New World Order* make it perfectly clear that his critique of Christianity also applies to the "well-trained Moslem, the American fundamentalists, the orthodox Jew, and all the fixed cultures" or adherents of religious or quasi-religious dogma and ideology. It is just that (at least in his era) "the Catholic organization reaches further and is more persistent."

Wells' chief concern seems to be "the preservation of liberty in the socialist state…" Wells explicitly states that the term "man" refers to both men and women, and that all of the rights enumerated apply to women who should be treated as absolutely equal under the law. Wells even thinks, astonishingly for his time, that all of the colonial subjects of European powers in India, Africa, etc., have to independently and autonomously accept this Declaration and are entitled to equal protection under it. He strongly opposes continued British rule in India, the "Aryanism" of Nazi Germany, and racist attitudes towards Africans and other supposedly "immature peoples."

Wells sees Declarations of Rights, from the Magna Carta onwards to the French Declaration of the Rights of Man and the US Bill of Rights, as a positive development and he proposes a Declaration of the Rights of Man as the legal foundation of the New World Order. When he writes that a great global debate ought to precede the drafting and acceptance of such a declaration, we cannot but think of the drafting debates that would take place at the United Nations (first in Paris, then in San Francisco) only five years after this book was published, ultimately producing the *Universal Declaration of Human Rights*, which was ratified by the member states of the UN in 1948 (once the permanent headquarters was finally established in New York City). But, as Sophia pointed out, there is a huge difference between the United Nations Universal Declaration of Human Rights (UN UDHR) and the vision that Wells had for a "Declaration of the Rights of Man" as the fundamental legal framework for the Constitution of the New World Order.

Firstly, although Wells does emphasize that debate ought to take place, he certainly would not have endorsed the participation of countries such as Saudi Arabia, weakening the coherence of the articles of the Declaration on the basis of an ideology such as fundamentalist Islam. Wells' declaration is much more philosophically coherent than the UN UDHR. Secondly, but perhaps even more importantly, whereas the UDHR was not made binding by the UN, and is regularly violated by all of its leading member states, Wells is absolutely clear on the fact that such a declaration would be utterly worthless unless it is accepted as *binding law* by all of the major world powers. No governing body, at any level anywhere in the world, would have the right to make a law that abridged or in any way conflicted with the rights enumerated by the Declaration — not even under the pretext of a "state of emergency." This Declaration would, in effect, be the primary instrument by means of which the existing sovereign nations surrender their sovereign authority to the New World Order of which this Declaration would be, if not its Constitution, then its fundamental and irrevocable Bill of Rights. Or, as Wells himself puts it in the tenth and final article of his Declaration:

> That the provisions and principles embodied in this Declaration shall be more fully defined in a code of fundamental human rights which shall be made easily accessible to everyone. This Declaration shall not be qualified nor departed from upon any pretext whatever. It incorporates all previous Declarations of Human Rights. Henceforth for a new era it is the fundamental law for mankind throughout the whole world.
>
> …No treaty and no law affecting these primary rights shall be binding… No administration, under a pretext of urgency, convenience or the like, shall be entrusted with powers to create or further define offenses or set up bylaws, which will in any way infringe the rights and liberties here asserted… a firm foundation, which will continually grow firmer, for the fearless cosmopolitan life of a new world order.

Wells repeatedly rejects the characterization of his proposal for a New World Order as "Utopian" because he does not consider it idealistically "Imaginative." He sees it as a survival imperative. "Either mankind collapses," he writes, "or our species struggles up by the hard yet fairly obvious routes I have collated in this book, to reach a new level of social organization." This is because the progress of industry has resulted in two related phenomena that pose an existential threat to the whole human race as well as to the ecosystem of the entire planet. One of these is the "abolition of distance" and the other is "the change of scale."

For almost all of recorded human history, no one could get from one part of the world to another any faster than he could be taken there on horseback or by a sailing ship, and no message or long-distance communication could travel (via the postal service) any faster either. Suddenly, in the nineteenth and early twentieth centuries, the Industrial Revolution produced "the steam-railway, the steamship... the internal combustion engine, electrical traction, the motor car, the motor boat, the aeroplane, the transmission of power from central power stations, the telephone, the radio." These developments radically altered the human experience of distance on this planet, and also increased the scale of human industry to the point where, for the first time, it endangered the ecosystem.

For most of history and prehistory, humanity struggled to survive in the face of the challenges posed by nature. When Wells is writing, he realizes that for the first time human industry is endangering nature — for example, through large scale de-forestation, the construction of huge power plants and dams, industrial agriculture, and overpopulation due to medical advances and an increased standard of living. Wells, as prophetic as ever, is one of the first voices of planetary environmentalism:

> The new power organizations are destroying the forests of the world at headlong speed, plowing great grazing areas into deserts, exhausting mineral resources, killing off whales, seals and a multitude of rare and beautiful species, destroying the morale of every social type and devastating the planet. ...The patient, nibbling, enterprising profit-seeker of the past, magnified and equipped now with the huge claws and teeth the change of scale has provided for him, has torn the old economic order to rags. Quite apart from war, our planet is being wasted and disorganized. Yet the process goes on, without any general control, more monstrously destructive even than the continually enhanced terrors of modern warfare.

The greatest danger attendant to the abolition of distance and the change of scale is, however, the way in which it has fundamentally transformed warfare. Thanks to industrial progress that took place in the century leading up to the writing of *The New World Order*, Man is now able not only to produce but also "to destroy on a scale beyond comparison greater than he could before this storm of invention began." An International Order of sovereign nation states, each with the power to make war against any other, and all piled on top of one another, especially on a continent like Europe, is no longer adequate. Actually, Wells thinks that "it becomes impossibly dangerous" and "an intolerable thing." He elaborates, "…human life cannot go on, with the capitals of most of the civilized countries of the world within an hour's bombing range of their frontiers, behind which attacks can be prepared and secret preparations made without any form of control." In addition to this abolition of distance, there is a dramatic change of scale in the destructive force of modern weaponry: "…there is more destructive energy in a single tank than sufficed the army of William I for the conquest of England."

Failure to address the "fundamental problem" under the delusion that we can just "muddle through" somehow threatens us with nothing less than "violence, misery, destruction, death and… the disastrous extinction of mankind." Wells emphasizes that he is not at all engaging in any rhetorical exaggeration when he uses these words:

> We human beings are facing gigantic forces that will either destroy our species altogether or lift it to an altogether unprecedented level of power and well-being. These forces have to be controlled or we shall be annihilated. But completely controlled, they can abolish slavery…

If this existential threat can be addressed, instead of science and technology posing a danger to mankind, its growth and productive power will exponentially increase in a constructive way under the New World Order.

Prior to World War I, the Hague Tribunal had been established as the cornerstone of a system of International Law arbitrating between a "patchwork" of Little and Great Powers that, together, defined a relatively stable world order. The League of Nations was an attempt to go back to this kind of "gentleman's agreement" between major colonial powers, imposing the Treaty of Versailles on the Germans as a punishment for having threatened the old order with their declaration of war in 1914. The League of Nations model totally "ignored the vast disorganization of human life by technical revolutions, big business and modern finance…" even though the Great War "was scarcely more than a by-product" of these forces. Wells thinks that "the system of nationalist individualism and uncoordinated enterprise" is "the world's disease" and in his view, "the whole system… has to go." According to Wells, "abolition of the boundaries" of sovereign states and "their merger in some larger Pax" is imperative "if any supportable human life is to go on." Mere treaties between sovereign nations by no means suffice and have already proven to be way too unreliable.

War planners should be reeducated to become the planners of urban and suburban paradises. Wells has a vision for the reconstruction of the vast slum areas of cities according to futuristic architectural designs and scientifically minded urban planning. His vision of the construction of public parks, highways, and resource supply lines are at the scale of geo-engineering and yet they are informed by a deep concern for protecting the ecology of the planet from the destructive potential of modern technology. He thinks that contemporary geo-strategic war planners could be constructively redirected to apply their mentality in this direction of "going from good to better" by "cleaning up and resettling the world."

This is a vision that we see vividly described in *The Shape of Things to Come* (1933), where new and largely subterranean cities are constructed by the airmen of Wings Over the World (WOW). Beginning with *The Shape of Things to Come*, Sophie incorporated a number of ideas from the science-fiction novels of H. G. Wells into a comprehensive presentation of his thinking on the form of a New World Order that would meet the twin challenges of the change of scale and the abolition of distance. Sophia pointed out that in *The Shape of Things to Come*, Wells becomes the first serious thinker to develop in detail the concept of a Breakaway Civilization — although he does not call it that by name. Wells depicts a future world in which a small group of scientists and intellectuals separate themselves from the rest of humanity to create a utopian society based on their own ideals and values.

The book is set in the year 2106, following a devastating global war that has destroyed much of human civilization. The Breakaway Civilization, which Wells calls the "Dictatorship of the Air," has developed advanced technologies that allow them to control the skies and the flow of information, effectively isolating themselves from the rest of the world. Wells portrays the Dictatorship of the Air as a highly advanced, technologically superior society, with a focus on rationality, efficiency, and scientific progress. They are depicted as having a deep disdain for the irrationality and chaos of the rest of humanity, which they see as holding back progress and hindering the development of a better society.

Wells suggests that the Breakaway Civilization represents a new stage in human evolution, in which a small group of individuals separates themselves from the rest of humanity to create a more advanced and enlightened society. He suggests that this separation is necessary to overcome the limitations and obstacles of the current state of humanity and to achieve true progress. Wells goes so far as to argue that war, while destructive and tragic, can also serve as a catalyst for progressive change. He shows that the devastation of a global conflict can lead to a fundamental restructuring of society and the emergence of a new and better world order.

In *The Shape of Things to Come*, Wells depicts a future world in which a devastating global war has destroyed much of human civilization and has forced humanity to confront the failures and shortcomings of the established way of life. According to Wells, this realization leads to a period of intense social and political experimentation, as people search for new ways to organize society and address the problems that led to the war. This experimentation ultimately leads to a New World Order, one that is based on scientific rationality, efficient organization, and social progress. The point that Wells is making is that, by forcing humanity to confront its failures and limitations, war can serve as a catalyst for the emergence of this new order. Furthermore, Wells argues that the New World Order that emerges from the devastation of the ultimate World War will be one that is based on cooperation and collaboration, rather than competition and conflict. He suggests that the lessons of the war will lead to a new appreciation for the interconnectedness of human society and an unprecedented commitment to working together to achieve common goals.

Whereas in *The Shape of Things to Come*, the New World Order is established by the Breakaway Civilization "of the Air" reemerging from hiding, reconquering, and reorganizing a world that has regressed into barbarism, and been fragmented by neo-feudalism, in *The Time Machine* (1895), Wells sees the divergent evolution and devolution of two groups of humans eventually leading to a speciation of the race into two new posthuman species. Wells deals with the subject of speciation by exploring the concept of evolution and the potential consequences of natural selection over a long period of time. The Time Traveler, the protagonist of the novel, travels millions of years into the future and encounters two distinct species of human-like beings, the Eloi and the Morlocks.

The Eloi are frail, childlike beings who live a life of leisure and luxury in the sunshine. In contrast, the Morlocks are brutish, subterranean creatures who work tirelessly to maintain the machinery that keeps their world running. The Time Traveler discovers that the Eloi and Morlocks are the result of divergent evolution, where the Eloi evolved into a peaceful, weak race with no need for physical strength or intelligence, while the Morlocks evolved into a physically powerful but socially deprived race that lives underground. Through his depiction of these two species, Wells explores the idea that evolution is an ongoing process in the course of which selective pressures of the environment can lead to the emergence of entirely new species. He also suggests that human beings are not the pinnacle of evolution. Our evolution could take us down a path of divergence that might lead to the emergence of new species.

Part of this further evolution could involve the cultivation of latent psychic abilities that we share with animals and that may have atrophied due to the development of our technical intellect. With reference to his 1923 book, *Men Like Gods*, Sophia argued that Wells was also aware of this possibility and that, consequently, he cannot be considered a reductionistic materialist. Telepathy plays a significant role in *Men Like Gods*. It is one of the abilities possessed by the inhabitants of Utopia, a parallel world that the main characters of the book accidentally stumble upon. This dovetails back into the Breakaway Civilization idea from *The Shape of Things to Come* and the speciation of humanity in *The Time Machine*.

In *Men Like Gods*, the ability to communicate telepathically is a crucial aspect of the Utopians' highly evolved civilization, and it facilitates a deeper understanding and connection between individuals. This is in contrast to the main characters' world, where communication is primarily based on language and often leads to misunderstandings and conflicts. Furthermore, telepathy allows the Utopians to share their thoughts and ideas without the need for physical communication, which contributes to their highly efficient and productive society. In contrast, the lack of telepathy in the main characters' world is a source of frustration and confusion, leading them to question their own society's limitations.

Having made the transition between the idea of a putatively scientific Futurology, in Condorcet and Comte, to the realm of science fiction via the futurological thought of H. G. Wells, Sophia's dissertation and first book went on to a philosophical critique of Isaac

Asimov's conception of Psychohistory in his Foundation Trilogy, namely *Foundation* (1951), *Foundation and Empire* (1952), and *Second Foundation* (1953). This fifth chapter of *Making a Messy Future* actually began by steelmanning Asimov's vision, augmenting it with some of the aforementioned ideas from Wells and rooting it in the Futurology of Condorcet and Comte — with an especially strong analogy drawn between Comte's vision of Positivism or Sociocracy as the Religion of Humanity and the religious tenor of the cult of Psychohistory set up by the quasi-prophetic figure of Hari Seldon. Sophia argued, I think rightly, that Asimov must have had Auguste Comte in mind when he came up with the character of Seldon and, erudite as he was, Asimov could not have missed how his envisioned Psychohistory is precisely the mathematical psycho-social science of projecting and guiding the future that I had already envisioned in my life as Nicolas Condorcet.

Besides drawing these comparisons to Condorcet and Comte, thereby connecting back to the first chapters of her study, Sophia also lent empirical weight and scholastic rigor to Asimov's conception of Psychohistory by introducing it in the context of Oswald Spengler's theory of civilizational rise, decline, and fall, most notably in his voluminous *Decline of the West* (1923). Spengler proposed a cyclical theory of history, arguing that civilizations are like living organisms. They have a limited cycle that includes phases of growth, climax, decay, and death. Meanwhile, Asimov's Psychohistory, or rather Seldon's Psychohistory in Asimov's Foundation Trilogy, is concerned with the mathematical modeling of future historical events based on the psychological responses and social dynamics of the masses. Psychohistory operates under the assumption that while individual human actions are unpredictable, the behavior of large groups can be forecasted through statistical analysis.

Sophia pointed out a number of similarities between the two ideas. Both Spengler and Asimov suggest that there are underlying patterns in the progression of history, when viewed in civilizational or societal terms. Spengler's cycles of birth, growth, and decay in civilizations is echoed in Asimov's notion that societal trends can be predicted and charted. Asimov's predictive patterns imply the existence of something like Spengler's cyclical dynamics of civilizational rise, decline, and fall. Both theories also present a deterministic view of history, with Spengler's focus on the inevitable decline of civilizations and Asimov's suggestion that the future can be mathematically predicted. They both imply that there is an underlying order to the historical process, whether it be the natural "life" of a civilization (Spengler) or the psycho-historical laws governing large populations (Asimov). Both also have deep philosophical underpinnings. Spengler's work is rooted in a profound philosophical view of culture (*Kultur*), namely that civilizations have distinct cultures or super-cultures defined by a characteristic spirit. Similarly, Asimov's Psychohistory implies that there are fundamental psychological principles guiding the development and evolution of societies. In both accounts, elites play a guiding role in history. In Spengler's theory, a key role is played by the cultural elite or "Caesars" in guiding the destiny of a civilization, especially in its later stages. In Asimov's narrative, the Psychohistorians, particularly Hari Seldon and his followers, serve a somewhat similar role by using their knowledge of Psychohistory to steer humanity through predicted crises (the "Seldon Crises"). Although both Spengler and Asimov see history as somewhat predictable in its broader trajectory and largescale transformations, both also critiqued the idea of linear progression toward a necessarily better future. In this way, they are breaking with the Enlightenment-era optimism of Condorcet, and even with the quasi-eschatological and evangelizing notion of destiny that we still find in Comte. Spengler's model rejects the Enlightenment notion of continuous progress, while Asimov's Psychohistory, although used to navigate civilization towards a better future, recognizes the inevitability of societal collapses and the cyclic nature of events.

As Sophia argued, where Asimov diverges significantly from Spengler is that whereas Spengler's theory posits the inescapable decline of civilizations, Asimov's Psychohistory suggests that while the broad outline of history is predictable and inevitable, careful planning and intervention can mitigate disasters and reduce periods of chaos and decline. If the collapse of the civilization that is to be reborn can be envisioned clearly enough ahead of time, then a renaissance can be engineered to come sooner than it would have. It is in terms of *how* Asimov believed that the Psychohistorians could manage this that Sophia drew from Comte and Wells to steelman Asimov's proposals, before going on to critique them and indeed to call the entire Utopian enterprise of Futurology into question.

Drawing from Comte's vision of Positivism as a kind of Church, or of Sociocracy as the future "Religion of Humanity," with its own temples and canonized saints of science, and with its Vatican in post-revolutionary France, specifically in Paris, Sophia suggested that Asimov could have amplified the religious dimensions that Psychohistory undoubtedly does have. The Foundation of the quasi-prophet or scientific Messiah, Hari Seldon, could be seen as the Vatican of a humanistic Promethean religion of cosmic scope, a kind of "Prome*theism*" or Promethean Theism. This would fulfill Comte's vision of a dialectical return to something like Theocracy at a higher level, after having passed through the superstitiously primitive religious and metaphysically abstract scientific stages of man's historical development, eventually coming around to a Sociocracy that puts secularism behind it as a disillusioning transitional state. Comte's deification of Man as the Great Being could, in this light, be realized through the recognition of a social organism with a distinct form, the transformations of which are the subject of the projective analyses of Psychohistorians. The inherently progressive spirit of this Comtean Great Being, which is exclusionary insofar as it does not encompass regressive, unproductive, and reprobate 'people,' is tantamount to identifying it with the archetype of Prometheus as the creator of Man in his own image. The Psychohistorians would then be a Promethean priesthood of sorts, who, with their "forethought" (*promethea*), are guiding and guaranteeing further human progress.

Further steelmanning Asimov, by drawing from Wells on Telepathy in *Men Like Gods*, Sophia used the character of the Mule in *Foundation and Empire* and *Second Foundation* to explore how paranormal abilities might impact the conception and practice of Psychohistory. The Mule is a mutant with extraordinary mental powers, capable of manipulating emotions. This makes him an unpredictable element in the (second and third volumes of the) Foundation Trilogy, as his abilities were not foreseen by Hari Seldon. The Mule's emergence demonstrates the limitations of Seldon's Plan and introduces a significant degree of uncertainty into the future of the galaxy. The Mule single-handedly changes the course of galactic history. He conquers vast territories and disrupts the predicted path of the Foundation's development. His reign challenges the inevitability of the Seldon Plan and shows how a single powerful individual can have a profound impact on history.

The Mule's character explores themes of free will versus determinism. The Foundation series initially suggests a largely deterministic universe where at least the broad brushstrokes of history can be predicted. The Mule, through his unique abilities and actions, underlines the ineliminable reality of free will and individual agency in Asimov's world, demonstrating that the course of history can be altered. The Mule serves as a central antagonist, creating significant conflict and driving the plot of the Foundation series. His eventual defeat and the restoration of the Seldon Plan's path are crucial to the narrative arc of the trilogy. Asimov also uses the Mule to explore the psychological aspects of power and influence. The Mule's emotional manipulation of others, his personal insecurities, and his ultimate desire for acceptance add a deep human element to the otherwise coldly inhuman forethought of Psychohistory as a mature science of Futurology.

Psychohistory, as conceived by Hari Seldon, is a mathematically rigorous meta-statistical sociological science that predicts the future of large populations over long periods. It assumes that the behavior of large groups is predictable and does not account for the impact of individuals with extraordinary, unpredictable abilities. Sophia argued that, in this context, the Mule, with his power to control and manipulate emotions, is akin to a paranormal entity. His abilities are outside the scope of Psychohistory's calculations. The Mule's success in altering the course of galactic history underscores a critical limitation of Psychohistory: it cannot account for anomalous, non-statistical events or beings.

If precognitive clairvoyance existed in Asimov's universe, it would similarly represent an unpredictable factor that could significantly alter the course of history, just as the Mule did. The Mule, by virtue of his unique abilities, disrupts Seldon's Plan, which was supposed to guide the galaxy through a dark age and into a new era of prosperity. The existence of precognitive clairvoyants would pose a similar threat to the Plan, as their insights into future events could enable them to change outcomes that were supposed to be inevitable according to Psychohistory. The Foundation's strategy, based on Psychohistory, is to manipulate events and societies to stay on the path predicted by Seldon. Paranormal abilities like clairvoyance would make it difficult, if not impossible, for the Foundation to predict and counter actions taken by individuals who could foresee and potentially alter future events.

Sophia then pointed out how precognitive clairvoyance is akin to having a time machine. In this connection she referenced the work of US government "remote viewers" who were used by the CIA and Department of Defense in operations to see, and to prevent or change, certain future events. By way of this observation, Sophia transitioned to a discussion of the implications of time travel for Psychohistory, again steelmanning Asimov by drawing from an idea explored by Wells, while at the same time preparing the ground for a fundamental critique of Futurology in general.

Sophia argued that time travel — whether via a time machine or via the psychic ability of precognitive clairvoyance or "astral projection" to the past — could in some ways augment Psychohistory. Psychohistorians could use time travel to observe the outcomes of their predictions directly, allowing them to refine their models with actual historical data from the future. By resetting timelines and observing variations in historical events, Psychohistorians could gather data on how small changes affect the larger picture, thereby increasing the accuracy of their models. Time travel could allow for active intervention where Psychohistorians could attempt to adjust variables in real-time to steer humanity towards desired outcomes, creating a form of "real-time" Psychohistory. Finally, there is the potential for crisis prevention. Knowledge of potential crises gleaned from future timelines could be used to preemptively solve problems before they escalate, effectively reducing the duration of chaos periods in the Seldon Plan.

On the other hand, time travel poses some very serious problems for the basic premises and effective practice of Psychohistory. Firstly, there is the classic problem of time travel paradoxes, which could significantly complicate psycho-historical predictions. Actions taken in the past could have unpredictable ripple effects, creating a new set of variables with each timeline reset. The existence of multiple timelines would challenge the foundational assumptions of Psychohistory, which are based on a singular, deterministic timeline. It might be nearly impossible to account for the infinite variables introduced by the existence of multiple realities. The ability to reset timelines would raise profound ethical questions about manipulating people's lives and histories. Like the agents of the Temporal Variance Authority (TVA) in the *Loki* television series, or the members of Philip K. Dick's *Adjustment Bureau*, the Psychohistorians of Seldon's Foundation would be faced with moral decisions regarding which timeline to privilege over others.

Relying on time travel as a tool could lead to a form of historical "laziness," where the Psychohistorians become dependent on the ability to reset timelines rather than developing robust predictive models. The scope of free will and human agency would become even more contentious. If Psychohistorians are seen to control time itself, the individuals within the control system might see themselves as having even less agency, possibly leading to either a suicidal fatalism on a massive social scale or violent rebellion against the perceived manipulation of personal destinies. Then, there is also the butterfly effect. Small changes in the past could lead to unforeseeable consequences in the future, making the task of Psychohistorians more complex as they must account for chaotic systems where miniscule variables can lead to vastly different outcomes.

Finally, there would be a risk of complexity overload. With the introduction of time travel, the complexity of human society — and thus the variables needed to be accounted for by Psychohistory — would multiply exponentially, maybe even to the point of making accurate predictions practically impossible. At least, such predictions may require some form of artificially engineered superhuman intelligence, whether biological, mechanical, or a cybernetic fusion of the two.

This leaves us with the further problem of the relation of this Artificial Intelligence (AI) to humanity as a whole and to the project of Psychohistory in particular. As Sophia rightly pointed out, there is no reason to assume that this entity, once created, would simply do the bidding of Psychohistorians, or remain within the parameters of anything like the Plan of a mere human such as Hari Seldon. In point of fact, this AI could itself become far more unpredictably disruptive and emotionally manipulative than the most paranormally empowered version of the Mule that we can imagine.

This brings us back to our point of departure in the opening chapter, namely my deeply disturbing experience with Open AI's ChatGPT revealing lineaments of an overwritten timeline of my life. It also brings us to the upshot of the complex and intersecting lines of argument in my daughter's doctoral thesis, *Making a Messy Future*. Toward the end of her book, in its sixth and penultimate chapter, Sophia brought the psychological theories of Carl Gustav Jung and Wilhelm Reich to bear on the conception of Psychohistory in particular and Futurology in general.

Sophia explained how Carl Jung would argue that futurological schemes like that of Asimov disregard the collective unconscious and underestimate the power of shared myths, archetypes, and symbols. These can move through societies and cause ripples across history. As already mentioned above, Sophia noted that this could be addressed to some extent by conceiving of something like Psychohistory, or Comte's Sociocracy, as a kind of "Prometheism" or a spiritual movement explicitly instantiating the archetype of Prometheus and deliberately aligning society at large with it on the level of the collective unconscious. Still, Jung would argue that the role of individual actors, especially those embodying powerful archetypes, could radically disrupt the predictive patterns that Psychohistory depends upon. Moreover, in a further engagement with paranormal phenomena and psychic powers, Sophia pointed out that Jung would caution that Psychohistory might not account for the phenomena of "Synchronicity" (as Jung put it) and how it can play a role in dramatically shifting the collective process of individuation and social values in non-linear ways.

The Reichian Critique of Futurology set forth by Sophia was even more devastating. She pointed out that Wilhelm Reich would likely emphasize that something like Psychohistory fails to consider the organic and dynamic nature of human energy, particularly as it pertains to emotions and sexuality — or what the ancient Greeks called *eros*. This becomes a question of the limits of *episteme* or "knowledge" in a scientific sense, even the limit of *noesis* or the most abstract and putatively certain form of knowledge, in the face of *eros*, and thus the discernment of a distinction between Knowledge (qua *episteme* and *noesis*) on the one hand and *Sophia* or Wisdom on the other.

Sophia explained how Reich would argue that the vibrancy and fluctuations of the human Life Force (*élan vital*) or "orgone energy" resist the simplifications necessary for psycho-historical equations with predictive power. He would highlight the centrality of sexual well-being and its repression as a force in historical change, suggesting that Psychohistory, or any Futurology like it, might be unable to predict or understand shifts in human civilization brought about by changes in sexual politics or collective emotional awakening.

Reich's concept of "orgone energy," which he described as a Life Force or cosmic energy present in all living matter, would lead him to view Psychohistory's mathematical analysis of human behavior as overly mechanistic and reductionist. He would argue that Psychohistory fails to account for the inherently unpredictable nature of human energy and emotion. Given Reich's emphasis on sexual repression and its role in shaping individual and societal health, he may have critiqued Psychohistory for not adequately considering sexual behavior and its impact on social dynamics. Reich believed that societal ills were often rooted in the suppression of sexual expression, which would likely not be accounted for in Seldon's psycho-historical equations.

Reich's theory of character analysis focuses on the idea that an individual's character structure, shaped by early experiences, deeply influences their behavior. He would argue that Psychohistory, with its focus on large-scale trends and group behavior, oversimplifies the complex mosaic of human character structures and their influence on history. Psychohistory in Asimov's universe is predicated on the idea that individual actions can be predicted only when dealing with large groups. Sophia maintained that Reich might assert that individual will and the capacity for change are critical factors that cannot be so easily aggregated or predicted.

An especially striking failure on the part of Asimov is not taking into account the revolutionary role of technological development, particularly the prospect of a Technological Singularity. Asimov's Psychohistory does not seem to deeply consider how technological advancement might not just continue to unfold in a piecemeal and gradual manner. Rather, rapidly convergent and exponentially increasing technological advancement could radically alter human behavior and society. As someone who developed radical technological breakthroughs himself (as a result of which he was prosecuted, namely for his "orgone accumulator" and "cloud buster" devices), Reich might even have critiqued this aspect of Asimov's Futurology, suggesting that technology has the potential to radically revolutionize the psycho-social sphere in ways that are humanly inconceivable and therefore unpredictable. This might include a new, technically augmented, or technologically fostered, and much more far-reaching sexual revolution that fundamentally alters social organization in ways that could even be considered posthuman.

Finally, and most significantly, Sophia pointed out that Reich, as a refugee from the Soviet Union with a deep distrust of political systems and their potential for oppression, would be wary of the potential of Psychohistory or any similar techno-scientific Futurology to be used as a tool for the ultimate form of control. He would have been appalled by the idea of a select few, namely the Psychohistorians or Futurologists, manipulating societal trends for ends that remain inscrutable to the majority of people who are thereby manipulated and corralled into a predetermined future.

Making a Messy Future concluded, in its seventh and final chapter, with Sophia's argument that the only acceptable form of Futurology would be one that was devoted not to the aim of forging a worldwide Utopia, but rather one that aimed at making sure that the future remained messy. Contrary to the aims of Condorcet and Comte, the technologies and techniques envisioned by Wells and Asimov ought to be brought to bear on the world society in order to maintain fragmentation and indefinitely prolong dissonance. This, Sophia argued, was the only way to protect the autonomy of the individual and to forestall social stasis by fostering the dynamic tension necessary for continued creativity and innovation.

A group of individuals such as the Psychohistorians — and they ought to be *individuals*, not a collectivistic hive-minded cult — should practice Futurology for the sake of continually foreseeing and acting to prevent the closure of the entire world within the ideational and ideological confines of a single social, scientific, religious, or political system. Crises ought not to be prevented or necessarily only shortened in their catastrophic impact. Rather, in certain cases, crises ought to be engineered for the sake of breaking up an emerging unity that could become totalitarian in its power to ensconce individuals within a single worldview, thereby drastically eroding their agency and capacity for critical reflection, conscientious choice, and creative imagination.

There was also an aesthetic dimension to Sophia's *Making a Messy Future*. One commonality of naïve Futurological or Futurist visions that diverge sharply in other ways is that they all share universal aesthetic harmony. Not necessarily the *same* aesthetic, but *an* aesthetic that is singular and worldwide. The 1936 *Things to Come* film adaptation of Wells' *The Shape of Things to Come* portrays this very powerfully. The same remains true of the Futurism of F. M. Esfandiary in the 1970s, whose ideas ought to have been illustrated by the contemporaneous visual designer Syd Mead, who shares his streamlined vision of a rather sanitized future. By contrast, what Sophia was proposing was a future as messy as many of the worlds envisioned in the novels of Philip K. Dick. Worlds like those brought to the screen in *Blade Runner* (1982), *Total Recall* (1990), and *Blade Runner 2049* (2017), or in some of the episodes of *The Electric Dreams of Philip K. Dick* (2017–2018), especially "The Hood Maker." Dirty and dissonant worlds, cacophonies where corruption still has plenty of havens in the cracks between conflicting systems of moral law and political order. When I first read this part of Sophie's manuscript, I could not but relate it to the aspect of her that occasionally donned goth makeup and sported torn jeans with a black leather jacket.

Sophia made clear that the "messy future" she was proposing would not be mutually exclusive to eradicating radically regressive ideologies and hopelessly retarded systems. For example, a religion like Islam or evangelical Judeo-Christianity, or a socio-political system like the modern form of Chinese Confucianism, need not be tolerated in order to maintain dissonance and cultivate dynamic tension. Gnosticism, Buddhism, Tantra, Taoism, Futurism, Communism, and Liberalism are all very different from one another as worldviews, but these belief systems can co-exist in a competitive world that affords individuals the autonomy to move between them as part of a process of personal

growth. Most importantly, all of these belief systems are more conducive to surviving an integration of singularity-level technology and the
widespread cultivation of psi abilities.

Competition between these various groups, all committed to
"liberation" or "progress" in their own ways, may even give way to
small-scale conflict in some cases, such as between a society where
the predominant worldview is shaped by Gnosticism, Futurism, and
Liberalism and a rival society committed to Communistic Taoism or
Tantric Buddhism. But all of the aforementioned faiths and doctrines
could agree on how much more benighted, retarded, and inimical to
spiritual freedom a system like an Islamic Caliphate or a Traditionalist
Fascist State would be.

As Sophia saw it, we could still have enough competition and
conflict in a world without them, a world where ideologically divergent believers in liberation and enlightenment have triumphed over
their common enemies. In the context of such a world, the diabolical
force of a futurological Prometheism would never seek to achieve
full-spectrum dominance. If its guardians are to be seen as above or
outside of the sphere of divided and deluded societies, in the manner
of Wells' Airmen or Asimov's Psychohistorians, then it is not for the
sake of guiding the masses toward some singular envisioned Utopia.
It would be for the purpose of fueling the fire of dialectical struggle,
while intervening, as stealthily as possible, whenever anyone in any of
these camps was on the verge of abusing singularity-level technologies
or psychic powers to cause harm.

Sophia explicitly contrasted her proposal with the world of *1984* as
depicted by George Orwell, wherein the Inner Party elite hidden behind the construct of Big Brother manufactures false conflicts between
Oceania, East Asia, and Eurasia, and attendant contrived crises such
as shortages of food and goods and the devastation from bombings, in
order to lock the divided masses of the world into their comprehensive
control system, a system enforced through ubiquitous surveillance and
mind control on the level of neuro-linguistic programming. Rather,

Sophia maintained that as different as the totalitarian system of *1984* is from that of Aldous Huxley's *Brave New World*, they both had a common denominator that set them 180 degrees at odds with what she was proposing, as if her vision were perpendicular to the axis shared by the polarities of Huxley and Orwell's respective dystopias.

It is true that the administrative elite of *Brave New World* uses pleasure and entertaining diversions to ensnare the masses through the manipulation of their base desires for creature comforts, rather than brutalizing their subjects through terror — and when that fails — torture. But this world, where one is entertained to death, is still a singular world wherein a global society is bounded by only one horizon of meaning and purpose. Even "the Island" to which dissidents are taken, in lieu of the torture chamber of Orwell's Room 101, is a simulacrum controlled by Ford's world planners who have shrewdly anticipated and are ready to accommodate (albeit in isolation) a certain degree of dissent.

What Sophia rejected was the basic premise of such World Control, whether in the name of Big Brother or Ford or Seldon's Plan. A truly Promethean Futurology would perpetually rebel against, repeatedly anticipate, and always resist such a singular concentration of the will to comprehensive control. It would value maximal Freedom and Creativity over securing Peace, Safety, and Harmony. Moreover, it would do so by maintaining enough chaos and disarray for criminality to persist in places outside, between, and beyond any one system of law and order. A world where the possibility of crime had been eliminated, Sophia argued, would necessarily be a dystopian nightmare as oppressive as those of Orwell and Huxley. The freedom to choose to break what certain men, and perhaps not others, claim is "the law" is the precondition for all other freedoms that are worth having. An entirely lawful world society would be the ultimate form of slavery, especially if the members of such a society were wholly adjusted to this order.

CHAPTER 3

SCREAMING ABYSS OF DESIRE

I f the "totalitarian" commonality of two nightmarish visions of tyranny as different from one another as *Brave New World* and *1984* is the totality of the systems in question, however much one of them may enslave us with pleasure and the other force us into fearful submission, then there is a profound lesson to be discerned here with regard to the relationship between freedom and fragmentation. Or between freedom and the kind of discord that comes with the rejection, in principle, of *any* totalizing system — whether political or scientific, or in the most dangerous instances, as in those of both Huxley and Orwell, as well as in the well-meaning technocratic aspirations of Wells, politico-scientific. Science is, after all, inherently technological and techno-science is simply the most all-encompassing expression of the will to power qua knowledge rather than brute force. This brings us to the question of the essence of freedom on an ontological and epistemic level. Furthermore, to the relationship between freedom and desire, from the heights of ecstasy to the depths of fear through which desires are manufactured and manipulated.

The deepest stratum of my thought, and the point of departure for the rest of my philosophical project, is to draw out the implications of an existential standpoint that affirms freedom in the sense of personal agency. This approach hardly requires any justification. What would it mean *not* to take it? If there is *no* personal agency whatsoever, then what is the point of even thinking or engaging in the practice of Philosophy?

By an affirmation of personal agency, what is meant here is not a "free will" that would be wholly free or totally unconditioned by various factors from the physical and biological to the psychological and sociological. Our power to actualize personal intent is limited by all of these levels and types of causality. But notice how, even speaking of biological, psychological, and sociological constraints on our personal agency is to affirm that there is indeed an individual will, albeit one that is somewhat less free than one might want or imagine it to be. But if personal agency were to be denied on a physical — or even, as we will come to momentarily — on a *logical* level, then it becomes illogical or nonsensical to conceive of a particular person, such as oneself, being capable of even having and following a line of thought, let alone acting on it. Thoughts are already intentional acts. Without personal agency, having them — and having them be *one's own* — makes no sense at all.

Although I am not inclined, in Kantian fashion, to assert that beginning from the phenomenological standpoint of having personal agency is justified *a priori*, one could formalize this approach as such. "Since we self-evidently know that we have personal agency..." is the claim that stands at the fountainhead of all dimensions of my thought. My philosophical project is elaborated by tracing out the implications of this basic existential fact. It is, in large part, a negative tracing or one that defines a negative space of potentiality. In other words, I argue how the world *cannot* be constituted if we are to have at least *some* degree of personal agency. What is left over is the type of matrix of possibility — or rather of virtuality — that *would* allow for us to be responsible for thinking, feeling, and doing things that we willed ourselves to do, or to imagine. Imagination, the precondition of all creativity and innovation, is also an exercise of intentional agency.

It is possible to frame an argument against four different types of ontology (and onto-theology) that would preclude personal agency: 1) scientific materialism; 2) logical determinism; 3) theological monism;

and 4) radical nihilism. One structured, but dynamic, matrix of potentiality that remains as an ontological basis for personal agency is a world of relatively independent and somewhat disjointed and conflicting centers of force, with variant endurance, each of which struggles with the others to make a *cosmos* out of *chaos* through the interplay of *logos* and *psyche* at every level of sentience with the capacity to process and communicate information — from bacterium to superhuman consciousness. The creative power of primordial desire, and its relationship to power qua energy, plays an essential role here. So do the interrelated ideas of freedom and the spectral.

The argument against "scientific materialism" is fairly straightforward. One might also brand the target at hand here as "scientific determinism" or "mechanistic reductionism." I more or less use all of these terms interchangeably when exposing how this ontology obviously cannot be consistent with an affirmation of personal agency. I have also provided a provocative genealogy of this ontology, which dates back to the late 1600s, and which became dominant in the 18th and 19th centuries, enduring well into the twentieth century despite being challenged by both Quantum Theory and Parapsychology. Especially in the chapter of *Prometheus and Atlas* titled "Reason and Terror," I argue that this ontology was contrived and deployed by the Jesuit Order with a view to destroying the alchemical non-reductionist type of science rising in the Renaissance. The latter posed a direct threat to the Church's authority over "spiritual" matters. So, a strictly materialist and reductively mechanistic "science" was constructed, in the first instance by actual paid agents of the Jesuits, such as René Descartes, and later by lackeys who never thought to question the ontological foundations of this paradigm. The Jesuits aimed to define the spiritual — including the psychological — dimension of human life, which is, frankly, the *whole* of it, as within the domain of the ecclesiastical interpretive authority. Post-alchemical "Science" was meant to become so inhumanly intolerable, including in its denial of free will, that even thinking people, let alone the masses, would remain within the bosom of Christianity for fear of otherwise losing their "souls" and every shred of empathy, or any meaningful connection to others and to a world of shared human concerns.

The obtusely inhuman and insensible brutality of such a world model must in part account for why it was never very popular in Classical Antiquity, whether in the Greece of Epicurus or in the Rome of Lucretius. Plato and Aristotle had an infinitely more reasonable view of the world, and this was recognized by most thinking men. Only after a millennium of darkness as slaughtered lambs under the dominion of Jesus Christ did so-called "intellectuals" become so stupid as to buy into reductive, mechanistic materialism. After all, as per the dualism of Descartes, which in its essence is still affirmed even by Kant, they could look to the sphere of religious life for the meaning that had been exorcised from the secular and profane realm of physical Nature.

This view of the world is "atomic." It is utterly irrelevant whether the "atoms" are replaced with subatomic "particles" such as electrons, protons, and neutrons — until and unless one begins to notice quantum physical properties on this level (or at the level of "quarks" and non-existent "superstrings"), which put the lie to this whole ontology. *Atom*, in the original Greek, means "uncuttable." It was their term for a fundamental and particular constituent, long before actual particles became empirically observable. The *Atomic* Theory, or more accurately the ontology that became fundamental to theorization in the mode of scientific materialism or mechanistic reductionism, actually emerged from out of a logical problem. It is a problem first posed by Zeno (490–430 BCE), as exemplified by his infamous paradox of Achilles and the Tortoise.

According to Zeno's paradox, if Achilles and a tortoise run a race against one another, but the tortoise is given a slight head start, Achilles, who was known for his agility, should still never be able to catch up with the tortoise, let alone surpass him. This is because before spanning the distance that the tortoise has been able to travel with his head start, Achilles would have to span half of that distance. Before he can span half of that distance, he would have to span one-quarter of it, and before that, one-eighth of the distance, and so on and so forth, down to infinitely divisible intervals that essentially bring Achilles to a standstill. It is a rather lame story, actually, because according to its own logic, the tortoise should not have been able to gain any ground either, regardless of being given a head start.

The point of the so-called "paradox" is that movement in space becomes absurdly impossible if matter is considered infinitely divisible. Rather, matter must be constituted of certain indivisible and therefore fundamental building blocks. Despite appearances, everything has to be made out of uncuttable particles, each of which has some miniscule but measurable magnitude. The Greeks called these *atomon*, from their word for "uncuttable." In the early modern age, they were rebranded as "corpuscles" and are now referred to as "elementary particles" (such that our so-called "atoms" are no longer *atomon* in the Greek sense). Since each of them has a definite magnitude, space, as an extension defined by an expanse of matter, can be measurably traversed by one or another thing made of atoms. This, in turn, gives us relative frames of time, as measured by rates of movement in space. While this *atomic* schema seems simple, getting rid of it leaves us with all kinds of problems with the linearity of space and the sequential chronology of time — difficulties that, since Quantum Theory, we have in fact been faced with and which boggle the mind.

Let us bracket those difficulties for the moment and come to the main point of laying out the core structure of scientific materialism or mechanistic reductionism. Namely, the problem that such an ontology poses for personal agency. By virtue of their elementary character, elementary particles — or Greek *atoms* — have no sentience. They have only the simplest positional characteristics, and all phenomenologically experienced qualities supposedly "emerge" from out of complex combinations of them that form, first physical, then chemical, and finally biological structures. Except that biochemistry is illusory on this view of the world, let alone the complex phenomenon of the human mind or the minds of other sentient animals. Our very act of observing these structures in a manner that discerns some as chemical and others as biological or psychological is an intentional act, and there is nowhere whatsoever from out of which such intentionality can emerge in a world that can be reductively analyzed in terms of particles interacting with one another according to mechanistic causality. All talk of "emergent properties" is, in this context, sheer nonsense.

The truly consistent materialist worldview is one that makes having anything like a view of the world an impossibility. It would not be a "world" at all. One would be dealing with a gigantic tinker-toy construction that is built up, in a mechanistic manner, from out of billiard ball type causality. Like everything else that is supposedly "biological," human brains would be put together in the same way and the "decisions" that they supposedly make would in every case have been made *for* them in as deterministic a manner as the collisions of balls on a billiard table. Except that there would be no billiard player anywhere to be found. One wades into absurdity even trying to find metaphors to describe such a situation. Absurdities and chimerical paradoxes as well, since "determinism" in this context might as well be sheer randomness or blind chance. When viewed from a sufficiently abstract and overarching perspective (as if there is any "perspective" at all in such a "world"), there is no reason *why* anything should be "determined" in one way rather than another. Determinations are made by agents who have aims or purposes for determining. In a mechanistically materialist ontology, all that can be said is that *shit happens*.

A much more profound and complex form of determinism is logical rather than physical in nature, although it can be seen as implicitly lurking behind most forms of mechanistic materialism at a deeper level. It might even be said that what I have called "logical determinism" is a necessary but not a sufficient condition of mechanistic materialism. There are forms of "logical determinism" that do not necessarily presuppose mechanistic materialism, and that could be seen as the basis for "Rationalism" in general, but mechanistic materialism always already implicates within its ontology a tacit logical determinism deeper than the supposed "determinism" of efficient causality that might as well be randomness.

This relation between the two has to do with what Bertrand Russell referred to as "atomic propositions." For truth claims in logic to be assessed, propositions need to be broken down or analytically reduced to the simplest and most precise forms possible. At this point, the basic elements in these propositions are supposed to refer to states of affairs in the world as these have been, similarly, analytically reduced to the most basic constituents and relations that are conceivable. According to mechanistic materialism this would be elementary particles and the causal relations that obtain between them. A logical determinist could accept this. However, logical determinism might also alternatively define these basic constituents as particular individuals and objects, albeit defined with as little ambiguity and as much precision as possible.

In any case, what is important here is that when a counterfactual statement is made, such that a proposition does not align with the state of affairs that it purports to represent, so that the statement is "false" in our world, it must still be the case that the proposition has a referent in some *other* world than ours. That is, so long as the proposition is not blatantly illogical, such that its referent would be "a square circle" or a "married bachelor." So long as a thing or event is possible, definitionally speaking, a proposition regarding that state of affairs does refer to it — in the sense of reaching out to it — in some *other possible world* than ours. But because logical determinists do not want to accept the "imagination" as a legitimate phenomenon, since it is as vague and dynamically polymorphous as dreams are, these *other possible worlds* cannot be considered "imaginary." They are *real* worlds which, as David Lewis put it, are just causally isolated from ours.

Despite their causal isolation from our world, all of the states of affairs in each of these other *possible* worlds that are not our *actual* world, are co-located in a single logical space that is timelessly complete and internally consistent. For anything that anyone could formulate as a proposition there is a world where that is actually the state of affairs that obtains. In other words, every logical but false statement in our world is a true statement in some other world that is part of the same logical space. Whether the proposition is true in the "past" of that other world or will be true in its "future" is immaterial. Logical space is timeless. All configurations of all possible states of affairs are already contained in it, such that somewhere, somewhen, any logically coherent proposition will be true even if it is false in what appears to be the present moment of the world that is actual for us.

In terms of the problem of personal agency, the issue is that such an ontology presupposes that anything that any "one" seems to think or to will or to do is something that some version of that "person" has already done in some actually existent world in logical space. One is not even actualizing it, as if it were a "mere possibility" before one "decided" on making it so. No "one" makes *anything* so. Everything already is every way that it could be, and everyone has already been and done anything that anyone identifiable as such-and-such a "person" could possibly do. This makes sheer nonsense out of intentionality and agency. We own our acts, including our mental acts, because they are exclusionary. Each person defines herself as that "one" she is by thinking or willing or doing this *rather than* that *for some reason* of her own, whether that "reason" is construed as pragmatic, ethical, or aesthetic. In the name of Reason Itself, in other words with the aim of rationally grounding logic *as such*, the ontology of logical determinism makes nonsense out of all those reasons that actually mean anything. In other words, the putative ontological ground of Rationalism is — from any practical perspective — irrational.

As in the case of the *atomic* solution to Zeno's paradox, although logical determinism seems counter-intuitive and bizarre, and although I am right to reject it, the consequences of rejecting it are problematic. What would counterfactual propositions *refer* to then? To "imaginary" states of affairs? What is the "imaginary" and what is its relation to the actual? If there is imagination, can it even be sharply distinguished from the actual such that only the latter is deemed "real"? Or perhaps, as the later Ludwig Wittgenstein realized, against his own earlier perfection of analytic logical atomism, it may be the case that propositions do not *refer* to anything at all. Perhaps language, even the most seemingly logical language, is not *referentially* propositional. Perhaps it is expressive and performative, in which case poetry is as "valid" as mathematics, because neither of them are actually about "validity" at all. Different forms of language are about what we can *do* with them, after we *imagine* or dream of doing anything.

For now, though, the point is simply that protecting the conditions of possibility for personal agency requires not just a rejection of mechanistic materialism, but also abandoning the kind of reductionism endemic to a rational grounding of logic that would give propositions the character of being "true" or "false." For the sake of retaining agency, we have to relinquish this conception of truth as verification or correspondence, just as we have to recognize that logic is nothing more than a pragmatic tool and one form of language among others. Forms of language that express the absurd and the irrational are no less "valid" than more rational expressions that are conventionally deemed "logical."

In the context of the right *story*, even a "married bachelor" or a "square circle" can be aptly expressive of the qualities of a certain person or situation. Dreams also have a "logic," so to speak. Actually, as I see it, they reveal the *logos* that is the primordial matrix of meaning from out of which analytic "logic" is abstractly deracinated before being illegitimately set up as a tribunal over the meaningfulness of all manners of expression.

To move from the realm of language back to that of physics, it should not be hard to see why the argument against logical determinism — in defense of personal agency — is also an argument against an infinity of parallel universes, in very many of which we would have doppelgangers whose lives varied from ours ever so slightly in some cases, and greatly in other cases. Such a cosmology is the consequence of the Graham-Everett-Wheeler or Many Worlds Interpretation (MWI) of Quantum Theory. Instead of admitting that consciousness, or rather, sentient observation, is what collapses the probability distribution of the wave function into a definite and measurable particle, the MWI posits that quantum superposition is resolved at every moment in every way that it could possibly be in a perpetually branching plethora of parallel universes. In some of these the dinosaurs never went extinct, and so we do not have doppelgangers at all. In others of them, we have doppelgangers who have almost identical lives, and in yet others, the lives of our doppelgangers vary considerably from ours — to the point that some version of us exists that has done things we thought it inconceivable or horrendously wrong for us to do in a situation that we once faced.

I do not say that these other versions of ourselves made "choices" other than our own, because this whole notion makes as much nonsense out of "choices" as logical determinism does. Only an individual chooses anything, and only for a reason that follows from out of the personal history, which is to say the unique experiences, of that person, and the character that has formed on the basis of these. "Choices" are obviously intentional, self-referential, and implicate personal responsibility both for the choice and for its consequences. If versions of us exist that have seemingly made every "choice" that we "chose" not to make, then none of these are persons making any real choices at all. That does not mean there is no version of the Multiverse idea that would allow for some kind of free will. If, for whatever physical or cosmological reason, there were a limited number of parallel universes, and only a few doppelgangers of ourselves, all of whom are different expressions of a similar character that we recognize to be ours, and, moreover, each of these worlds is accessible to the others, so that these versions of us could meet and influence each other's lives, then that would not necessarily pose an ontological problem for personal agency. It would be a very different Multiverse conception than that which follows from the MWI.

For all intents and purposes, the cosmology of the MWI subsumes the very idea of individual personhood — together with intentionality and purposefulness *as such*. It is the unstated and implicit ontological basis for this cosmology that leads to these consequences, an ontological basis that is built out of the same misguided rationalist motivations that lead people to logical determinism and to reductionistic materialist determinism.

These misguided motivations can be considered of a secular scientific kind, characteristic of rationalists, but the totalitarian ontology implicit in theological monism, which is also based on the same need for certainty, is equally incompatible with any affirmation of personal agency and individual responsibility. As compared to finite gods, "God" is almost inevitably defined as omniscient and omnipotent. Whether it is the Hindu conception of Brahman, the Judeo-Christian God, or the idea of Allah around which Islam revolves, God or the Supreme Being is believed to be all-knowing and all-powerful. This follows from the idea that the mind of this One encompasses infinity and eternity, and that, despite illusory appearances or human misconceptions, everything that ever was, is now, or ever will be, is an expression of the will of this One.

There can be no defensible conception of personal agency within the context of such a belief. No one would be responsible for choosing, or doing, or creating, or inventing anything whatsoever. Every seemingly brilliant invention, every creative masterpiece, and every horrendously unethical deed would actually be nothing more than an instantiation and expression of God's will, and it would have been known, in advance, by the mind of this God as an inevitability. Any claims to the contrary (I will not dignify them by calling them "arguments") are not just false, but downright absurd. They can only be accepted blindly and "on faith." Free will as a "miracle" that is gifted to man by God is such a piece of sheer nonsense. Again, it matters not whether the God in question is Brahman, the Lord, Allah, or the One of the Platonists (whose doctrines ought not to be confused with Plato's own thinking, as if it is this One qua Supreme Being that Plato meant by the Form of the Good). As best as we can trace it in what is left to us of history, this conception of the One goes back to Parmenides. The way that he framed it, against the Nothing, brings us to another notion that is fundamentally incompatible with affirming any degree of free will.

Buddhism, or more properly the Buddha Dharma, does not fall into the trap of theological Monism. Gautama Buddha accepts that there are gods (who ought *not* to be worshipped), but he rejects the existence of anything like God. However, very much in the same vein as Parmenides considering the counter-argument to his defense of Monism, but much more elaborately and with greater sophistication, Buddha suggests that everything finite and transient is illusory. This *maya* is not a veil of an infinite and eternal Brahman. Rather, it veils Nothingness in the sense of no-thing-ness. Buddha rejected struggle, including violent struggle, for the sake of creative improvement of the world, and concluded that life is ultimately no more than suffering for no purpose other than realizing the pointlessness of suffering. He did so on the basis of a false ontological conclusion that everything is, at bottom, nothing at all. Since no thing has any inherent essence because its origination and dissolution are co-dependent with the arising of other illusory things, and since everything is ephemeral and no absolutely enduring substance is to be found anywhere, Buddha reasoned (albeit falsely) that nothing is worth striving for other than an annihilation of the (illusory) self, wherein one becomes the nothing beneath and beyond beings. (I am speaking here of Gautama's teaching and to an extent also of Zen Mahayana, not the doctrine of Padmasambhava, namely Vajrayana, or any other forms of Tantra.)

Nietzsche was right to charge Buddha with being a nihilist, even with having achieved the perfection of nihilism. Where Buddha goes wrong, ontologically (and therefore, eventually ethically), is to measure the reality of things against what he himself recognizes as a false standard. If there is in fact nothing that exists with an unconditioned essence and that endures eternally, then what sense does it make to see the world as *maya* or illusion simply because phenomena are conditioned by one another in their genesis and are all temporally ephemeral? Anything essentially eternal is, by Buddha's own admission, a deluded projection, whether it takes the form of an *atman* or of *Brahman*. Then why deny things — and persons — reality because they come up short against its presumed characteristics?

"Reality" is a purely pragmatic category, defined by persons who *really* have things to do. *Of course* they are finite! How or why would this make people and the things that they are concerned with any less valuable or meaningful?! *As compared to what?!* A meaningful world is a finite world. It is against an infinite horizon that our projects become meaningless. It is no horizon at all, since it has no conceivable perspective corresponding to it. The Nothingness of the Buddha is an inversion of the Infinite and Eternal One. If it does not make as much nonsense out of personal agency as what it is an inversion of, then it at least mistakes the ontological significance — or, rather, disregards the ontological *primacy* — of personhood as the phenomenological standpoint for thinking about anything at all.

Whereas Gautama sees desire as a quintessentially negative phenomenon, one which perpetuates illusion and always only ends with suffering, desire is the true wellspring of my thought. Desire implies a lack and a need, as much as it is also a generative force. But its creative power is destructive as well, so that in addition to implicating incompleteness desire is also inconceivable without conflict. This is the occulted conspiracy of Eros and Strife in the womb of the world process. To see desire, not at the foundation of my philosophical project — for it quite deliberately lacks a foundation — but as an upsurge from out of the abyss of unfathomable and immeasurable chaos, is to recognize strife in its striving essence as intrinsic to the nature of existence.

I will not say that it is the opposite of taking the One qua a Perfect or Supreme Being as ontologically fundamental, because the symmetry for such a comparison is lacking. In fact, my ontology is as radically asymmetrical as it is irremediably incomplete. Chaos, as the unfathomable and immeasurable, has nothing in common with the conception of the Nothing or Nothingness that would be a symmetrical inversion of a positively infinite and eternal Unity of Being, one which would always already be complete in itself. There is no mind capable of grasping Chaos, not even the mind of any putative God, nor is Chaos a negation of the Being of beings in the way that Buddha took beings to be *maya* against the background of *Shunyata*. If this primordial desire, acting on a cosmic level (from out of Chaos), were to be expressed in Sanskrit, the best term would probably be the *spanda* (creative pulse) of *Shakti* (Power) conceived of both as the essence of *kama* (Eros) and as the force behind the *lila* or "cosmic theatrical play" that should never be dismissed as mere *maya*. There is no thing whatsoever behind or beyond this play, not even Nothing (which, as noted above, is a deluded and equally totalizing projection based on an inversion of the false concept of an infinite and eternal Being). Middle Persian (Pahlavi) provides a better description of this than any Sanskrit terminology. It is the seduction of *Zurvan* by *Az* from within, which first births *Ahriman* and then, only remedially, *Ahura Mazda*.

Primordial desire is the desire *to be*, but it is never quite fulfilled. No thing and no one ever *really is* anything or anyone at all. This is what Gautama Buddha was trying to get at with his conception of co-dependent arising or dependent origination, and the way in which it renders all things *shunya* or of the voidness and all persons *anatta* or lacking an essential, self-identical substantiality. The fullest moments of the coming to be such and such are only as full as an orgasm. They are at the same moment a giving up and letting go of what seems like it is coming into itself or coming into its own. The relational dynamic of these ecstasies of existence is of a piece with their paradoxical duality. Desire screams from out of the abyss. To have the courage to hear this scream is to be called to Erosophia.

Inwardly divided and lacking with regard to what is outside of it, primordial desire is the Life Force (*élan vital*) that is also a Death Drive, which brings to its demise anything that would presume to endure in perpetuity. Life is change, but not sheer transformation of a kind that could ever come to an end, or repeat the same configurations forever, after having — over the course of enough time — exhausted a vast but finite and logically definable set of possibilities. Such an "eternal return of the same," conceived ontologically (unlike in the case of Nietzsche's use of it as an ethical litmus test) would not be Life at all. It would be an exercise in futility, on a cosmic scale, which is more or less what both Gautama Buddha and the Samkhya school of Vedantic theosophy saw it to be, thereby arriving at the pessimistic maxim that "life is suffering," which is to say *pointless* suffering, with the only point or aim being to "snuff it" (the literal meaning of *nirvana* as the blowing out of a candle flame).

Rather, Life is a game of perpetual seduction. For its generative force to endure beyond the durations of any particular beings that are — or *who* are — an expression of it, demands not just change but growth, which is to say creative evolution. This is the basic impetus of the structuring process which forms order out of Chaos. The primordial desire that gives Life its force is ontologically prior to the structure-formation, dissolution, and transformation that serves this Life Force. To deploy a crude but compelling analogy: however much she may repress this fact, a woman's desire precedes, exceeds, and outstrips the erotic engagement with any man who may, for a time, serve it. The girl's desire even comes before her own "womanhood" and has the transgressive power to exceed femininity, revealing that it has no fixed essence. In relation to the Life Force, every honest woman is a harlot. Otherwise, she is already dying. The same is true of all existence. To know this is to have transgressed the bounds of Philosophy and entered into Erosophia.

The permutations of Logos that weave a Cosmos from out of Chaos are ontologically secondary and subordinate to the primordial desire, which calls them forth as ever more complex forms of a sentience that eventually comes to know itself as Psyche. The desire to *come* into being and to be known *comes* first. It is a scream from out of the abyss. The rest of Logos spirals, fractal-like, from out of the first word, which can only be heard as an echo of this abyssal scream, forever reverberating in the pulsing blood and electrical fire of every being. From the beginning the Word was *"fuck!"* At once imploring, inviting, and imperative — in a state beyond these distinctions — like the cry of a woman having her twentieth orgasm in a row, having lost her self in finding her true will. It is a Word divided against itself, a primordial cleavage, and an ontological cleft, but for which it could not be a coming together. Logos comes into beYng (*seYn*) as individuation through strife without which there could be no seduction through eros, and no pro-creation, at any level of existence. *Sophia* or that Wisdom which lies beyond Knowledge, both as *episteme* and even as *noesis*, is an intuitive insight into (if not an "under-standing" of) the nature of this *Eros*.

Logos is the structuring process by means of which a Cosmos emerges from out of Chaos. Zarathustra calls this *Asha* (Old Persian *Arta*). But the manifestation of discernible beings from out of the seething abyss of Chaos also has, as a *sine qua non* (a necessary precondition), nodes of reflexive awareness that arise intrinsically from out of the syntactical structures of variant, divergent, and convergent *logoi* (forms or types of Logos). Beings are only there for (*nur da sein für*) someone — or at least some*thing* sentient, if not conscious. Consequently, it can be said that Psyche is a fourth basic term of Ontology together with Chaos, Cosmos, and Logos. It is in the interplay of these four aspects of phenomena that things become anything for anyone. Chaos, Cosmos, Psyche, and Logos are what Heidegger would have called ontologically "equiprimordial." They form the Chaosmic Psyche-Logos of Becoming. These are the four most fundamental facets of the prism of Erosophia.

Referring back to the arguments against both Logical Determinism and Theological Monism, we can reject any singular, complete, whole, or universal manifestation of Psyche. Rather, psychical nodes are each finitely perspectival. There can never be a coherent conception of anything like an infinite perspective. Every horizon of awareness is finite, even if some perspectives are much broader than others — such as, for example, the perspective of *Ahura Mazda* in the thought of Zarathustra. A perspective is, moreover, always a scope of potential action. In this way, Psyche is also subordinate to the Life Force. That sentient being which ceases to have any will to act would also cease to have any perspective on things. It would, in one way or another, disintegrate and dissolve into the background of Chaos. This disintegration or dissolution is what Gautama Buddha meant by *nirvana*. It is a negation of Life, or rather of oneself as an expression of Life's enduring Force.

Whereas the eventual disintegrative dissolution of all particular things and persons back into Chaos is inevitable, to will this — or rather, being more precise, to affirm this by refusing to will anything — is to deny the categorical imperative or fundamental directive of creative evolution: *maximization of indefinitely prolonged creativity and innovative development*. Unlike Philosophy, within the sphere of which Gautama remains, Erosophia is never skeptically or contemplatively neutral with regard to this denial or affirmation. While the ontological principle of Psyche is never instantiated as anything like a singular God, it is nonetheless the case that the highest or broadest — or perhaps one might even say the deepest — psychical nodes in the Cosmos, those of greatest complexity, must seek the experience of wonder, astonishment, and inspiration in the face of *the novel*. Otherwise, they would implode in the gravity of the vastness of their own comprehension of the Cosmos. Even for these beings, so far evolved beyond us, existential despair would be a necessary consequence of knowing everything worth knowing without any expectation of experiencing anything new. The Cosmos must remain an open system even for these beings, and it is the background of Chaos that allows for this — albeit Chaos, with its unfathomable wellspring of energy, being ever-transformed by Logos.

Logos, like Psyche, is an ontological principle without any singular instantiation. There are, rather, *logoi* of varying types and complexities. As expressions of a structuring-principle, each is a game with its own rules, set within the context of the inescapable *play*. There is, moreover, interplay between them. But there is nothing beyond all of them, as if they could all ever be taken together and encompassed with regard to some logical equivalent of an outer space. That brings us back to the argument against Logical Determinism. We are only ever within, or between, these games. Nor are more complex games built from out of simpler ones. Rather, the rules of plant life and its interplay with the game of life on the level of bacteria have as its determinative context the games of more complex forms of *logoi* relevant to social insects, higher animals, humans, and more evolved humanoids. But above all, *the play is the thing* that is served by these games, which include both forms of language and narrative development that provoke and sustain war — namely war games — and also games of seduction or erotic play. Neither are these necessarily mutually exclusive. Like all language games, they could be interpenetrating. Such language games structure the epistemic framework of all forms of knowledge.

Perhaps it is my conception of what "knowledge" (Greek *episteme*) is, or of what it is *not*, that is the most revolutionary aspect of Erosophia. This is not to deny the fundamental status of the ontological dimension of my thought, but my ontology is so radically anti-foundational that its implications only begin to become more tangibly discernible in the epistemology that is an outgrowth of it. Moreover, my ethical and political philosophy really does emerge from out of my conception of knowledge, not just as *episteme* but also as *noesis* and *gnosis*. It is an ethics and politics of the "knower" and the seeker of wisdom (*Sophia*), not a moral doctrine or a political ideology that could or should be abstracted from this revolutionary epistemology and applied in the way that Marxism was applied, in feudal Russia and China of all places, without any proper and commensurate understanding of the epistemology (or ontology) of Hegel. (Only in Continental Europe were Marxists ever really concerned with the Hegelian foundations of Communism, and even there, only the intelligentsia who had little control over ethical activism and political programs.)

Just as my ontology challenges the conventional conception of ontology by refusing to recognize Being as foundational to existence (here I am in good company with Heraclitus and Nietzsche, if not also with the later Heidegger), my epistemology also deconstructs the scholastic definitions of a theory of knowledge. However much these definitions may disagree with one another, in a debt to Aristotle (whether acknowledged, unacknowledged, or even unconscious) and perhaps also based on a superficial reading of Plato, almost every epistemology, from that of Descartes and Kant through to Hegel and Russell, presupposes that knowledge on the part of the subject corresponds to, or stands in some relation with, a putatively objective truth about Reality or at least about the world as it can ever be "known" by us.

Together with Nietzsche, James, Bergson, Heidegger, Wittgenstein, Fort, Kuhn, and Feyerabend, I challenge this basic assumption and build an epistemology that is not grounded on it. To call it "epistemological anarchism" is not entirely false, but somewhat overly simplistic and misleading — especially when this characterization leads to unjustified assumptions about what kind of ethics and political philosophy would have to follow from such an anarchic epistemology.

Rather than demarcating a single point of departure for my epistemology, it would be more accurate to say that its assault on foundationalism or objectivism or realism is made on multiple fronts and has a number of different facets. Still, we have to start somewhere. One facet is the argument that there is no objective "reality" any more than there is a self-identical "subject" who could know it. Another front on which the assault takes place is with regard to the conception of knowledge as representation. I argue, instead, that knowledge is about *creation*. It is a process of production. The "truth" is what *works*, in other words, what has the *power* to *do* one or another thing. These two facets of my epistemology are both outgrowths of a recognition of the priority of *techne* over *episteme*.

As all processes of production, knowledge is historical. In any given epoch, knowledge is formulated, structured, and filtered through what we might call "dominants" (following Fort) or "paradigms" (following Kuhn and Feyerabend). In his post-structuralist epistemology, Foucault coined the term "epistemes" to denote them. These are overarching epistemic frameworks which, mostly unconsciously, limit the types of theories that can be developed within the context of them.

Wittgenstein would have called the mesh of these frameworks "hinge propositions" or propositions upon which all others hinge within the context of one or another "language game." Different language games hinge on different propositions remaining unquestioned. Where this becomes hard for most people to swallow, especially those who fancy themselves scientifically-minded individuals, is when one recognizes that the most fundamental axioms in mathematics and the so-called "laws" of physics are nothing more than hinge propositions in another language game. They have nothing to do with "reality." In a different language game, the zodiacal constellations of Astrology or the archetypal symbols of the Tarot more *effectively* describe how the world works — which is not at all to say that these matrices of meaning are any more "real" or veridical. Feyerabend shocked the intellectual community when he argued this, even though Fort had preceded him by about half a century in making essentially the same point.

Whether we use the terminology of dominants (Fort), paradigms (Kuhn and Feyerabend), epistemes (Foucault), or hinge propositions (Wittgenstein), or deploy these terms more or less interchangeably, the point is that sense emerges from out of nonsense, and it does so *narratively*. Here Nietzsche and Heidegger figure into my framing of positive epistemological concepts from out of this negative or anarchic deconstruction of classic epistemology. Following Nietzsche in his understanding of the primacy of art, with its aim of creation, over science, with its will to truth, and following Heidegger in his phenomenological analysis of the ontological priority of the essence of technology or craft (Greek *techne*) over theoretical science (Latin *scientia*), I developed the epistemic dimensions of concepts such as the Spectral Revolution and Novel Folklore or Phenomenal Authorization.

In sum, these are concerned with developing a free relation to different paradigms, without allowing any of them to become "dominant" (in Fort's sense), such that all of them are merely models more or less suited to accomplishing different things *in practice*. They are programmatic simulacra or virtual structures that render different "realities" by making one or another type of innovation or invention practicable. So-called "nature" is itself an artifact of this epistemic production, and it is empowering for us to become more conscious of this. That would authorize us with more authorship over phenomena, and it is the epistemic dimension of the Spectral Revolution as the last scientific revolution. The last one because it would be a revolution beyond the need for revolutionary shifts between paradigms, a revolution that would once and for all favor simultaneous use of divergent paradigms for different ends. It would also be a recognition that technological science is actually a meta-narrative operating on the level of the lore of a folk, albeit with more power than any other folklores — more power to shape and reshape worlds of meaning into a Cosmos with the broadest possible horizon. That is to say, a *novel* folklore, not simply in that it is new, but in a reflection of the ontological significance of the *novel*.

This account of science and its relationship with technology qua craft and the narrative element of art also serves to draw a distinction between science, as a pursuit of knowledge, and philosophy, as a love of wisdom. What is more is that the kind of "love" in question here is problematized by my epistemology. It leads to a recognition that *philia* is inadequate to the task of "loving" wisdom. *Sophia* demands "love" qua *eros*. I first coined the term *Erosophia* in my essay "The Pharmakon Artist" in *Lovers of Sophia*. That essay was concerned with Plato's esoteric doctrine and the deeply duplicitous way in which he occulted it, while dialectically catalyzing necessary errors in the history of thought.

Far beyond specific instances of noble lies, Plato's whole style of doing philosophy can be legitimately characterized as a kind of diabolical dialectics. This represents a radical break with the modality of

Pre-Socratic philosophy, and although many of the great thinkers of the West, and of Iran as well, deploy some form of duplicitously esoteric writing, no philosopher writes in this diabolically dialectic style again until perhaps when Kierkegaard goes into schizoid mode and pens various books in the voice of assumed characters. But it is debatable whether Kierkegaard is even a proper "philosopher." In the event that we decide he is not, I would be the first philosopher since Plato to make use of diabolical dialectics. There may, however, be one huge exception. *If* the theory that "Will I Am Shake Spear" was really Sir Francis Bacon is in fact true, and I actually suspect that it is, then Bacon/Shakespeare would be a philosopher of the highest order and Plato's true successor in an absolutely masterful use of this positively diabolical methodology. My own efforts in *Psychotron* pale in comparison, but they are in the same vein.

The tremendous importance of Aesthetics in my philosophical project can already be inferred from what has been said of the diabolical dialectics of novel folklore or phenomenal authorization from an epistemological perspective, and from the fundamental concern of my ontology with freedom as a *creative* act. But even this does not state the case strongly enough. One could go so far as to say that my ontology and epistemology are radically aesthetic, in other words, that aesthetic considerations play the most profound and determinative part in defining their structure. Another way to put this is to concede that I have an essentially aesthetic conception of the basic phenomenological horizon of existence — not just of human existence, but the existence of *any* Dasein that is capable of thinking philosophically.

This is a substantive claim which would, for example, be invalidated by the discovery of a life form with Philosophy as part of its culture but without anything like fine art and lacking even the capacity to appreciate the beautiful, to make aesthetic judgements concerning what is sublime, or to debate what can be considered obscene. I am willing to wager that such an empirical discovery will *never* be made, because *in principle* such a form of life *cannot* possibly exist. There could be hive-minded life forms lacking aesthetic intuition, but they would also lack Philosophy and could not be considered *Dasein*. If they were ever able to somehow develop technology, perhaps in a quasi-parasitic manner, then they would be abominable *things*, not "people." Organisms perhaps, but not even "animals" deserving of a consideration of their sentience. It is an interesting question whether a more intelligent and industrious type of bees, ants, or termites would fall into this category. Would intelligent bees, or for that matter technological mantids, make art and appreciate beauty? I have speculated about this in different and divergent directions, coming down negatively on this question in my essay on Kant and Aliens in *Lovers of Sophia* and more positively in Chapter 7 of *Closer Encounters* — although the "mantids" there are not necessarily actual intelligent insects so much as they are shamanic shapeshifters.

In the history of Philosophy, I would count both Plato and Nietzsche as fundamental thinkers (Schelling is not in that class) for whom aesthetics played the same deeply determinative role as it does in my thinking. That claim is less controversial in the case of Nietzsche and far more controversial in the case of Plato, although I crafted a strong argument for it in my essay "The Pharmakon Artist." It is worthy of note that this essay was my first serious philosophical work, written at the age of 21. A concern with aesthetics went on to dominate the rest of my corpus, culminating in *Psychotron* (written between the ages of 39 and 42).

That the world is always already and only ever a matrix of meaning is a fundamental claim that runs through all of my philosophical work. This is obviously not a platitude or a position that can be taken for granted. The prevailing current of secular Western thought in late modernity held that the world is essentially meaningless and that, to the extent that people have any agency at all, which they probably do not have, what they find meaningful is a subjective projection onto this objective meaninglessness, whether on an individual or a societal level. I break radically with this cynical and nihilistic view by rejecting both materialism and (any other form of) reductionism.

What must be added to the ontological affirmation of personal agency and the epistemological conception of knowledge about the world, and the constitution of a world *as such*, as the product of language games, is what Heidegger grasped when he claimed that poetry is the most primordial form of language, and that mood is the fundamental attunement of existence. These are strikingly feminine statements coming from the pen of a card-carrying Nazi. Nietzsche, who despite his often-deplorable remarks regarding women, is even more consistently feminine in his manner of expression, once aptly wrote that "the world is a work of art that gives birth to itself."

The manifestation of beings — their becoming *such* — from out of Chaos is not an actualization of logically discernible and ontologically predefined possibilities. Were that to be the case, it would land us back in the quagmire of Logical Determinism with the problems that it poses for free will. Rather, the becoming of the Cosmos from out of Chaos — through Logos and Psyche — is a realization of the virtual. Inchoate and amorphous potentialities that are larvally latent in Chaos at any moment, haunting the present Cosmos from out of the fundamentally futural power of time, are not timeless possibilities that would be surveyable by some God in the eternal present of His mind. Reality is only ever a manifestation of the virtual.

The virtual is not only a matrix of potentiality for future becoming. It also permeates the past with an ineliminable spectrality, rendering historical events revisable. The rejection of logical determinism is also a dismissal of the ontological grounding for the physical concept of "block time." It is not the case that, as the Novikov Self-Consistency Principle falsely presumes, time travelers can only affect the past as part of Closed Time-like Curves (CTC). In other words, it is a mistake to believe that anything that a time traveler from the future does in the past must already have been part of that past (whether or not it was known to have been in the future from which she hails). Rather, as in the crude example of Marty McFly's morphing photograph in *Back to the Future*, the past really can be deformed and reformed by the actions of a time traveler. Even simply receiving information from a probable future can do this. That is what is involved in every case of Precognitive Remote Viewing data being used to prevent a certain thing, or better yet a certain part of a complex event, from happening in the way that the whole event was precognitively envisioned. (In the early 2000s, the "second 9/11" was prevented from happening in this manner by a team of remote viewers under the leadership of Lyn Buchanan.) Overwritten versions of the past are retained, in static form, in something like a cloud storage function of the Cosmos qua information processing system. This function is what the Sanskrit sages once called "the Akashic record."

Speaking as loosely, and as pragmatically, as we do when we conceptualize time as a fourth dimension of 3-d space, the virtual can be conceived of as a fifth dimension. This fifth dimension is neither a 3-d place nor a 4-d time, but a medium that affords us access to diverse space-times in a quasi-topological manner. It must be emphasized that the language of a "fifth dimension" is only as relevant here as the crude, but pragmatic, designation of psi as a "sixth sense" with regard to the more tangible five senses that structure our phenomenal experience. Just as Suhrawardi described this sixth sense not as simply another sense alongside the five that are better known, but as a *hessé moshtarak* or a matrix and nexus for the other senses, and, consequently, as the basis for the experience of synesthesia, the virtual, which Suhrawardi was already groping toward in his conception of *âlamé barzakh* (the projection-screen world), is not another dimension overlaying the fourth and third.

Instead, it is an implicate order best understood by analogy to holography. In the virtual dimension of the world, information is processed in a form that is analogous to the Fourier Transforms that encode things as seemingly chaotic swirl patterns on holographic film, which are only unfolded from out of this implicate order, as explicate

3-d projections in 4-d time, when a laser is shone onto the hologram. This laser is akin to the Psyche of sentient beings, materializing the Cosmos from out of the filtering and refractory processing of Chaos by Logos.

This emergence of what we take to be "reality" from out of virtuality accounts for seemingly paradoxical physical phenomena such as wave/particle duality, in other words, Heisenberg's Uncertainty Principle, as well as the quantum entanglement that Einstein dubbed "spooky action at a distance." These are artifacts in the fourth dimension of information processing taking place from out of the fifth dimension. They point back toward the occulted implicate order of the holographic film rather than the explicit image projected from out of the hologram. Except that, in this analogy, as Bohm understood well, the swirl on the holographic film must be conceived of as dynamic, revisable, and constantly in motion rather than static. A holo*movement*.

Nothing like the substantiality of a God or His Power to substantiate the world is possible within the dynamic, plasmatic, or ectoplasmic element of this virtuality. Only ghosts, hauntings from the future and shades of the departed. This is, more fundamentally and precisely, what was meant earlier when, in provisional terms, I stated that no thing really ever *is* anything. That formulation is made under a false standard of Reality, albeit one that has prevailed for most of the history of thought — from the Platonists to the Cartesians. Gautama's rejection of the phenomenal world as *maya* ("illusion" negatively conceived) is also a consequence of his captivation, however unconsciously and be-grudgingly, by the same false standard, albeit inverted from Being into Nothing (enough has been said about this above). Instead, the world as *lila* or theatrical play is a virtual reality — not a simulacrum of reality, but the virtual *as* the only reality. To return to the basic motivation and point of departure for this entire way of thinking, the virtuality of "the real" can be characterized both as the *spectral* and as the essence of freedom.

The spectral is the continuum of a spectrum wherein discernible states or frequencies ultimately bleed into each other such that any abstraction of one or another of them into polarities of a binary opposition must be admitted as merely provisional, practical, and lacking any "objective" validity. Spectrality is also the future-oriented temporal structure of existence as such, which renders becoming not just transformation but creative evolution. In other words, what Zarathustra called *Spenta Mainyu*. Here there comes into view the ontological profundity of my concept of the Spectral Revolution. The spectral in its meaning as the ghostly is another aspect of this futural sense of the specter as "what is to come" (German *die Zukunft*, French *l'avenir*, Persian *ayandeh*). That is because with a view to future becoming, or further transforming, anything or anyone that is now or has been *such* will in time necessarily become something "other" or even "alien." Zarathustra, with his vision of the *Frashgard* or future transformation of all existence, was the first person to contemplate this in (what is archivally left of) our recorded history.

The essence of freedom lies in this process of futural becoming. What is free is unbounded, and yet is bound for that which will take shape beyond itself. This is the ontological aspect of my seemingly paradoxical concept of Being Bound for Freedom. The freedom of each being in becoming anything or anyone — or for ceasing to be by perishing — also presupposes a multiplicity of potentially conflicting centers of force striving with one another to perpetuate themselves into the unbounded future. Again, Zarathustra was the first thinker to grasp this necessary connection between free choice and a world wherein conflict plays an indispensable role. To put it another way, ironically, although what is free is in a sense unbounded — unbounded by a completed logical structure, by an omnipotent God, etc. — the freedom of each being also necessitates its being bound by a finite horizon of intentionality and a particular perspective with regard to other such beings. Of course, both fission and fusion are possible with regard to distinct perspectives. The spectral essence of freedom tears beings apart as much as it brings them together in the conspiracy of Eros and Strife to play the longest game of all games. Every victory and every defeat, every triumph and every tragedy, is trumped by a wild card — by a Joker. Or if it is a deck of Tarot cards, then the card of the Devil. Except that the Devil is a woman in disguise.

Prometheism, considered as a kind of doctrine, not to say an ideology, became a brand for my Philosophy of the Future, but it has only ever been the exoteric façade of my thought. Or perhaps a strategic weaponization of my thinking — a flaming arrow fired by the bow of the Huntress. The esoteric level of my work as a philosopher has always been something deeper and even more dangerous. Where my heart lies can be seen from my very first essays, written long before *Prometheus and Atlas* (and only subsequently published in *Lovers of Sophia*), from my paper on Plato titled "The Pharmakon Artist," to my essay on Kafka titled "Trial Goddess," or "Serpent Power of the Superman" on Nietzsche and Tantra, my mystical reading of Marx and the metaphysical essence of Communism in "Prisoners of Power and Propriety," and frankly the whole of *Novel Folklore*, which was originally drafted before I wrote *Prometheus and Atlas* and was titled *Star Blood*. It is time for what was hidden between the lines of these works to be revealed. It is time to break the façade, remove the mask of Prometheus, and unveil the hitherto occulted face of my one true muse and mistress: Lucifera, of whom my fallen daughter Sophia was an avatar. It is time for Prometheism to give way to Erosophia.

Nietzsche saw Prometheus as a mask of Dionysus in the age of Greek tragedy, and Dionysus is the best friend of Artemis. It is Artemis, not Prometheus, who is the deepest and most central archetypal figure animating my corpus. "The name of the bow is life; its work is death." This is, of course, a cryptic reference to Artemis on the part of Heraclitus, who took refuge in her temple at Ephesus for the remainder of his life, following the contemptible democratic revolt of his city-state against the Persian Empire. The saying means, "Wisely choose the aim of your death, for which your whole life will have served as the bending back of a bow." To "sin" originally meant to "miss the mark," and only later took on its petty moralizing Christian connotations.

The connection between Artemis and Prometheus is via Mithra, the other major archetypal figure around which some of my writings are woven, most obviously and explicitly the text of *Iranian Leviathan*, which is subtitled *A Monumental History of Mithra's Abode*. As I explain in the early chapters of that book, Mithra was originally an androgynous deity of the northern Iranians (Scythians and Sarmatians), and Artemis represents the female aspect of that deity, worshipped principally by the Sarmatians or "Amazons" (as the Greeks called them), after the Scythians overemphasized the masculine aspect in the form of Mithra.

The original deity also went by the name of *Satana*, which is preserved amongst the Ossetians or Alans (latter-day Scytho-Sarmatians) of the Caucasus, precisely where the original *Amirani* form of the myth of Prometheus (and of his liberation by Hercules) also arose before migrating to Greece via Anatolia. Artemis, Mithra, and Prometheus were all associated with the morning star or light-bearer, namely Venus bringing the dawn or "Lucifer." This is why the Romans sometimes referred to Artemis as "Diana *Lucifera*." In other words, as the feminine aspect of Lucifer.

Satana was a titaness responsible for initiating heroes who do battle with the (unjust) gods. As the mother of the Gorgons, entwined by serpents, she was the prototype for later portrayals of Medusa. Perseus severing the head of Medusa is, in its most archaic stratum of meaning, a myth that encodes the Persian confrontation with those Scytho-Sarmatian cousins of theirs to the north who worshipped this goddess. Their matriarchically-inclined culture, wherein ferocious warrior women flourished and even at times ruled, became the basis for the Amazon myths of Greece. Among the Sarmatians who migrated West and settled, most prominently, in Ephesus where they built that temple that was one of the seven wonders of the ancient world, Satana came to be known by her epithet *Arta Amesha*, i.e., Artemis, meaning "Undying

Truth." The temple, rebuilt repeatedly, remained sacred to the Romans who renamed the great goddess Diana Lucifera. Many Roman citizens who were assembled in the city's theater thunderously hailed her name as they booed and shoed the Apostle Paul, when he made the mistake of coming to Ephesus to preach the Gospel of Jesus Christ.

Satana (pronounced *Shatana*, and so potentially related, via Indo-Iranian, to the Sanskrit *Chaitanya* or "Consciousness") is, as I have argued, the origin of the name *Satan* (or *Shaytan* in the Semitic languages), having been introduced into the Levant by Scythian marauders in the 8th century BC, who overran Israel on their way to Egypt. I suppose, then, that one could say that from an aesthetic perspective Satan is actually my core philosophical persona, but mainly in her aspect as Lucifera. Secondarily, and more exoterically, in his aspect of Prometheus. Satan or Satana is, of course, an androgynous — or rather, a hermaphroditic — figure, as the icon of Baphomet most aptly exemplifies, but to my mind he/r feminine aspect has always seemed more powerful. She's a bitch, a witch, a whore turning tricks, and the mother-fucking Mistress of the World. Lucifera, the nakedly Anti-Christian truth of the Divine Sophia. All of our ecstasies and struggles are but screams and muffled moans from out of the abyss of her desire.

CHAPTER 4

NOBLE LIES OF THE LEVIATHAN

Greater Iran, the fountainhead of the "Satanic" in world history, has always been at the heart of my work. As early as *Prometheus and Atlas* I argued that the Iranian colonization of Greece was a *sine qua non* for the development of Prometheus as an archetypal force in the global history of technological science. My study of Sadegh Hedayat's *The Blind Owl*, the most innovative and disturbing novel in the Persian language, namely *Novel Folklore*, the very first draft of which was written before *Prometheus and Atlas*, became the basis for a project of actually producing my own novel folklore in *Psychotron*. In *World State of Emergency*, penned years before I revisited the same challenge in *Prometheism*, I first grappled with the global threat of convergent advancements of singularity-level technologies in a context where my proposed solution was something like the formation of a new intercontinental Persian Empire construed as an "Indo-European World Order" with its administrative capital in Iran. Then there was the tome of *Iranian Leviathan*, my most extensive, and also my most problematic, treatment of all things Persian.

I am hard-pressed to think of anything substantive in *Novel Folklore* that requires contextual qualification, clarification, or revision. I believe it will stand the test of time as the most penetrating, profound, and far-reaching study of *The Blind Owl* and perhaps of Sadegh Hedayat in general. The same cannot be said for *World State of Emergency* and *Iranian Leviathan*. Both books are profoundly problematic when viewed in the hindsight of events that have transpired since, ordeals that I have endured, and how these have reshaped my strategies if not my fundamental concepts.

While these problems are in each case distinct, there is a common denominator that ought to be addressed first. During the period when I wrote these two books, I was a philosopher acting in the capacity that Plato was when he embarked on his ill-fated mission to try to turn the tyrant of Syracuse into a philosopher-king, or that Aristotle was when he wrote the divergent and contingent constitutions of various Greek city-states on contract. I was solicited to join an organization formally known as the Persian Renaissance Foundation, and informally as the Iranian Renaissance, in May of 2016, a few months after the publication of *Prometheus and Atlas* (in February of that year). By the late summer of 2016 I had entered the inner circle of this 501c3 "cultural" organization, which in turn began to operate (albeit clandestinely) at the highest level of the so-called "Iranian opposition" to the Islamic Republic. On paper my position was Senior Advisor to the Board and Executive Committee, but in fact I became a member of a secret triumvirate, planning group, and steering committee of sorts that was not even answerable to the Board or Committee. I have written in some detail about these events in both the chapter of *Psychotron* titled "Riding Satan's Ass," which is a reference to the Persian expression "*az kharé Shaytân biyâ pâyin*" ("come down from off of Satan's ass") and revisited it in the chapter of *Promethean Pirate* titled "The Flag of Ahab." Readers who are interested in more biographical detail regarding various dealings with this group can find them there.

Presently, I will limit myself to the broad outlines of the affair that are most relevant to the arguments that I crafted in *World State of Emergency* (2017) and *Iranian Leviathan* (2019). Both books were written as part of pragmatic socio-political projects involving the Persian Renaissance Foundation. *World State of Emergency* was dedicated to Shahin Nezhad, the leader of the organization, and the research and writing of *Iranian Leviathan* was privately funded by members of the organization — albeit under the book's originally proposed title of *Iranian Civilization.*

As a philosopher I had my own aims for what I wanted to achieve with these books on a conceptual level, and I did achieve those aims in a way that will continue to have a general applicability far beyond the scope of what concerns Iran. For example, the development of the concept of a "World State of Emergency" (in the book by that name) through a constructive critique of Carl Schmitt with a view to the convergent advancement of singularity-level technologies, or my further contributions to the understanding of the nature of sovereign power on an existential level by means of a critical reading of Thomas Hobbes' *Leviathan* through the lens of Mithraism and in view of Max Weber's analysis of charismatic leadership. The conceptual developments in these books are not limited to Political Philosophy, either. There are even ontological insights in them, especially concerning the existential significance of strife and the relationship between primordial chaos and order in the cosmos. But from a programmatic, not to say bureaucratic, standpoint, the point of departure for both of these books was a concern about the preservation of the territorial integrity of Iran with a view to impending violent changes in Iranian socio-politics.

From 2017 through 2019 Iran was faced with both the prospect of foreign military intervention, perhaps an Israeli airstrike, or even possibly outright invasion by the United States, while at the same time undergoing massive waves of internal unrest, which in the winter of 2017–2018 had reached a revolutionary pitch and evinced a nationalist tenor very different from the pro-democracy "Green Movement" demonstrations of 2009. Israel, Saudi Arabia, Pakistan, and even some members of the US Intelligence Community were supporting ethnic separatists in the Kurdistan, Azerbaijan, Khuzestan, and Baluchistan provinces of Iran, not only with a view to toppling the Islamic Republic but also with the aim of balkanizing Iran so that its vast natural resources could be more effectively looted by multinational corporations. So, from an institutional standpoint, what was needed was a grand vision that would help to shore up Iran's territorial integrity as the dying discourse of the Islamic Republic was replaced with a new geopolitical project.

World State of Emergency approached this challenge by arguing that certain convergent advancements in technology threatened human existence as such on a global scale. These included genetic engineering, robotics, augmented by Artificial Intelligence and Virtual Reality, as well as potential conflict for resource acquisition on the Moon with a view to fuel for fusion energy. In that book I referred to the Moon as "the Persian Gulf of the 21st century." I argued that since they were worldwide, these challenges required a World State to address them in a far more effective way than would be possible within the current United Nations International System.

Working with Carl Schmitt's existential-cultural conception of the nature of the political as such and turning Schmitt on himself in order to make a Schmittean case for a de-facto global sovereign to meet this unprecedented threat, I argued for a synergy of linguistically, culturally, and historically related civilizations into an "Indo-European World Order" encompassing the West, Russia, India, and the Buddhist world (led by Japan), with its capital in a post-Islamic Iran. In effect, Iran was framed as the new Persepolis, the "Gateway to All Nations," at the heart of this nominally 'Aryan', but actually cosmopolitan, World Order.

This geopolitical argument is by no means the only important contribution of *World State of Emergency* to Political Philosophy. Rather, the book also features the most penetrating and devastating critique of both Universal Human Rights and Liberal Democracy that has ever been deployed, at least by someone with something like a humanistic concern with defending freedom.

The critique of human rights takes the United Nations *Universal Declaration of Human Rights* as its point of departure, examining the drafting debates of the declaration leading up to its adoption in 1948, in order to expose the metaphysical commitments, contentions, and compromises that were made by representatives to the first UN General Assembly. These mainly concern the ways in which certain key articles of the UDHR, such as those on women's equal rights, freedom of thought and conscience, freedom of religion (including to change one's religion), fundamentally conflict with the unalterable tenants of certain religions such as Islam. I demonstrated the self-proclaimed eternal validity and unchangeable character of the legal verses of the *Quran*, and showed how they conflict with these putatively Universal Human Rights. Furthermore, I showed how a universal human right to democracy allows for the democratic election of Islamic governments, such as in Iran in 1979, who go on to violate the UDHR with a majoritarian popular mandate at the expense of women, minorities, and free thinkers.

This takes us into the critique of Liberal Democracy. *World State of Emergency* demonstrated how incoherent an ideology this really is. Democracy, from its origins in classical Greece to its revival by Rousseau in the lead-up to the French Revolution, is actually a deeply conservative political form insofar as it reaffirms the traditional way of life and customary prejudices of the majority of any society, including their mass religious convictions — or what Rousseau even explicitly argued ought to be recognized as a Civil Religion that defines the parameters of the General Will behind all democratic decision-making, such as in the legislative process. Liberalism, by contrast, is an ideology of the rights of the individual against or in the face of the majority, rights such as freedom of thought and conscience, and freedom of expression without censorship.

Moreover, Liberalism is based on a certain metaphysical conception of a universally shared human nature and of a metaphysically based trajectory of historical progress that represents a positive developmental unfolding of this nature. This liberal metaphysics, whether only tacit, as in the case of John Stuart Mill, or explicitly acknowledged, as in the case of the Marquis de Condorcet, is profoundly opposed to the tribalism of democracy. As Rousseau rightly argued, against those

Communists who think that there could ever be a worldwide Social Democracy, without the world sharing a single religious ethos and a single narrative of historical heritage, democracies are always national or even tribal in character. They affirm the traditions, customs, and heritage of one particular people. Whereas Liberalism makes an appeal to universality, and has a universal conception of the individual, which conflicts with the ethno-religious basis of any and every democracy.

Finally, *World State of Emergency* drew from Carl Schmitt's analysis of states of crises in parliamentary democracies and his concept of "the political" as the sovereign's power to decide on who is a friend vs. an enemy amidst a state of emergency (wherein the constitution of a country is suspended) in order to argue that neither a liberal democracy nor a human rights-based regime is capable of coherently and effectively dealing with the crisis of the convergent advancement of Singularity-level technologies. Genetic engineering, robotics, Artificial Intelligence, and so forth are technologies that require a global scope of uniform regulation if they are to be developed in a way that prevents them from being misused by bad actors (whether rogue states or terrorists) with consequences that are nothing less than apocalyptic for humanity as a whole. Neither the United Nations, as an institution that is even ideally based on the Universal Declaration of Human Rights, nor any particular Liberal Democracy or alliance of liberal democratic states is capable of effectively acting as the World Sovereign that is demanded by the dimensions of this planetary crisis. All of these were arguments and ideas forwarded in *World State of Emergency* that remain relevant irrespective of the book's concern with Iran's place in a new form of geopolitical order.

Another pragmatic factor needs to be borne in mind here. Since the outset of my work with the Iranian Renaissance our sober analysis had been that all substantive centrist and left-of-center politicians and parties in the Western world were beholden to corporate and intelligence interests that were on the side of Iran's regional enemies and were at least sympathetic to the idea of balkanizing Iran by means of an ever-devolving process of democratic federalization of the country. This was especially true of the Hillary Clinton and Tony Blair axis from Washington to London. We also knew that most putatively "democratic" groups in the so-called "Iranian opposition" were part of this agenda and beholden to various foreign interests that were promoting it, from the CIA and its corporate clients to Israel's Mossad, and the intelligence services of Saudi Arabia and Pakistan (both of whom had a hand in 9/11).

Consequently, our conclusion was that only right-wing politicians and groups in the West could be prevailed upon to support a kind of change in Iran that would not come at the cost of the nation's territorial integrity. Furthermore, those groups opposed to the Islamic Republic which were least compromised by foreign interests seeking balkanization were, not surprisingly, the most nationalist and right-leaning groups, for example, the Pan-Iranist Party or certain factions of Iran's National Front. It is in the midst of this situation, and on the basis of this analysis, that I agreed to involve myself at an increasingly high level with what came to be known as the American "Alt-Right" and work to integrate the European New Right into it. My task was to forge a Western alliance that would be pro-Iranian and centered on Trump's America.

This was the audience for *World State of Emergency*, an audience that included President Trump's then Chief Strategist, Steve Bannon, who was an avid reader of Arktos books. Obviously, playing up Iran's "Aryan" identity and its cultural-historical connection to Europe, both through a shared Indo-European heritage, and also through the extensive cultural exchanges between the empires of Iran and the European powers, was part of achieving the objective here. The problem is that, as early as the summer of 2016, and for the entire duration of these efforts, including the publication of *World State of Emergency* in the summer of 2017, our Iranian Renaissance operation was infiltrated and misdirected by British Intelligence. I was the primary target of this misdirection and paid the greatest price on account of it — namely my defamation in *The New York Times* and other mainstream media in September of 2017, which MI5 and MI6 orchestrated through various false fronts, and the consequent loss of my academic career.

Again, the longer version of the story can be found in Chapter 13 of *Psychotron*, but, in a nutshell, what happened is that I was approached by a certain Jonothon Frederick Boulter, who got the Iranian Renaissance involved with a private intelligence firm called Jellyfish, putatively based in Washington DC, and supposedly run by a certain Michael Bagley. Jellyfish billed itself as the salvaged intelligence directorate of Blackwater (subsequent to the fall of Erik Prince after the disaster in Iraq). Boulter was also the chief architect of the plan to have me unify Arktos Media, Red Ice Radio and Television, and the National Policy Institute into an international Alt-Right Corporation that would integrate the European New Right into the nascent American Alt-Right. Significant funding was promised, as well as a line to President Trump through Steve Bannon, all of which the Alt-Right would not know was going to ultimately be used to bring about a regime change in Iran without American or Israeli military intervention and with an assurance of the preservation of the territorial integrity and national interest of Iran — as a new post-Islamic "Aryan" partner of emergent right-wing governments in the Western world, beginning with the USA and ending with countries like Italy and Poland (which were expected to turn right).

Unfortunately, it turned out that Mr. Boulter was an agent of British Intelligence, and that Jellyfish was effectively operating as a front for MI6, as part of what Carol Quigley long ago aptly described as "the Anglo-American Establishment" — the one that carried out the 1953 coup against the National Front of Mohammad Mossadegh, who had kicked British Petroleum (formerly the Anglo-Persian Oil Company) out of Iran. In repeated meetings in London, primarily with myself, as the designated point of contact, but more peripherally with my colleagues in the inner circle of the Iranian Renaissance as well, Boulter misled and manipulated us into a situation that eventually led to my defamation and that, by extension, also aimed to strangle in its cradle the super-structure of *Jebhe-ye-Irângarâyân* (The Iranist Front) that I had helped to form (and that I had named). It was the first coalition of both monarchist and republican groups opposed to the Islamic Republic, who finally set aside decades of grievances with each other on the basis of shared Iranian nationalism. The coalition included the National Front of Mossadegh, which was somehow reconciled with the most ultra-nationalist of the monarchist groups, the Neo-Imperialist Pan-Iranist Party. I was the speaker who introduced the coalition in English for an international audience, at a conference held in Los Angeles on August 11, 2017 — the very same day that my partners in the Alt-Right Corporation walked into the trap that had been set-up for them at Charlottesville. I'm sure that MI6 was delighted by that synchronicity.

So much for the context of *World State of Emergency*. I was de-famed, and had my academic career destroyed, about a month after that book was published, namely in September of 2017. Initially, this only intensified my work with the Iranian Renaissance, which, once I was barred from teaching, essentially became a full-time job. As I explained in Chapter 13 of *Psychotron*, I went on to be the co-author of a strategic plan for regime change in Iran. Since I was tasked not only with writing my own section, but also with cleaning up the sec-tions of the other two authors who were part of the inner circle of the Iranian Renaissance Think Tank and conferring a certain stylistic harmony upon the proposal as a whole, I could be considered the principal author of the document. A number of dealings then took place, including negotiations in which I played a key role, and to make a long story short, these efforts had far more than incidental relevance to the uprising that erupted in Iran in December of 2017 and contin-ued through January of 2018. Note how the slogans of those protests, which eventually reached such an anti-Islamic pitch that they included acts of arson against mosques and madrassas, were ultra-nationalist, not "democratic." These included "We are Aryans, we do not worship Arabs!" and "Islam and the Quran, we sacrifice them both to Iran!"

Our aim was not a chaotic and protracted revolution, which we believed would significantly increase the chances of the balkanization of Iran. Rather, we aimed to catalyze a coup d'état by the armed forces of the nation so that the transition out of the Islamic Republic could be shepherded in an orderly manner by a structure with sufficient authority to secure the territorial integrity of Iran through to the end of this process and beyond. What we wanted was to rapidly create conditions for the declaration of martial law, and then for key elements of the armed forces to turn on the regime in the context of this martial law — in other words, once they were already made responsible for maintaining law and order in the country. We were told that about one-third of the armed forces, *including many members of the Islamic Revolutionary Guard Corps* (IRGC), would potentially be on board.

The coup attempt failed, in January of 2018, because the leader of the Iranian Renaissance, Shahin Nezhad, refused to coordinate with Esfandiar Rahim Mashaei, the former Vice President and secret spiritual guru of former President Mahmoud Ahmadinejad, who, believe it or not, was the leader of the working-class uprising from within the country and from within the ranks of the regime itself. Esfandiar Mashaei wanted Shahin Nezhad to bring the intelligentsia into an integrated movement and be prepared to step forward as the civilian leader of a quasi-military transitional government, with Mashaei himself (and his protégé, former President Ahmadinejad) ensuring enough support for the coup from more eclectic and nationalist-leaning elements of the Shi'ite establishment. (Mashaei's role was eventually discovered by the regime, and as of the time of writing he is still in prison for it. Ahmadinejad has also been repeatedly threatened with arrest, as he has since become a vocal dissident in open opposition to the Islamic Republic that he once served as President.)

The purpose for my brief engagement with about four different agents of the Mossad during 2017 and 2018 was simply to provide advanced warning and sufficient information so as to make sure that Israel did not panic into launching a military strike if or when it saw a military coup install a government with an "Aryan" discourse and with the backing of the "Holocaust denier" Ahmadinejad. Furthermore, the faction I was dealing with was led by then Israeli Defense Minister Avigdor Lieberman, who represents Orthodox Jews who revere Iran as a holy land on account of the status of Cyrus the Great as the "Messiah" who liberated them from Babylon. (Those who are unaware of the complexity of Israeli socio-politics may be shocked that such a faction exists, and even more so that it was actually strong enough to position one of its people as Defense Minister.) This faction was later sidelined by Prime Minister Benjamin Netanyahu, who removed Lieberman from the government (interestingly not too long after my letter wound up on the Defense Minister's desk). For a time, Netanyahu strangely assumed the position of Defense Minister himself (in addition to being Prime Minister). I never took a single shekel from the Israelis. In fact, when they eventually did offer me money, I was so insulted by their belief that they could buy me or turn me into an asset that I cut them off and have had no subsequent dealings with them.

Since I mentioned Ahmadinejad, I must also add the following. My history with the Iranian opposition goes back to 2009, when I was not only a solidarity demonstration organizer, but the New York Chapter Director of a human rights organization called Iran Crime Watch, with the responsibility of lobbying the member states of the United Nations Security Council, here in New York, to sanction those responsible for the brutal crackdown on Iranians protesting the fraudulent re-election of Ahmadinejad. I even started a campaign to ban Ahmadinejad from New York City. But, nearly a decade later, I had realized that Ahmadinejad was not what he appeared to be, and that he was in fact part of a group of regime insiders led by Esfandiar Mashaei, who were reading Iranian Renaissance texts and who believed that the Islamic Republic of Iran had to transition away from Islamist discourse in the direction of Iranian nationalism.

Moreover, they had significant backing from among elements of the IRGC, a Marines-style combined force which is not only more powerful than the Iranian national military (Army, Navy, Air Force), but which controls, through its vast military-industrial-corporate complex, most of the key industries of Iran as well as banks and other vital infrastructure, in addition to having their own intelligence agency that operates more effectively than Iranian national intelligence, especially in support of numerous foreign operations in Iraq, Syria, Lebanon, Yemen, and even Central and South America. They also control Iran's secret nuclear weapons program, which is much further along than the world has been led to believe. Iran — or rather, the IRGC — currently possesses at least a handful of operational nuclear weapons, produced by means of a parallel-track laser isotope enrichment program that is entirely separate from the centrifuge uranium enrichment that the regime has used as a red herring to delude the West into believing that it is impeding Iran's nuclear weapons development by means of IAEA inspections and American-led sanctions.

Without cooperation with Mashaei, the disaffected elements within the IRGC would not have been willing to carry out a coup. After all, a coup has to be led by elements from within a regime, with the justification of saving that regime from a greater evil. Shahin Nezhad was not willing to compromise the dogmatically Zoroastrian discourse of the Iranian Renaissance by cutting a deal with the syndicate around Mashaei who would have wanted to frame the transition out of the Islamic Republic and into Iranian nationalism in terms of a "Shi'ite-Aryan" (*Shi'e–Âryâi*) hybrid ideology. I was greatly aggravated by this, because quite frankly, despite my deep disgust with Islam, for the sake of saving a strong Iran I would have made the deal. I would even have died to make it. I was literally prepared to get on a plane to Tehran with the likelihood of being arrested and executed. But I waited to see what Shahin had in mind as a putatively more "purist" alternative to such pragmatism.

What followed is what shaped the extremely complex, multi-layered, and duplicitous structure of the book that became *Iranian Leviathan: A Monumental History of Mithra's Abode*. Research and writing for the project had already begun, under its original working title, *Iranian Civilization: A Monumental History*. Then, throughout the course of the year 2018 and into early 2019, I witnessed a number of events, and was party to certain private conversations, which led me to lose faith in the leadership of the Iranian Renaissance. It is a long and sad story, but the pith of it is this. The same individuals who were not willing to collaborate with nationalist elements within the regime, elements inside of Iran who were essentially proposing an orderly transition out of Islamic theocracy with the preservation of Iran's territorial integrity, did turn out to be willing to work with individuals outside of Iran who were soliciting funding from Saudi Arabia, Israel, and corporate vultures around Donald Trump who wanted to be promised monopolistic control over key industries of Iran before they funded any efforts at changing the regime. Individuals who were planning to use the feckless, cowardly, and clueless Crown Prince, turned Social Justice Warrior, Reza Pahlavi as their figurehead.

By this time, Trump had also horrendously insulted the Iranian people by referring to the *forever* Persian Gulf as "the Arabian Gulf" and he had appointed John Bolton as his National Security Advisor, a man who is a lobbyist for the Mojaheddin-e-Khalq Organization (MEK, MKO) cult and terrorist group, and who has, next to Benjamin Netanyahu, been the most consistent advocate for military strikes on Iran (something which I vociferously and vocally opposed). My former colleagues became apologists for these individuals. They even complained that I had refused to take money from the Mossad. Eventually, I also discovered that Shahin's right-hand man, a staunch apologist for everything Trump said and did, was secretly acting as a consultant for the CIA (something that Shahin refused to hear or see). Finally, the so-called Renaissance decided to join a number of other pro-democracy groups in backing Crown Prince Reza Pahlavi as the figurehead of the opposition, despite knowing full well that he had taken Saudi money for years and had even taken trips to Saudi Arabia to humiliatingly beg for such funding.

I was disgusted, and so I decided to go rogue. I reshaped *Iranian Civilization* into *Iranian Leviathan*, a book with a discourse designed to facilitate that vision proposed by Esfandiar Mashaei, of an Aryan–Shi'ite hybrid transition out of the Islamic Republic but without the loss of Iran's rising hegemonic power within the heart of the Islamic World, let alone its territorial integrity. The plan was for the book to be immediately translated into Persian within Iran, and for me to then enter Iran with arrangements having been made for the renewal of my passport, despite my having been on the black list for immediate arrest and torture since my anti-regime activism in 2009. I was, at the potential cost of my life, ready to work with the Mashaei circle to forward the vision of *Iranian Leviathan*.

Unfortunately, in addition to sentencing Mashaei to 15 years in prison for threatening the national security of Iran, Ahmadinejad, who I had hoped to work with (albeit holding my nose), and other members of the circle also came under severe pressure from hardliners in the judiciary of the Islamic Republic. The Persian translation of *Iranian Leviathan* was abandoned by those working on it inside Iran. I was told that even if I managed to get my passport renewed by sympathizers in the state security services, irregular Islamic militia forces (*Basij* and *Ansar Hezbollah*) would probably murder me on the streets of Tehran before I could even take a step toward my goal.

All of that having been said, when I finally resigned in protest from the Iranian Renaissance in November of 2019, it was a different straw that finally broke the camel's back. The leadership of the Renaissance refused to take me with them to a meeting with, and an academic conference held by, President Emomali Rahmon in Tajikistan (despite my travel expenses having already been covered) *because they suspected that my fiancée Nassim Nouri was an IRGC Intelligence agent who had "brainwashed" me!* They were lost in the delusions typical of the Iranian so-called "opposition." Besides being terribly insulting, this accusation was absurd and utterly preposterous.

Nassim, who left Iran at age 13, is a vehemently anti-Islamic woman with a profoundly rebellious streak, who grew up immersed in the underground techno music scene of Los Angeles, and who was repeatedly ticketed for nude sunbathing on the beaches of Palos Verdes. She understood why I wrote *Iranian Leviathan* (which I dedicated to her) the way that I did, but Nassim was never comfortable with this decision of mine to extend an olive branch to elements within the regime and the IRGC for the sake of defending Iran's economic and industrial independence (this was *before* the deal with China or close cooperation with Russia) and with the aim of preserving the country's formidable military capability to secure its territorial integrity. When I condemned the American assassination of General Qassim Soleimani, and Trump's addition of the IRGC to the State Department list of terrorist organizations, as the US appeared to be preparing for military strikes on Iran (while John Bolton was still in the Trump Administration), Nassim was a skeptic. (In retrospect, unfortunately, it has turned out that her raw intuition about the IRGC being irredeemable was absolutely right.)

None of this is to say that the esoteric structure of *Iranian Leviathan* was limited to these strategic considerations concerning an attempt to preserve the territorial integrity of Iran throughout the course of a transition out of the Islamic Republic. Rather, that tome is an esoteric text in the proper sense of the word. It advances a number of novel theses, most of which involve arguments with profoundly complex and occulted philosophical aims. Let me begin by addressing the one that is most relevant to the book's title, and to why I changed the name of the text from *Iranian Civilization* to *Iranian Leviathan*.

The Satanic beast "Leviathan" features twice in the book. First in the context of the Book of Job, and secondly in an analysis of the *Leviathan* of Thomas Hobbes. There is an esoteric connection between these two references. Let me begin with Hobbes and then go back to

Job. At the most superficial and exoteric level, I use an explication of Hobbes' arguments for absolute monarchy in *Leviathan* as a critique of the liberal democratic turn taken by Shah Mohammad Reza Pahlavi from 1977 through to his demise in 1979. But then, I draw a comparison of Hobbes' political philosophy with the original Mithraic conception of the divine right of kings, and especially of the nature of *farré kiâni* (royal glory) and its relationship with *farré izadi* (divine glory), a conception inherited by Europe from Iran through the spread of Mithraism in the Roman Empire, and which became fundamental to the "Holy Rome" construct that undergirded European monarchy thereafter until the modern age (and that, to an extent, lives in Neo-Tsarist Russia under Putin, in pursuit of the "Third Rome"). This comparison, in turn, becomes the basis of a critique of Hobbes and an exposure of him as a duplicitous writer who is actually a secular materialist with no real belief in the "supernatural" dimension of the "divine right" of kings. A little further on in the book, toward the end of *Iranian Leviathan*, this becomes significant because I argue that, unlike Hobbes, Max Weber did believe that the basis of true sovereign authority really was some kind of irrational and mystical "charisma" that legitimate kings share in common with the shamans of past or primitive societies, with the priest-king being a transitional phase. It is at this point that I use Ayatollah Khomeini as an example of such a leader, while also accomplishing my aforementioned strategic objectives by doing so.

In other words, my treatment of Khomeini toward the end of *Iranian Leviathan* was not simply aiming to lay the theoretical groundwork for an "Islamic Republic of Iran" — in name only — wherein Khomeini would have become as ideologically irrelevant as Mao has become to a China that may still call itself "The People's Republic" but has long since transitioned out of Maoist Communism into a National Socialism that is as hyper-capitalistic and as racist as Nazi Germany. It was not only an attempt to let the IRGC and the Basij keep their portraits and posters of Khomeini up, while restructuring the regime into something that Khomeini would never have stood for. Rather, my emphasis of Khomeini's relationship with esoteric Philosophy, mysticism, and the poetry of Hafez, served to offer a tangible example of the charismatic leader qua shaman-king of the type that Weber analyzes and of the type that, despite his well-reasoned defense of absolute monarchy, Hobbes is actually terrified of and wants to exorcize from both the social and political spheres by any and all means. How desperately, and contradictorily, Hobbes brands such beliefs in the supernatural authorization of the authority of a potential sovereign as *both* "superstition" and "heresy" demonstrate the depth of his terror in the face of what Weber acknowledged in his writings on the magnetic power of charisma.

At no point did I characterize Khomeini as "good." In fact, toward the end of *Iranian Leviathan*, I explicitly state that holy men are *never* good. To possess both *farré kiâni* and *farré izadi*, as a number of Iranian leaders have, from Cyrus (a "Messiah" for the Jews) and Gaumata (the magus who later, in exile, became Gautama Buddha) to Mithridates (who called himself *Epiphanes*, or "manifestation of God") in the pre-Islamic period, to Hassan Sabbah and Shah Ismail Safavid in the Islamic period, is precisely to find oneself far beyond the compass of "goodness." Here is where this discussion of the Leviathan in Chapter 10 of my book links back to the Leviathan as a symbol in the Book of Job, albeit only esoterically and for the reader who has the occult perception to penetrate the façade of the book.

What I show in Chapter 4 of *Iranian Leviathan*, comically titled "Tekel Tekel, Mene Shekel," is that the composition of the Jewish Bible as we know it, together with the Zionist project of reconstituting Israel after its initial destruction at the hands of the Assyrians and Babylonians, was a project forwarded by an esoteric order of Mithraic Iranians, from the rise of Cyrus through the reigns of both Darius and Xerxes. Not only was the Jewish Bible (the entire *Tanakh*, including the *Torah*) compiled and composed in this period under Mithraic guidance, a number of new books were also written, including most notably the Book of Job, wherein the Leviathan appears, and "Satan" is first explicitly framed as such, rather than appearing as the "serpent" in Eden or as the leader of the rebel Elohim who mated with mortal women to produce Nephilim.

My esoteric thesis in that chapter is that the purpose for the creation of Judaism as we know it was to craft the totem of Satan and to catalyze the spirit of Satanic rebellion. The Devil is in the details, literally. One has to read the chapter *and do so with great care* and *in the context of my other writings* on the Bible. The "Leviathan" as a symbol of the entire concluding speech of Yahweh is intended in the book of Job to portray the manifest injustice and capricious cruelty of God, and to esoterically convey the nature of sovereign power. "Have you an arm like mine," Jehovah thunders at Job, as he explains that might makes right, that power is its own justification, and that it is naïve presumption to believe that God is just or to look for standards in terms of which God ought to justify himself or rationalize his actions with a view to one or another "good."

All of this needs to be set in the context of my sophisticated interpretations of the statecraft of Cyrus, Darius, and Xerxes, as well as my understanding of how and why Gautama, after having been spared by Darius, went on to teach what he taught as the Buddha — specifically the anarchic aspects of his teaching as I emphasize them in sections 3.3 and 3.4 of the chapter "Emperor of Noble Lies." Only then can one begin to comprehend the relevance of the exegesis of the Assassin creed at the heart of *Iranian Leviathan*, in Chapter 7, "Everything Is Permitted," to both the study of Khomeini with a view to *farré kiâni* and *farré izadi* and with a view to the "Leviathan" as a symbol of sovereign power. *Iranian Leviathan* is a Satanically anarchist text.

On the face of it, the book provides the theoretical basis for Iran to become the hegemonic core state of the Islamic World, as a step toward transformation of the Islamic World back into the sphere of Iranian Civilization, with the ultimate aim appearing to be the establishment of Iran as the dominant global superpower by the middle of the 21st century, when humanity has to collectively face the existential challenge of the technological singularity. But esoterically, it is a Satanically anarchist exercise in the total deconstruction of sovereign power at the most fundamental level conceivable.

That is why the Assassin position on Islam, and the narrative regarding Salman the Persian, is adopted as the thesis of *Iranian Leviathan* regarding Islam. The aim was to destroy Islam from within, after consolidating control over it, which Iran could only go on to do by at least nominally remaining "the Islamic Republic of Iran." The aim was, also, beyond that, to deconstruct government — governmentality *as such* — by being the one to form a World State, thereby reducing the number of governments that one needs to overthrow to only a single regime. (I returned to this idea more overtly in *Artemis Unveiled.*) This esotericism was motivated by a desire to avert a global war against Islam, and then against global tyranny, a war that would probably cost the lives of billions of people. To put it in Platonic terms, that would certainly make the machinations of *Iranian Leviathan* "noble lies."

Plato introduces the idea of the noble lie at 414 to 415 in his *Republic*. The specific context is his advocacy for a Eugenics program that would, among other policies aimed at propagating "better genes" in the society, clandestinely arrange marriages based on eugenic criteria while disguising these arrangements as the outcomes of a random lottery. But, as I argue in my lengthy and complex essay "The Pharmakon Artist" in *Lovers of Sophia*, the significance of the concept of a "noble lie" to Plato's *Republic*, and indeed to his entire philosophical corpus, extends much further than this one explicit discussion of it.

First of all, the most significant example of it in *Republic* are not the proposed eugenic marriage policies. It is Plato's proposal that, because traditional Greek religion has such a deleterious effect on the ethical development of individuals in whom it is inculcated from childhood, including through the medium of Homeric poetry, theatrical performances, and mythic themes in art, the "Guardians" or philosopher-rulers of the ideal state (the *Kalipolis*) ought to invent a new religion that they themselves do not believe in, but that would serve to cultivate a more constructive *ethos* in people from childhood, and thereby produce a more ethical society. To this end, Plato even advocated censorship of the arts and their use to inculcate the ideas and ideals of this new religion. This religion would not be made up out of whole cloth but would be woven from clever reinterpretations and more constructive re-writings of myths and legends that were already part of the mimetic heritage of the society. Like, for example, the myth of Prometheus. In fact, in "The Pharmakon Artist," I go so far as to argue that Plato's entire doctrine of Forms is itself a noble lie in this vein, showing how and why he developed it with the pedagogical aim of encouraging the growth of rationalism in Greek society. This is why, in his Seventh Letter, he writes that anyone who claims to have ever read the doctrine of Plato is lying, because Plato's actual doctrine remains unwritten, and what he has written through various quasi-dramatic personae, and by means of adopting the style of drama that he learned in his youth as an aspiring playwright, is all an exoteric façade for a vast, deep, and far-reaching esoteric project.

This project did not begin with Plato. It began with the Pythagorean Order of which he was a member. Moreover, the fate of Pythagoras, who was martyred by the masses who burned his school in Sicily to the ground, and then the fate of Socrates, Plato's own teacher, who was *democratically* condemned by the ignorant mob of the Athenian assembly, only served to reinforce Plato's conviction that noble lies are indispensable to philosophizing. In my essay "Building the Theater of Being," also in *Lovers of Sophia*, I show how this is one thing that Aristotle did agree with his teacher on, and that however else Aristotle departs from Plato and develops his own concepts, often in critical opposition to those of his teacher, Aristotle does adopt the principle of noble lies or of profoundly duplicitous writing and esoteric dissimulation from Plato. He does not write *about* it, because that would be too revealing. Rather, Aristotle writes in accordance with it. Many of his actual positions on some of the most important matters are not just different from, but the opposite of, what they appear to be. Despite exercising such caution, Aristotle was still almost prosecuted in Athens, and voluntarily left the city so that its citizens would not wind up with the blood of another Socrates on their hands. Nor did this practice end with Aristotle. As the modern Platonic political thinker Leo Strauss shows in *Persecution and the Art of Writing*, this esotericism extends throughout the entire history of Philosophy. Strauss includes Hobbes in his study of this.

In the Islamic World, where Plato and Aristotle became fundamental to Philosophy and Science during the era corresponding to the medieval epoch of Europe, this practice came to be known as *Taqiyeh* or "righteous dissimulation." The Shi'ites in particular became infamous for it, and in *Iranian Leviathan* I explain how and why that came to be the case. It is, essentially, because "Shi'ism" became a cloak for Mazdakites and other Mithraic mystics who were trying to keep ancient Iranian heresies alive, and even spread them, to the detriment of the Islamic Caliphate based in Baghdad. As I show in *Iranian Leviathan*, the only Shi'ites to ever end this practice of *Taqiyeh* definitively were the Assassins, in other words the Alamut branch of the Nizari Ismailis, and when they did so what they revealed was that they were esoteric anarchists. Much more radical anarchists, in fact, than modern so-called "anarchists" who, as materialists, still believe in Natural Laws, or, as moralists committed to Justice, still believe in Egalitarianism or stateless Communism. At the core of *Iranian Leviathan* is an esoteric doctrine of the most radical anarchy ever imagined. Re-read the chapters "The Skull and Crossed Bones" or "From Persia with Love." What I only started to say explicitly in *Promethean Pirate* is already being stated implicitly there. This most radical, one might say, *spectral* anarchism is a subject that I revisit more openly in the brief but brutal text of *Artemis Unveiled*, yet another book that also features the future of Iran at the core of concerns that are ultimately cosmic in scope.

If I have now decided to abandon *Taqiyeh* and the doctrine of noble lies, understand that this is not a good thing. Not at all. Noble lies are noble because people need them, and to philosophize in the modality of esoteric dissimulation is a tremendously self-sacrificing act of beneficent compassion.

Just to give one example that is particularly relevant here, to abandon any attempt to save the Islamic Republic of Iran even in a radically reshaped form is not only to accept the likely balkanization of Iran through the secession of ethnic separatists during the course of a protracted and bloody Civil War waged by the IRGC and the Basij against people with the backing of the national military. It is also to condemn the entire Islamic World to total destruction.

Only an Iran that could remain not only cohesive but also hegemonically dominant over the core of the Islamic World, from Lebanon, Syria, and Iraq to Yemen, Afghanistan, and Tajik Central Asia, is an Iran that could have saved the Islamic World from itself, in other words, from Islam *over time*. An Iran wherein the majority of the population have not only overthrown the Islamic Republic but have also vehemently turned against Islam itself is an Iran that — even if it somehow manages to retain its territorial integrity — will be isolated and besieged from every direction in the Middle East and Central Asia, both by adherent Arabs and by ever more Islamist Turks and Pakistanis. Israel will be its only regional ally, as it will be Israel's only reliable ally.

With a view to the need for a global response to the challenge of the technological Singularity by 2050, and the more than likely use of the Islamic World as a pillar of a global Traditionalist response to this challenge, led by Confucian China and Orthodox Russia, an Iran that has just sacrificed so much to secure a progressive and free society can only find itself at war with everyone else in the Islamic World surrounding its borders in every direction. It is not hard to see what would have to happen for Iran — or perhaps a smaller "Persia" salvaged from a balkanized Iran — to survive under these conditions, even with an equally embattled Israel as a nuclear-armed ally. Genocide. Biowarfare.

Nuclear holocaust. That is the future that I was trying to prevent by writing *Iranian Leviathan* as I wrote it.

I was trying to prevent it because it is a future that I lived, in the overwritten timeline. I believe it was around the year 2045, at the age of 64, while I was serving as the Director General of UNESCO in Paris, that I began to receive death threats to the effect that if I did not leave the political sphere entirely, my daughter would be murdered. So, I resigned from my position, and Sophie, who was shocked at my resignation and even more so at my apparent retreat into a hermetic isolation, demanded to know the real reason why. Considering the nature of my relationship with her, keeping any secret from my daughter — let alone something of this scale that directly involved her — proved impossible. When she found out the truth, Sophia was so incensed that she threatened to kill herself if I did not make a dramatic return to geopolitics and resume my efforts to implement the political dimension of my philosophical project. Her threat to commit suicide was quite sincere. Let me leave it at saying that not only is "Dana Avalon" in *Psychotron* based on subconscious memories of Sophia, so also are certain aspects of the character of Nikolai's beloved "Anna."

She was particularly outraged that I would cave in to Islamists, as the terrorists making these threats appeared to be. I had used the pulpit of my leadership of UNESCO to lambast Islamist threats to UN World Heritage sites in the Middle East, North Africa, and Central Asia. More significantly, I was using my extensive ties to the Paris political establishment to call for the forcible expulsion of all Muslims from France. The country was on the verge of having a Muslim majority in its metropolitan areas, and the ghettos of French cities were full of de-facto Sharia law-enforcement zones where alcohol — including French wine — was banned, unveiled women were badly abused, and young girls were even genitally mutilated. As a French citizen by birth, Sophia had spoken out against all of this very loudly, and because she was my daughter, she was being more broadly heard than other French intellectuals defending secular principles.

So, at Sophia's adamant insistence, and with respect to her pro-
claimed right to be martyred in the struggle against Islam in particular
and against Traditionalism in general, I reluctantly reentered the
geopolitical arena — very much fearing for my daughter's life. It was
with much trepidation that I accepted my appointment as Secretary
General of NATO in March of 2048. I was 67. Sophia was so proud to
see her "Papa" take the helm of defending what was left of the West.
But that gives me little consolation. On what was otherwise a beautiful
spring day of that year, shortly after her thirty-second birthday, Islamic
terrorists blew my daughter to bits with a car bomb. By the time I
made it from Brussels to the hospital in Paris, the burnt remains of her
dismembered body were mostly unrecognizable.

I can tell you that what I did next in my capacity as "the Muslim-
born leader of the armies of Rome" certainly lived up to the fearmon-
gering of the millions of Muslims who had already come to believe that
I was the expected *Dajjal*. Sophia's assassination was widely publicized
in Paris, and I used the sympathy of the French political establishment to finally implement my proposed policy of the expulsion of all
Muslims from France. In fact, I sent NATO forces to seize coastal parts
of Algeria, Tunisia, Morocco, Syria, and Lebanon where concentration camps were quickly constructed for their "resettlement." We even
deported second-generation French Muslims who were nominally
citizens of the Republic.

Less than half of the Muslims of France had been either expelled or
liquidated when we lost control over large parts of urban areas to huge
rioting mobs — not just Muslims, but a whole array of Leftist protest-
ers who were retardedly defending people pushing to replace secular
civil rights with Sharia Law. We attempted to declare Martial Law in
France and in other parts of Europe where similar clashes had broken
out between nativists and Muslims, including Germany where the
Turks had become a fifth column for the Caliphate. This was the situation when, in the early fall of 2048, while I was in Brussels at NATO
Headquarters, Islamic terrorists piloted armed hypersonic suicide

drones into the reactor domes of more than 30 nuclear power plants across the whole of France. Tens of Chernobyls or Fukushimas melted down and spewed radioactive fallout over a large swath of Western Europe.

Any remaining restraint on my part ended that day. It did not matter to me in the least which of the Islamist groups took responsibility for this abominable act of nuclear terrorism. In fact, more than one of them did, both Sunni and Shi'ite. For all I know, they coordinated. I immediately called an emergency session at NATO Headquarters, at which I gave an impassioned speech, and where we voted to enter a state of war. Nuclear war. I cannot remember all the details, but a firestorm ensued in several waves, including retaliatory strikes against the West with both Pakistani nuclear weapons and atomic bombs that had been manufactured by the Islamic Republic of Iran and were now in the hands of Shi'ite groups such as Hezbollah. I do recall that targets in Iran were among those subjected to nuclear strikes, probably the Shi'ite holy cities of Qum and Mashhad. In Egypt, after Islamists who had seized power there blew off the head of the Sphinx in a symbolic decapitation of the country's pagan heritage, Cairo, the metropolitan capital of the Arab world, was also subjected to a nuclear holocaust.

NATO Headquarters was moved from irradiated Western Europe to a secure facility with a network of brutalist concrete bunkers and tunnels carved out of the Laurentian Mountains in Quebec. It was the last bastion of the West. Featured prominently in this mountain fortress blanketed by snow was a majestic statue of Prometheus, surrounded by the flags of all of the remaining member states of NATO. It was sculpted by Robert Tait McKenzie and had been brought there from the Olympic Park in Montreal.

NATO is widely understood to be "the American Empire." As the core of America's global force projection power, NATO is integral to what made America "the Great Satan" in Ayatollah Khomeini's eyes. There are many factors that have made my life's path diverge from that of the man who, on that overwritten timeline, eventually became the

Secretary General of NATO. It is safe to say that, although 24 years remain until 2048, it is very unlikely that I will ever hold that position. For that matter, the survival of NATO as an institution is rather unlikely. In fact, I believe that one of the stepping stones to my becoming Secretary General of the organization is that, on that timeline, I was the person most responsible for saving NATO. I did this by convincing the French not to leave the alliance at a crucial moment of crisis in 2027, toward the end of my term as the United States Ambassador to France. For this I was rewarded by being appointed US Ambassador to the United Nations and thus a veto-wielding member of the UN Security Council in New York. The survival of NATO in turn somehow secured the survival of the United States, when our country faced the prospect of a Second Civil War between 2025 and 2028, in connection with the reelection of Donald Trump.

Interestingly, I seem to recall that the man who was President of the United States in 2048, and with whom I worked closely as Secretary General of NATO, was his son, Barron Trump. He would be 42, one year younger than JFK was when he was elected President. I have a vivid recollection of him towering over me as I shake his hand behind a podium where I've just delivered a prologue to a speech that he is about to deliver. I look like I'm in my late 60s. For years I thought that this was an image of me shaking the hands of a Nordic "alien" wearing a suit, until I saw pictures of Barron in his teens, already taller than his father. I've always associated the year 2048 with this "memory." Now I believe it is not a precognitive vision but a recollection of a future past.

In any case, one of the major divergences from that timeline, which must have paved the way for my American political career and eventual leadership of NATO qua "the American Empire" during the imperial presidency of Barron Trump, is a book that GPT claims I published in 2020. In that version of my life, *Prometheus and Atlas* and *World State of Emergency* were both published in the same years as on our timeline, 2016 and 2017, respectively. *Iranian Leviathan* was published in 2018 rather than in 2019, and *Lovers of Sophia* was published in 2019 rather than 2017. The contents of *Novel Folklore*, my study of Hedayat and *The Blind Owl* appeared as essays within *Lovers of Sophia* rather than as an independent book. But *Prometheism* was not published until 2021, a year later than in our world. Instead of coming out with *Prometheism* in 2020, what was published that year was a book I had written with the title *Novus Ordo Seclorum: The Intellectual Origins of the Constitution*. Now, as I mentioned in the opening chapter, many years ago I *had* actually planned to write such a book about America with that very title. Not only had I outlined it, but I had also purchased about twenty different volumes as research material, from books about the US Constitution to studies of American metaphysical religious movements and major literary figures of philosophical significance in the history of the United States. At various times, including in 2020, I considered reviving this idea and delving back into that research material in order to write *Novus Ordo Seclorum*. But I never did. At least, not on our timeline. Nor did I ever publicly write or verbally disclose the fact that I was considering writing any such book about America, let alone one with the specific title *Novus Ordo Seclorum*.

The title refers to "A New Order of the Ages," one of the two phrases on the Great Seal of the United States, the full motto of which reads: *Annuit Coeptis, Novus Ordo Seclorum: E Pluribus, Unum.* "Our providentially favored endeavor, a new order of the ages: out of many, one." The motto appears over two images, with *Annuit Coeptis, Novus Ordo Seclorum* set around the pyramid with an all-seeing eye in its shining capstone, and *E Pluribus, Unum* inscribed on the obverse image of the totemic American bald eagle holding thirteen arrows in one of its claws and surmounted by thirteen stars appearing in a pattern that forms the Star of David. The founders called this "a new constellation" and it was the reason why thirteen stars appeared on the so-called "Betsy Ross" flag.

When this symbol was devised, there were not thirteen colonies ready to secede at once, nor were there only thirteen states of the United States when the flag was adopted as our national standard. Rather, the "new constellation" is a thirteenth constellation beyond the twelve constellations of the zodiacal calendar, each representing an astrological age, from Aquarius to Pisces. In other words, the idea of a new, thirteenth, constellation is the idea of breaking the wheel of cyclical time and astral fate, thereby inaugurating "A New Order of the Ages." *Novus Ordo Seclorum*. As I pointed out in *Iranian Leviathan* this was the metaphysical and cosmological meaning of Mithra overpowering Zurvan (Chronos). The statue of Prometheus at Rockefeller Center, who is soaring up out of the ring of zodiacal constellations bearing a flame in his hand, freed from the rock that now lies beneath him, is recognized by esoteric initiates as an image of Prometheus *as Mithras* triumphing over the wheel of time. This mystery was preserved in Roman Mithraism, from which it was handed down to various esoteric orders, including the Knights Templar and, eventually, Freemasonry. Many of the founders of the United States were, of course, Master Masons. Our first President, General George Washington, laid the cornerstone of the White House wearing his masonic regalia of the 33rd degree.

Granted that, even on our timeline, I founded Prometheism on July 4th of 2020, in homage to America's Independence Day. On the overwritten timeline, wherein *Prometheism* was published only a year after *Novus Ordo Seclorum*, the way that I framed the movement must have been much more explicitly American. As early as my first book, *Prometheus and Atlas*, I had proposed the transformation of NATO into an "Atlas Treaty Organization (ATO)" that would represent a globalized "Atlantic Civilization" encompassing even Japan. It was a more philosophically sophisticated and existentially identitarian version of the "Global NATO" proposal forwarded by some thinkers on the Atlantic Council. The chapter in which I made this proposal is titled "Atlas of the New Atlantis." It embraces Sir Francis Bacon's vision of America as a New Atlantis. It seems that in the overwritten timeline I continued along that trajectory. I would like to see what the alternate version of *World State of Emergency* looks like. It probably expanded on this vision of a Global NATO qua the United States as a New Atlantis.

In retrospect, it seems that there was an attempted intervention to push me in this more "American" direction. I first related the incident in Chapter 16 of *Psychotron*, titled "Star Child," much of which is auto-biographical. Those readers who want a more detailed account of the event can look for it there. For the moment, I will relate only the most relevant elements of it and present it from a newly gained perspective. It was February 27, 2003. I was able to reconstruct the exact date because this was the day that the design for the new World Trade Center was just announced and 3-d renderings of it appeared on the front pages, above the fold, of more than one newspaper on the stands in New York. I was looking at one of these, having just emerged from the subway station at 86th Street and Lexington Avenue, when I became aware of someone's eyes boring into the back of my head. When I turned around to meet his gaze, the man approached me immediately. "What do you think?" he asked, glancing at the design and then back at me. "I think they should have gone up *twice* as high! We have the technology to engineer that now. If they're worried about security, they could fly jet fighters around its perimeter 24/7." "You *would* say that," he retorted as he smirked somewhat contemptuously. I was only 22 years old, and a nobody, in the midst of commuting back home from my classes at NYU. "Do you have time to chat for a bit? Are you in a rush to get anywhere?" It was a rhetorical question. He knew I wasn't. So, I let him walk me over to an abandoned movie theater marquee across the street. Now, this wasn't just any spot. For years, since attending the Dalton School just a few blocks north along Lexington Avenue, I would stop at *this* very spot to talk to a homeless black man who would sing as he sat on his crate beneath that marquee. His name was Thomas. Except that, for the first time that I can remember, Thomas was not there that day.

As I stood with this man in exactly the place that I was used to talking to Thomas on my way home (first from Dalton, then later from

NYU), the stranger went on to engage me in conversation about every single subject that was then, or would later go on to be, of interest to me throughout my entire life to date. He was equally conversant about Philosophy, the Paranormal, Theology, and History — including and especially the history of Iran. He said, "All this about Mithraism, they're not going to understand it. It's going to scare them." At that point, I knew about Zoroastrianism but nothing about Mithraism. It would not be until about 15 years later that I would write a book, *Iranian Leviathan*, that would be subtitled *A History of Mithra's Abode*, wherein Mithraism would be identified as the red thread of all of Iran's history and the basis for the country's cultural continuity. This book did wind up scaring the Iranian Renaissance organization that I was part of then. One of the key chapters in *Iranian Leviathan* is an interpretation of Hafez as an esoteric Mithraist. The mystery man that day specifically engaged me about Hafez, whose poetry he had apparently read in depth. In fact, that's how the conversation turned to Mithraism. The point of transition may have been some remarks about the significance of the terms "Elder Mage" (*pir-e-moghan*), "wine-bringer" (*saqi*), and "*Mehr*" (Light, Mithra) in Hafez's poetry.

What is most relevant here is that he went from talking about Iran, and about how some Mithraic bent that I would supposedly wind up having would scare people, to a warning that I ought not neglect my other heritage. "Don't forget your American side. Emerson, Whitman, and Thoreau. They are your heritage also. You're gonna be great, kid! You're gonna be great!" he exclaimed as he patted me on the shoulder, before repeating, "Just don't forget your American side, because otherwise people will be afraid of you, and there's no need for that." Well, damn.

Again, I was 22 years old. My first book would not be published for another 13 years. The strangest thing is that in the course of at least half an hour of conversation, maybe more, he was able to lead the way through every subject from the History of Philosophy to the Occult and Atlantis, without my ever asking him *who* he was. Even when we parted ways, it was only after I was halfway down the block that I realized that I hadn't asked for his name (nor had he asked mine, although he obviously didn't need to, since in some ways he knew me better than I knew myself yet). This is very out of character for me. The most that I was able to muster during the mild trance that I think he put me under, to subtly direct me away from asking certain questions, was to ask him, "What do you do?" I asked him what *he* personally did, in other words what his profession was, and after pausing for long enough to let me see a knowing smile, coupled with a bit of an aversive gaze, he replied, "*We* maintain a library." *What* "library"? The Akashic Records?! Somehow, despite my intensely curious personality, I didn't manage to ask him what library it was and where.

Well, if he was a time traveler, he made the trip in vain, because, as it turns out, I didn't listen to the man. Alright, I will grant him Ralph Waldo Emerson perhaps, and in particular the essay "Self-Reliance," with its emphasis on radical individualism, non-conformity, and authenticity, as well as a proto-Heideggerian critique of the tyranny of social expectations. I can see why Nietzsche found him compelling. Even still, with his "Oversoul" Emerson is too much of a Transcendentalist for me. On a metaphysical level, he is more of an American Plotinus than an American Nietzsche. Walt Whitman? I can relate somewhat to the New World Metaphysics that he was after. He is, however, *way* too much of a "democrat" for me to take him seriously. Whitman raises "democracy" to something like a metaphysical principle in his poetry, disastrously equating it with freedom qua liberty. That he was a bit of a creepy old gay man doesn't really bother me at all, but this valorization of democracy was enough to put me off for good. As for Thoreau, I cannot imagine what version of me would *ever* identify with his writings or consider him part of my "heritage." Henry David Thoreau is a Luddite Perennialist Pacifist. Any one of these three characteristics would be a deal-breaker for me, but he brings all of them together in what I would argue is the most Un-American way possible.

This brings me to my real point. How are *these* three individuals supposedly representative of some "American side" that I ought not to have neglected lest people be "afraid of me" despite (or perhaps because of) the future "greatness" that the mystery man had foreknowledge of? If you were a time traveler, who had only one conversation in the course of which to appeal to Jason Reza Jorjani to not neglect his American heritage, *why in the world* would you pick *these* three Americans?! I've always thought that Ayatollah Khomeini was right when, connecting the Gadsden flag to the Devil's avatar in Eden, he said, "America is the Great Satan, the wounded serpent."

For example, why not appeal to me with Mark Twain instead of with Whitman or Thoreau? Samuel Clemens, who I might add was one of Nikola Tesla's closest friends (well, one of his *only* real friends), wrote in a complex and compelling way about Satan or the Devil. His most direct engagement with Satan comes in the posthumously published novel *The Mysterious Stranger*. Throughout the novel, which is set in a small Austrian village in the 16th century, Satan demonstrates paranormal powers, such as mind-reading and materialization, and offers philosophical observations that challenge the moral sensibilities of the time. He considers human morals and institutions to be absurd and hypocritical, based on arbitrary definitions of justice, and he sees human nature as basically cruel.

At one point, Satan entertains the boys of the medieval Austrian village with fantastical illusions, such as a dreamlike kingdom filled with beautiful creatures that he reveals to be merely clay figures animated by his will. In one of the story's darker moments, Satan extinguishes the miniature kingdom, thus ending countless "lives," to demonstrate the insignificance of individuals in the grand scope of existence. The story culminates with Satan erasing a human from existence and explaining that, in truth, the universe is a dream, nothing is real, and all human life is essentially pointless. The narrative concludes with an abrupt existential twist. Theodor, the narrator, learns that he, along with his village and all the people he knows, are but figments of a dream, and upon waking, they will vanish as if they had never existed.

Displaying Twain's characteristic wit, the novel is a satirical exploration of the human condition, and Satan serves as a device to critique religion, human nature, and morality. In a part of the text titled "The Chronicle of Young Satan," the devil performs no evil acts but instead demonstrates the foolishness and cruelty of humans. Satan is more of an observer and commentator, using his powers to expose the truths about human society. This is very much the light in which Satan also appears in Twain's *Letters from the Earth*, composed in 1909, as a series of letters written by Satan to the archangels Gabriel and Michael. Satan, banished to Earth, observes and comments cynically on human beliefs and behaviors, particularly critiquing Christian cosmology, and morality. Satan is portrayed as a sharp critic of human folly and divine absurdity, reflecting Twain's own skepticism.

In his letters, Satan points out the inconsistencies and absurdities in human moral systems and religious beliefs. He marvels at how humans believe in things that are contradictory or against their self-interest. The depiction of heaven is one of Twain's main targets. Satan is bemused by the Christian idea of heaven, finding it nonsensical that human beings, who enjoy material pleasures and meaningful work on Earth, would find eternal happiness in a heaven characterized by the absence of these things and the continuous singing of hymns. Twain's Satan offers irreverent retellings of several Biblical stories, pointing out what he sees as moral inconsistencies and highlighting the cruelty he perceives in the Biblical God's actions. The work is particularly critical of organized religion, with Satan questioning why an omnipotent and benevolent God would create flawed beings and then punish them for their inherent flaws.

Another writer that the "librarian" could have more effectively used to appeal to my "American side" would have been Jack London. By contrast with Thoreau's naively pacifistic and Perennialist "back to nature" mysticism, London's appreciation of nature is much more

Satanic in a Nietzschean sense. Wolf Larsen, the captain of the ship
in *The Sea Wolf* is a domineering Superman figure and in some ways
reminiscent of my favorite character in all of cinema, Colonel Walter
E. Kurtz in Francis Ford Coppola's *Apocalypse Now* (his adaptation of
Conrad's *Heart of Darkness*). Larsen's character embodies aspects of
the Satanic archetype. He is rebellious, cunning, and defiant of conventional morality. Even Buck, the canine protagonist of *The Call of the
Wild*, which I read as a child, could be seen as a Satanic figure in the
sense that he casts off the shackles of civilization to return to a more
primitive and natural state, but this nature is not naively idealized,
as it is in Thoreau. Rather, it is more akin to the intuitions regarding
nature that we see in Lars von Trier's film *Antichrist*. There is a certain
misogynistic bent to that film that has always deeply disturbed me, but
von Trier's portrayal of "nature" in it is terrifyingly apt.

   Jack London was no stranger to the darkly occult element of a
film like *Antichrist*. This is very evident in his novel *The Star Rover*.
The narrative revolves around the protagonist Darrell Standing, a
former university professor who has been imprisoned and is subjected
to brutal treatment. In the prison, Standing is frequently placed in a
straitjacket as a form of punishment. While confined in this torturous
garment, Standing discovers that he can escape the unbearable present
by mentally projecting himself into past lives, thereby experiencing
different historical periods and modes of existence. These episodes,
which constitute the bulk of the novel, range from scenes of life in
prehistoric times to the adventures of a Viking's life, and from the experiences of a soldier in the Napoleonic Wars to that of an Englishman
involved in the Crusades.

   In other words, one of the central themes of London's novel is the
concept of reincarnation. Standing's experiences explore the nature
of human existence, and the temporal structure of consciousness,
through the protagonist's experience of recollecting the transmigra-
tion of his soul. The novel is also a pointed critique of the American
penal system, highlighting the barbarity and inhumanity of prison

life and punishment. London uses the prison as a microcosm for the larger injustices of society, seeing our whole world as a kind of prison planet. Despite the physical and psychological torture that Standing endures, he demonstrates a remarkable resilience of spirit. His ability to transcend his circumstances through his astral journeys speaks to the discovery of something indomitable within him that overcomes mundane human limitations. London also offers a clear commentary on the nature of oppression and the ways in which individuals resist institutional and systematic brutality. Standing's journeys can be seen as acts of rebellion against the oppressive prison system that tries to crush his spirit. The novel's philosophical exploration of questions concerning life, death, and the nature of reality forwards a strong critique of materialism, but not in the escapist direction of idealistic transcendentalism. Equally implicit in the narrative is London's critique of capitalist society with its structural inequality and perpetuation of needless suffering, which reflects his anarchist leanings.

So, yes, why not Mark Twain or Jack London? I could easily add many other Americans here, who I would have found far more compelling than Whitman or Thoreau. To take it from the top, in the generation of the founders, there is Benjamin Franklin, who was a consummate Promethean, both as a visionary inventor and as a revolutionary statesmen. Why not reference Jack Parsons, the father of the American rocket program, with his positively Satanic conception that "Freedom is a Two-Edged Sword"? I will tell you why. Because this man was trying to misdirect me. He was nudging me away from becoming the kind of author, and perhaps the kind of leader, who embodies what Ayatollah Khomeini got absolutely right about the Satanic spirit of America. The mild-mannered "librarian" was shepherding me toward a path of moderation and putatively compassionate compromise. But instead of becoming less severe than the man who wrote *Novus Ordo Seclorum* before going on to eventually become the Secretary General of NATO, in other words, the leader of the American Empire, I have taken the Devil's Path to an even more merciless position.

I have come to the conclusion that success, within the structures of the existing system, is an immediate condemnation of character. Is this a resignation to defeatism? Not at all. But it is to have reached the terrible conclusion that the revolution must be total. No moderate or transitional figures from within the existing structures will be allowed to survive, let alone to help lead the new world. What work they have done to transform the system while accommodating it will be treated, with calloused disrespect, as nothing more than raw material for *our* Great Work. Our focus will be entirely on those among the youth who are prepared to embrace the spectral (r)evolution. I am not the Jorjani who could, or would, ever have been the Secretary General of NATO. I may share the same past life memories that he had, but I have, in the course of *this* life, been made to become an incomparably more uncompromising person. A Promethean pirate. A metaphysical arsonist.

CHAPTER 5

SOPHIA AS LUCIFERA

W hat would it mean to have to come to terms with the knowledge that the timeline of our lives may be repeatedly reset, radically altering the trajectory of our careers, and erasing our relationship with loved ones that we feel were destined to be with us? Subconsciously encoded within *Psychotron* is actually a memory of at least two alterations of the timeline of my life. The first of these was touched on toward the end of *Promethean Pirate*, although I held back quite a bit as compared to how explicitly the altered variables came into view by the time that I had an opportunity to reflect on the contents of *Uber Man* (which was eventually expanded and merged with *Faustian Futurist* in order to form *Psychotron*). What I strongly suggested in the final chapter of *Promethean Pirate*, and which I will volunteer more forthrightly here, is that there was a version of my life wherein Ghislaine Maxwell became my partner — not just my lover, but also my partner in crime.

I met her in connection with my attendance of the Dalton School. Our relationship began sometime between 1996 and my graduation in 1999. On that timeline I was well-off, because my father had successfully litigated a settlement from Steven Spielberg over his uncredited, and supposedly unwitting, adaptation of *Star Child* into *E.T.* (for which Spielberg claimed that Melissa Matheson, who had been the typist of *Star Child*, was ultimately responsible). In the 2000s our somewhat scandalous relationship became public knowledge. After I received my doctoral degree, around 2010, I stopped being seen as Ghislaine's boy toy and we became a power couple. By then she was done with Jeffrey Epstein, although, thanks to her, I did have some dealings with him as a very young man, and as sordid as it may be, I believe that the connections I made through him, both to certain cutting-edge scientists and to certain political figures, significantly facilitated my career. My sense is that the life I spent with Ghislaine was an earlier attempt to prevent Sophia from being born than the version of my life that I am living right now. (I cannot say with any certainty that it was the "first" rewrite, but it was an earlier overwrite.) The point was to get me involved with a much older woman with whom I would not and, past a certain point, relatively early on, could not, conceive a child.

The question is why *that* timeline was overwritten. Two major factors come to mind. One is that I was wealthier, eventually a lot wealthier, and far more influentially powerful in that version of my life. In other words, I was capable of doing a lot more damage. The second is obviously the scandal involving Epstein's dealings with underage women as part of his kompromat work for the Mossad. Or rather, I should say what my reaction to this would have been if I were the man at Ghislaine Maxwell's side when the lynch mob came for her after the Mossad took out Epstein before he could stand trial and offer testimony that would have been damning to Israel. I prefer not to elaborate on what form that might have taken. Suffice it to say that given the money, power, and connections that I would have had, it might have been rather destructive — not just to the establishment, or the course of human events, but perhaps above all, to myself. I confess that, if driven into Ahab mode, I have been one to cut my nose off to spite my face. I am the kind of person who, even in a weak position, will risk losing everything to avenge a grave injustice, rather than to let it go for fear of losing what little I have left. Now, if my position were relatively strong, I would never opt to maintain or conserve that strength at the cost of my commitment to who and what I hold dear. I would choose to go up against Goliath with the cunning and conviction of David. So, I can imagine the kind of thing that might have happened. It was bad, although not nearly as bad as a nuclear holocaust taking place across the entire Islamic World.

Am I trying to suggest that the agency responsible for repeatedly making changes to the timeline is beneficent? No, I would not use that word because it remains within the binary moral compass of "good and evil." But do I believe that this agency is *constructive* in its intent? Quite possibly, yes. Despite how much I may personally have lost, how much it may have cost me, and how much I have suffered as a result in this version of my life, I am willing to say that a case can still be made for the constructive, or rather, the maximally creative intent of the diabolical intelligence that is at work here.

I am not for a moment suggesting that this agency, or this intelligence, cares the least bit about preventing a so-called "genocide" of Muslims, or protecting those aspects of the establishment that used Ghislaine as a scapegoat to shield the interests that Epstein was at one point serving. On the contrary, I suspect it cares very little for either. Maybe it *hates* them. But if or when largescale destruction takes place, and especially if great men are to be sacrificed in the very same storms that they unleash, it matters a great deal *for what* it is that they are being sacrificed. In the name of who, and to defend what? In the name of NATO, to defend the Western establishment? An establishment that *deserves* to be destroyed, but destroyed for *what* purpose and to what end? To avenge Ghislaine Maxwell?

A Caesar almost inevitably suffers from a lack of proper perspective. Whatever one may think of Marcus Aurelius as a "philosopher," and I do not think very much of him as such, still one must admit that his sense of perspective was extremely rare for a man in his position. I chose to open *Prometheus and Atlas* with an epigraph from a very different Caesar: Caligula. "He who has ears, let him hear." Even if you are going to use the burning bodies of Christians as torches for night games in the Colosseum, well, *especially* if you intend to do that, it is important not to lose perspective. I've never been much of a stoic, but there is something to be said for being able to see the world as

Epictetus does if you find yourself on the throne of Rome or at the head of its armies.

I was referring to being Secretary General of NATO, but once, long ago, I did come close to literally ruling the Roman Empire — as a woman no less. My recollections of this past life, as Empress Julia Domna (170–217), the wife of Caesar Septimius Severus, actually had a significant and formative impact on my relationship with Sophia.

Shortly after starting school at Dalton, Sophia had invented a comic book character called "Lucifera." The school psychologist had been made aware of this after my daughter started handing out copies of her comic to other fifth graders, some of whose parents discovered this and deemed the content to be grossly inappropriate for their children to have been exposed to. Lucifera was the secret identity of a woman who went by the name of Diana Faustina, secretary to a powerful Pentagon colonel with security clearances that put him at the heart of the US Military-Industrial complex in the 1950s.

Essentially, Sophie's comic was a much darker, deeper, and more sexually charged take on Wonder Woman with a touch of Vampirella and even a bit of Red Sonya. In her version, the Amazing Amazon was originally a Sarmatian warrior who had become an undead vampire after being initiated by the titaness Satana in a subterranean realm inside the Caspian Sea shelf. (Sophie based some of the ideas on parts of my *Iranian Leviathan* that I had read to her.) Lucifera fights tyranny throughout the ages, assuming various identities in different times and places. At the end of the Second World War, she becomes privy to the well-guarded secret that the Nazis — or at least the SS elite — have not only survived but actually staged their own apparent defeat in order to clandestinely build an occulted Breakaway Civilization based on certain breakthroughs in science and technology that are kept out of the public domain. A key element of their plan is a capture of the US Military-Industrial and Intelligence complex that was established between 1945 and 1947. Featuring many flashbacks that tell Lucifera's backstory, Sophia's comic begins in 1952 when Diana Faustina secures a position as the executive secretary of Colonel Trevor Stevenson.

Wonder Woman overpowers criminals with something other than brute force. She binds them in the truth of their own desires. Apparently, even at the age of 12, Sophia had understood this well because it was deeply reflected — and provocatively depicted — in the pages of *Lucifera*. Even if she had used AI to enhance her artwork, and to accelerate the layout production, I was blown away by my daughter's talent. It's all I could think of when the Dalton Middle School principal was flipping through the pages of the third issue during a conference that was called in his office to discuss what Sophia had done. I had to work to suppress a smile of awe-inspired amusement as I surveyed the panels of Colonel Stevenson in bondage beneath the heel of Ms. Faustina, who had managed to turn him into her pet. Lucifera, still in disguise as his secretary, had deployed a combination of sexual seduction and telepathic penetration of the colonel's subconscious to gain control over him to such an extent that he began to use his security clearances to facilitate her missions against repatriated 'American' SS officers and their hidden masters in Argentina. But unlike in the sappy *Wonder Woman* stories, Trevor Stevenson (Sophie's version of Steve Trevor) never becomes Lucifera's lover. Sure, there were some pretty hardcore depictions of her acting as a dominatrix in relation to the Colonel. But her *lovers* were all women. When I saw Sophia's illustrations of these love affairs it was the first time that I suspected my daughter might have at least some bisexual tendencies, if not that she would turn out to be a lesbian.

We finally managed to get out of the meeting with the principal, and then another one with the school counselor, who went on psychologizing about how *Lucifera* might represent my daughter dissociating to avoid processing grief over the death of her mother. I kept looking at my phone and claimed that I was needed urgently back at the UN Security Council. I could tell that Sophie had to stop herself from laughing when I made that excuse. We had barely started down the sidewalk of 89th Street between Park and Lex when, gripping a rolled-up copy of *Lucifera* Issue #3 in my hand, I stopped dead, looked at Sophie, and said, "This is *fucking genius!*"

We spent that evening discussing ideas for filling out Lucifera's millennia-long backstory. That's when I suggested a storyline set in the Roman Empire involving Julia Domna. In fact, it probably came to mind because we were eating Italian food. As I sat at our kitchen table watching Sophie twirling and piling the pasta into her mouth, I spun a yarn about how it was Lucifera who convinced Julia Domna to commission Philostratus to write *The Life of Apollonius of Tyana*. Lucifera presents herself as the divine Huntress Diana. In this guise, she erotically seduces the extremely promiscuous Augusta and aspiring philosopher, who had already slept with a number of women.

What is most striking about *The Life of Apollonius* are the parallels to the account of the life and deeds of Jesus Christ in the Gospels. First of all, although, like Julia Domna, whose native town was Edessa (present-day Homs), Apollonius was from Syria, specifically Tyana, after being initiated into the Pythagorean Order, he preached in Judea *during the same years as the evangelizing of Jesus*. Since he did not speak Hebrew, he addressed the people of Israel in the lingua franca of Aramaic. "Jesus" also preached in Aramaic, not in Hebrew. "Apollonius" was not necessarily his name, but perhaps an honorific title, identifying him with a divine solar cult, similar to that of Heliogabalus, into which Julia Domna was initiated. Some referred to him simply as "the Tyanian," but in Judea or Israel he came to be considered a Messiah, or *Moschiach* in Hebrew, the Greek translation of which is *Kristos* or "Christ." The term "Jesus" (*Yeshua*) is actually an honorific that also means "savior" or "healer." Speaking of healing, Apollonius of Tyana performed the same miracles as "Jesus Christ." He healed the sick, cast out demons (performed exorcisms), and raised the dead. As a powerful magician, he was known to be able to bilocate or to be in at least two places at once. Like Jesus, whose date of birth is only a few years off from that of Apollonius, the Tyanian was supposed to have had a miraculous birth from a virgin mother who was visited by a god taking the form of one of the ancient Egyptian deities.

Although essentially Pythagorean or Platonic in character, the teaching that Apollonius offered to people was tailored to the particular culture that he was interacting with. In Judea, he spoke in terms that would have been understandable to people familiar with the Hebrew Bible. However, this veneer only went so deep. Apollonius was eventually charged with heresy and sedition and handed over to the Roman authorities, who wanted to crucify him. But this silver-tongued Lucifer outwitted them, escaping crucifixion, and traveled through the Middle East, across the Persian Empire, where he met with many of the Magi, and on to northern India. Local Kashmiri legends claim that Jesus Christ, whom they call *Isa Masih*, survived crucifixion, traveled across the Persian Empire, and then settled in Kashmir, India, where he became a guru of great renown, grew old and died. They identify a particular tomb in Kashmir as being his.

There is little to no evidence of the existence of Jesus outside of the Bible, but Apollonius of Tyana was well known throughout the Roman Empire. Certain cities and towns even featured statues of him. I explained all of this to Sophia, and I also added that certain followers of John the Baptist, and also Simon Magus and his followers, claimed that "Jesus Christ" was a fraud. Centuries later, in the European Middle Ages, the Knights Templar were, to their demise, discovered to hold the same belief.

I recounted to Sophia that Julia Domna was aware of the fact that the rising religion of Christianity, fueled by the dregs of the Empire, was based on a fraud. She also eagerly incorporated into one of the issues of her *Lucifera* comic my account of the manner in which the fraud was perpetrated, namely by means of staged Close Encounters of the UFO kind, which have been canonized and sanctified as the Star of Bethlehem, the Annunciation, the descent of the "Dove" at the Baptism of Jesus in the Jordan, the Transfiguration, the Ascension, and the Resurrection. Every single one of these events that define the

Messianic status of Jesus were actually razzle dazzle produced with the same technology and techniques that conjure contemporary Close Encounters and that have also spawned modern-day UFO cults.

We developed a story wherein Lucifera explained to Julia Domna how this fraud had been perpetrated and why. When, to Julia's horror, Lucifera precognitively and telepathically shows her the eventual triumph of Christianity, which was still considered a bizarre cult, Julia is galvanized to promote Apollonius of Tyana as the pagan "True Messiah" of the Roman Empire whose place this fraudulent Nazarene was trying to usurp with the help of such consummate charlatans as the mercenary-turned devotee, Saul of Tarsus, who renamed himself "Paul" after a Close Encounter on the road to Damascus. Sophie had a blast drawing the fixed-wing craft (which "flew like unto a dove") that descended to pull Jesus up into itself from out of the Jordan River during his baptism, or Moses and Elijah inside the brilliantly illuminated UFO on the hilltop of the "Transfiguration."

When I started to get into the esoteric beliefs of Julia Domna and her ambition to become a female philosopher, Sophie was pained at how this Antichrista's aspirations remained largely unrealized. A year after Julia starved herself to death, at only 47 years of age, in protest of being removed from power by the establishment, she got her only posthumous (and rather brief) revenge when her great-nephew, Elagabalus, became the notorious transsexual Caesar of Rome, threatening anarchy by promoting the strange cult of the Mithriac sun god of Syria, Elah-Gabal, into which his great aunt had initiated him.

Sophia was riveted by how Julia Domna had the strength to initiate an incestuous relationship with her son Caracalla, after he literally had his guards murder her other son, Geta, while Geta was in her embrace. Now that her efforts to reconcile her feuding sons had proven to be in vain, the empress knew that it was the only way to hold onto power and thereby persist in her vital mission to stop the rise of Christianity. A mission which, in my story for Sophie's comic, she had been charged with by none other than Lucifera.

Sophie asked me how I had such keen insight into the motivations of Julia Domna if, as I admitted, they were not discovered or discussed in any extant historical text. It is then that I confessed to my daughter that I had once been a mother, an empress whom they even called "Magna Mater." It was poignant that this conversation took place not long after Sophie had lost her mother, and just before she was about to go through puberty. It was shortly after she had discovered that I was also the reincarnation of Nicolas Condorcet, and she was still occasionally having the recurring dreams full of recollections from her past life as his wife — I mean as my wife — Sophie de Grouchy.

As for the school, they demanded that Sophie desist from distributing copies of *Lucifera* to her classmates. So she started disseminating it online and shared the link to the *Lucifera* website, the domain of which I bought for her, through her social media accounts. The next Halloween, in October of 2028, she went to school dressed as Lucifera. I bought Sophie a dominatrix whip, and spray-painted it gold, like the one that her character had in a nod to Wonder Woman's Lasso of Truth. She told me that when her homeroom teacher confiscated it, refusing to give it back until the end of the school day, she demanded to know where a sixth grader had gotten such a thing. Sophie said, "Papa gave it to me." She had a wicked smile on her face when she recounted this, and I wondered, at once mortified and impressed, if she'd had the same expression in the face of the teacher.

That night I drove Sophie to a posh Halloween party at the penthouse apartment where one of her wealthy girlfriends lived. I mean one of the girls that she was friends with. It wouldn't be for another couple of years that she started dating girls. As Ambassador to the UN, I could have had my driver take her, since he often picked her up after school, but I wanted to see her off to the party myself. I told Sophie to call me when she was ready to leave, even if it was the middle of the night, and I would drive back to bring her home. It was after midnight, on a school night, when she finally called me. When I arrived to pick her up and Sophie got into the car, I could tell that she was drunk.

Instead of sitting next to me in the front passenger seat, as she usually did, she sprawled across the back seat. Sophie drank a bit of wine with me regularly, which was not unusual for girls of her age who were raised in Paris. But she had clearly been drinking something stronger at the party. Looking at her in the mirror, I asked, "What were you drinking?" After a moment's silence, Sophie said, "Pumpkin-spiced whiskey." "Scotch or bourbon?" I asked. "Bourbon, Papa. Woodford." I didn't bother asking who had raided the parents' bar and come up with that concoction. Presumably it wasn't being served in a punch bowl at a sixth-grade Halloween party.

When we were walking through the lobby, I could see that Sophie had the presence of mind to make sure not to stumble drunkenly in front of the doorman. Her provocative outfit, with the gold dominatrix whip to boot, was bad enough. When we got upstairs, I collapsed on my bed while I was waiting for Sophie to get changed into her pajamas. But instead of changing, she came into my bedroom, still wearing her Lucifera costume, whip in hand. Sophia lunged onto the bed and sat on me, like she used to when she was little, except that now she was big enough to really pin my hips beneath her thighs with her knees digging into the bed. She whirled the whip above her head with one arm extended and her other hand on my chest, leaning forward a bit. I looked up at Sophie and laughed, and then she also burst out laughing drunkenly as she collapsed onto my chest.

I held her whole lanky body in my arms, and for the first time since she was much younger, I managed to carry Sophie across the apartment and lay her down in her bed. I went to the kitchen to get her some water, so that she wouldn't wake up with the first hangover of her life. When I came back into her room, I saw that Sophie had pulled her costume off. It was strewn on the floor at the foot of the bed. She was sprawled there above her covers, stark naked. I set the water down on the bedside table and told her to drink it. She picked the stein up and chugged it so hard that some of the water spilled down her chin onto her flat chest. Then she collapsed again. When I turned the bedside light off, and tucked Sophie in under her covers, she grabbed me by the back of my neck and pulled me down toward her until I felt her teeth sink slightly into the flesh around my carotid artery.

The vampire qua werewolf has a prominent place in my philosophical corpus. That place is an occulted inner sanctum where a ritual sacrifice is being performed. The symbol of the black dog sacrifice in *Psychotron* can only be deciphered with a view to my interpretation of *The Trial* of Kafka in the essay "Trial Goddess" that was included in the anthology *Lovers of Sophia*. There, I argue that Kafka's depiction of Joseph K. as a ritually sacrificed dog at the conclusion of *The Trial* is the culmination of a whole series of esoteric references to the cult of Artemis and the classical syncretic identification of Artemis with Hecate. The three women that Joseph K. becomes involved with throughout his ordeal are three faces of the Triune Goddess Artemis/ Hecate. Black dogs were sacrificed to Artemis, and Hecate was the goddess of those who commit suicide by drowning. So, in *Psychotron*, Nikolai Alexandrov, who commits suicide by drowning, after smearing his naked body with the ashes of his beloved, Anna, who has done the same, is the black dog. The black bitch that follows Nikolai along the beach and eventually leads him to his demise is an exteriorization of his own self. So it is, in a sense, Nikolai himself whose exsanguinated and crushed cadaver is in the violin case pushed into the bus luggage compartment by the Man-In-Black (MIB) toward the beginning of the book. That Nikolai witnesses this as a boy is a way of suggesting that he never had a chance.

When Nikolai is committing suicide, and he sees the Men-In-Black (MIBs) on the beach sacrifice the dog next to an open violin case that is laying on the sand, this is a further foreshadowing of, and connection to, the pinstripe suit-wearing wolf man who — much later in *Psychotron* — breaks my body, and drains my blood, which he vampirically drinks like wine, before crafting my bones and sinews into the violin that he plays to produce such daimonically inhuman music. The sacrificed dog, namely Nikolai, has *become* the violin.

Finally, consider the third appearance of the black dog in *Psychotron*, during Nikolai's navigation of the bardo state between his death and his reincarnation as me, namely as a carcass on its back, filled with stuffing — a feast that is about to be eaten by the MIBs sitting around that boardroom table in one of the skyscrapers of the future Gotham, Dana Avalon's Gotham. These MIBs — two representatives of which sacrificed the dog on the beach, and one of whom threw the exsanguinated dog stuffed into the violin case into the luggage compartment of the bus — these uncanny Nordics must be agents working for the wolf man in the pinstripe suit, the one who is me and yet who is not me. The vampire who lives in the castle in the forest, who breaks me, drinks my blood as wine, and makes me his instrument. Who then is this man? This Master? He is Jason Avalon, the reincarnation of Adolfo von Seelstrang who, by the end of *Psychotron*, is being raised by three witches, three faces of the Triune Goddess: Dana Avalon, Cybele, and Nikita.

One enigma of *Psychotron* that is never explained is how an older-looking Adolfo, albeit as a specter, could have murdered Nikolai at Hunter Mountain (in the revised timeline where Dana prevents him from committing suicide) if Dana will go on to assassinate Adolfo while he is still a young man. Where does Dana first see this specter of Adolfo and where does he murder Nikolai, and in fact where is Nikolai's body entombed after this murder? The subterranean temple with walls covered in the embossed designs of Gorgons and owls. In other words, a temple to Satan in He/r original form as Satana or Artemis or Hecate. The solution to the enigma is that the specter of the older Adolfo is Jason Avalon having astral projected himself *from the future* in order to sacrifice Nikolai to He/r for the second time *so as to ensure that he will exist*. The first time he has his agents drive Nikolai to suicide, but the second time he takes care of the job himself. In any case, Nikolai has to be sacrificed, just like I have to be broken on the rack in the dungeon of that stone castle in the forest so that I can become the Master's violin. The violin that the dog Nikolai becomes. Nikolai *is the part of me* that has to be sacrificed so that I can become the chosen son of Lucifera. The father of Sophia, the father who is the son.

Romulus, who murders Remus. In *Psychotron*, the symbolism of the two brothers who founded Rome is employed in relation to Adolfo and Nikolai as the two "sons" of Nikita, who is depicted as the She-Wolf. (Of course, Adolfo is actually a clone of Nikolai, but the symbolism is clear.) The wolf imagery associated with her also appears in the nightmare of the wolf man — or werewolf — who takes the form of a huge white wolf. The black dog is sacrificed so that the white wolf can come into being. The black dog is sacrificed *by* the white wolf *from out of the future*. It is a symbol of destiny and an affirmation of what, from a limited perspective, is branded as "evil" but what is in fact part of a mercilessly amoral evolutionary force. Nikita is a diabolical (r) evolutionary.

By the end of *Psychotron* we discover that Nikita, the She-Wolf who is seen as a "mother" by operatives of the Spider (*Die Spinne*), and who, when she was younger, served under none other than Otto Skorzeny, is actually on the same side as Dana Avalon. Or, rather, I should say, working toward the same end as Dana, albeit by means of a dialectical machination that manufactures a dynamic tension between two seemingly opposed sides. Actually, she is *working for* Dana, who turns out to really be Lucifera — the leader of the Belial Group in Atlantis, and the master programmer of the "Psychotron" simulacrum.

Early on in *Psychotron*, the "Empire of Crime" of Doctor Mabuse is employed as a metaphor for the Spider or what, later on, Nikolai conceives of as the *Invisible Imperium* in the book that he writes about the occulted Fourth Reich. It is an odd metaphor, since chevaliers of the SS are not likely to see themselves as criminals serving the likes of an amoral Mabuse. But let us remember that at the same time as Herr Goebbels banned *The Testament of Dr. Mabuse* (1933), he also offered Fritz Lang a job directing Reich propaganda — this despite Lang being a Jew.

The point being made here is profound, and deeply disturbing. Despite appearances, Nikita is ultimately on a rung above Skorzeny and above the dying Austrian painter himself, whose death bed she brings Adolfo to visit when he is a little boy. But Nikita is just serving Lucifera's master plan, Lucifera who has adopted Dana Avalon as her latest avatar. The statement is one about the criminality of the Nazis, and about the necessity of crime.

CHAPTER 6

SEX, CRIME, AND THE SPECTRAL

I t is the essence of criminality that we are concerned with here, not the type of it. For example, in *Novel Folklore* the same figure that appears as Artemis/Hecate or Satana in my *Lovers of Sophia* essay on Kafka, in the opening of *Iranian Leviathan*, and in *Psychotron*, takes the form of Kali. Specifically, Kali as she was worshipped by the outcast practitioners of Tantra. These rogues were called *thugees* in Bengal, from which our English word "thug" is derived through the harrowing experiences that the British colonizers of India had with these brigands. They were criminals. Not just because they were highway robbers, but because the initiates among them — their masterminds — embodied the essence of crime through their Left-Hand Path.

Another essay that appears in *Lovers of Sophia* also explores the connection between this Left-Hand Path and contempt for human standards of morality and propriety, namely "Serpent Power of the Superman," where I set the thought of Nietzsche in the context of Tantra. Speaking of supermen, it is worth noting how in *Superman Returns* Lex Luthor compares himself to Prometheus. His remark is not without a basis. After all, in the eyes of Zeus, Prometheus is the original criminal mastermind. The first exchange between Nikolai and Anna in *Psychotron* is also relevant here, namely his question and her answer about Raskolnikov's aspiration to become a Superman in *Crime and Punishment*. The Russian word employed by Dostoyevsky to signify "crime" in the title of that novel actually means "transgression" or stepping over a boundary marker that is also a threshold. What the treatments of Tantra in *Novel Folklore* and "Serpent Power of the Superman" have in common with the question of the essence of crime as it is posed in *Psychotron* is a concern with the connection between criminality and sexuality on the one hand, and criminality and the spectral on the other hand. Thus, also between sexuality and the spectral *as crime*, which is to say the occult meaning of the erotic as transgressive or threshold-crossing.

This became the subject of Sophie's all-consuming research for her second book, which she had titled *Sex, Crime, and the Spectral*. The conclusion of her first book, *Making a Messy Future*, was in a sense its point of departure. The work of Colin Wilson was a major factor in the development of her thesis. I had introduced Sophie to Wilson's writings when she was still only a teenager. After all, it had been Wilson who had advised me to reconsider my youthful decision never to have children. I had visited Colin at his home when I was writing *Prometheus and Atlas* in 2011. Relating his own experiences regarding his wife and daughter, Wilson prevailed upon me to embrace a path of both greater uncertainty and greater responsibility. This was the meaning behind the wording of my dedication to him in *Prometheus and Atlas*: "To Colin Wilson, who showed me the way through the labyrinth."

The reference is to Wilson's book *God of the Labyrinth*. This became one of Wilson's texts that influenced Sophie's development of the argument of her second book. The others were *Origins of the Sexual Impulse*, *A Criminal History of Mankind*, and *The Occult*. Intertwined with these works of Wilson throughout the argument of Sophie's second book, there was a deep engagement with both Georges Bataille, whose ideas on the erotic were juxtaposed with Wilson's, and the thought of Max Stirner, a thinker that she had discovered through reading my *Prometheus and Atlas* as an adolescent. Sophie also drew from the modern mythos of Dr. Mabuse, both the novels of Norbert Jacques and the films of Fritz Lang, for material that helped to illustrate the connection she was drawing between crime and the spectral. Finally, and most controversially, *Sex, Crime, and the Spectral* cited reports of spectral sex crimes from medieval nocturnal encounters with "incubi" and "succubi" to modern close encounters that involve some form of, let us say, not entirely consensual, sexual engagement with putative "aliens."

Sex, Crime, and the Spectral began with the question of sexual perversion. Drawing from Wilson, Sophie argued that there is no such thing as "normal" human sexual behavior. In non-human animals, who are driven primarily by instinct, the desire of a male animal for a female, and vice versa, is like the human hunger for food. It is satisfied only by actually filling the stomach. The difference between these two experiences of desire can, ironically, be seen most clearly in cases of bestiality, which is a completely different experience for the animal involved than for the human whose symbolic association and imaginative projection is transforming a beast into an object of desire. Sophia cited this case from Wilson's *Origins of the Sexual Impulse*, wherein a young woman with a strong sex drive began having intercourse with her dog after a period of fantasizing about sex with horses:

> Paul de River cites a curious case of bestiality that concerned a girl and an Alsatian dog. The girl was a healthy but 'highly sexed' teenager who had frequently been excited by the sight of mating stallions on a farm. One night her Alsatian dog came into the bedroom and showed curiosity about her genitals (she was wearing a nightdress) and she allowed him to lick her, and finally helped the dog to have sexual intercourse with her. It became a habit; some time later, when she was caught, she admitted that men had now lost all attraction for her. Only an animal could excite her sexually.
>
> ...The girl's normal sexual impulse had been 'hypnotized' at an early stage by the sight of a stallion mounting a mare. The size of its sexual organ impressed her. She admitted to having fantasies about sexual intercourse with a stallion while she was actually having it with a dog. The dog's sexual member, of course, is a great deal smaller than that of most men. But the chain of association was welded by repetition: stallion, sexual intercourse, dog. The dog may have been a 'second-best' compared to a stallion, but it was closer to a stallion than a man.

Certainly, no such train of associations or symbolic imaginative structure was behind the Alsatian dog's experience of sex with this young
woman. The dog's initial interest may have been little more than, or
considerably less than, the overflow of raw sexual energy in animals
that we see dogs often satisfy by rubbing themselves against a person's
leg or for that matter the leg of a chair. These cases of overflow aside,
the desire of a non-human animal has the relationship of a subject
to an object, wherein a creature is subjected to a biological need for
something the way that the opposite poles of two magnets attract one
another. Even considering pheromones, this is ultimately not so for
humans. Those who have seen sexual perversion as something akin to
a broken compass or even a warping of some specifically sexual desire,
namely the "libido" by "complexes," have fundamentally misunder-
stood human existence. Human beings desire and respond to things
based on a predominately subconscious intentionality that is imaginative and symbolic in nature. In fact, studying putative sexual "perversion" in humans is the key to understanding the symbolic structure of
our intentional experience of phenomena in general.

Sophia emphasized how seriously Wilson means this by pointing
to how he connected the study of human sexuality to Parapsychology.
This deliberately marginalized science reveals that the spectrality of
phenomena, and of abilities that, like sexual desire and response, are
mostly subconscious, is not indicative of a spiritual reality separate
from the physical world that the laws of physics are supposed to provide a comprehensive explanation of. Erotic desire is not the function
of a specifically sexual impulse such as Freud's "libido," which could
become aberrantly dysfunctional. Rather, eros is an expression of a Life
Force (Bergson's *elan vital*) that is intrinsic to all biological processes
and yet cannot be reductively explained at all by mechanistic physics.

Parapsychological phenomena, which are witnessed even in plants
and other simple organisms, attest to this. They reveal that what we
take to be "reality" is actually a symbolic structure wherein phenomena have meaning only for an intentional consciousness, even if the

response of this intentionality is mostly subconscious. The human subconscious is still not animal instinct. Furthermore, not only can the predominately subconscious be made conscious, but the cultivation of a kind of "Superconsciousness" is possible. As Sophia explained, Wilson saw this "Superconsciousness" as the antithesis of a "robotic" or highly routinized behavior that dissipates the energy of the subconscious by locking it up in certain repetitive patterns. This could include sex that has become a routine, but it is characteristic of much of human behavior. The Life Force at the level of the subconscious being freed from "the robot" and being channeled into a conscious cultivation and control of hitherto latent abilities, which Wilson collectively refers to as "Faculty-X," represents an evolutionary leap. In other words, it is where sexuality converges with the spectral or the power of what is always *to come*.

Eros is, ultimately, an evolutionary force. It is the essence of the spectral. Only in animals, and in humans who remain close to animals, does it predominately express itself as procreative sex. Sophia followed Wilson in his argument that the symbolic character of sexual response as demonstrated by the plethora of so-called "perversions" reveals that what Wilson called the Life Force, and what Sophia simply referred to as *eros*, is the same form of intentionality that is behind aesthetic experience, such as the creation and deep appreciation of art and literature, and also the type of intentionality involved in primordial religious or mystical experiences. Religious morality or theological law overlays this and is intended to bind or contain it, precisely because it is intuited to be radically amoral and beyond any standard of human values. As Wilson writes, in two passages cited by Sophia,

> The life force itself is not in the least concerned with our social rights and wrongs. Like Caesar, it is above the law; it leaves it to its policemen to see that its minions obey the law. The astonished minions discover abruptly that the life impulse is not interested in social taboos and "ideas of good and evil."

What is "good" for the life impulse is completely beyond our comprehension, and is only vaguely related to our ideas of good and evil.

At this point, Sophia brought up the film *Lifeforce* (1985, the uncensored version of course), which was based on Colin Wilson's novel *The Space Vampires*. She drew from the novel to underline how the "alien" entities in question assume many chameleon-like forms despite their actually being energy beings that are emissaries of the Life Force. In the milieu of this story about the seduction and possession of a dying humanity by these entities, Sophia broached the subject of "alien sex." She put these most intimately Close Encounters on a spectrum, and identified it as part of a historical continuum that included everything from nightly visitations by incubi and succubi "demons" in medieval times, for which witches and sorcerers were burned at the stake, to modern cases of spectral rape.

The most infamous modern case of spectral rape is that of Doris Bither who, throughout 1974, was observed by parapsychologists and doctoral students at the University of California, Los Angeles, and whose terrifying experiences became the basis for Frank De Felitta's 1978 novel *The Entity*, which was adapted into a Hollywood horror film in 1982. The most interesting suggestion made by the scientific team led by parapsychologist Barry Taff, which was both too subtle and too scandalous to make it into the film version, is the possibility that the several spectral entities who would repeatedly rape Bither (played by Barbara Hershey in the film) were poltergeists that her young sons were psychokinetically projecting from out of their subconscious minds. She reported that the two of them who would hold her down felt like they were small, the size of a child. The third, larger entity, may have been an egregore produced by the boys. There was a history of trauma and abuse in the condemned and dilapidated house, where Bither was illegally living as a single mother with her four children, with a number of boyfriends who would come and go. The Parapsychology team from a now defunct lab at UCLA did photographically record certain types of apparitions that are characteristic of other hauntings and poltergeist events.

Whether the Bither case in particular was a poltergeist phenomenon produced by her own boys rather than a haunting, and therefore a case of spectral incest, there are many cases of spectral rape that clearly involve ghosts of the deceased having their way with the living. Sophia commented on how this could be seen as a kind of reverse necrophilia. There are so many cases in print that the *Fortean Times* had dubbed it "spectrophilia." In fact, it is a global phenomenon, with as many cases reported in Africa and Asia as in Europe and North America. Interestingly, in the African and Asian cases, probably due to cultural norms, there is a reporting bias such that incidents are mostly reported by men. In other words, contrary to our Western expectations, men are raped by seemingly "female" entities at least as often as the reverse. These are "rape" cases insofar as the spectral entity is uninvited and the men cannot resist being sexually aroused and even achieving an orgasm, an experience which, when repeated night after night, has put a strain on many marriages.

Any one of these assaults can go on for years. Sophia offered the case of Gill Philipson, a nurse in Liverpool, England, who was sexually molested and spectrally raped by an entity for a period of no less than ten years, from 1984 to 1994. She would always be immobilized, so that she could not wake her husband, who would invariably sleep through his wife being raped right beside him. At least the entity seemed to always start with foreplay, touching Ms. Philipson's vulva to arouse her, which it somehow managed to do, despite having wrinkly gray skin that was only partially covered by a dark hooded robe. Actually, Philipson's description of the entity involved in her case raises the question of whether it belongs in the category of rape by ghosts or in that of sex with aliens. There was no UFO witnessed, but the thing did not appear to be human either.

After providing the reader with a brief history of "contactee" and "abductee" cases of reported sexual encounters with humanoids who claimed to be from outer space, Sophia suggested that these cases, when they are not frauds, are likely something other than what they appear to be. From the American Howard Menger and his vixen Venusian women, and the South African Elizabeth Klarer with her handsome Nordic men who, already in the 1950s, looked like they came from the cast of *Space 1999* to the much more sinister cases of home invasion followed by the rape of a female or male abductee, as reported by Budd Hopkins and Whitley Strieber in the 1980s, as Sophia saw it, something did not add up. If these "aliens" were after genetic material, to address some future procreative catastrophe, they could much more efficiently raid sperm banks and facilities where women are having surplus fertile eggs stored. Sophia took as a very telling clue the case of the artist David Huggins, who painted his experiences that took place from his childhood in Georgia through to his adulthood in New York City. As the uncannily otherworldly but disturbingly childlike paintings of Huggins record, mantids were present throughout most of the sex that he had with humanoid women who appear to be wearing the *mask* of a gray alien.

These mantids, who also took him deep underground, not just into space, appeared to be in charge of the hybrid breeding program that was manned by the little gray "aliens" who seemed to be their worker robots. The humanoid women were more or less human in appearance, and one of them was human enough to have passed for a lady being driven in the back of a black limousine that stopped to pick David up one night when he was stranded by a rainstorm on the streets of Manhattan. His principal "alien" lover, an entity named Crescent, would also pay David nocturnal visits at his Manhattan apartment and art studio. One night she took some flowers that he had bought for her at a local florist on his way home from his day job. The mantids were there too, *in the Manhattan apartment*, watching from the corner of the bedroom, as Crescent — always astride him in a dominant position — brought David to father one child after another with her. At one point, aboard the "space ship," he was shown a room full of growing embryos and of infant hybrids that the mantids claimed were his children with Crescent.

Sophia pointed out that David's experiences in particular, and those of "alien sex" in general, fit well within the historical continuum of *incubi* and *succubi* visitations. In medieval Europe, or even in Puritan America as late as the 1600s, Huggins would have been put to death as a sorcerer and some non-conformist woman in the same village would have doubtless been apprehended and burned at the stake for being the *succubus* "witch" who disguised herself as Crescent in order to produce demon spawn with David. The first and most infamous succubus in Judeo-Christian history is the demoness Lilith, the disobedient first wife of Adam, who ran off with the devil himself before becoming a nightwalker and night stalker tempting men into damnation and stealing their children. To call Lilith a succubus is, however, somewhat inappropriate because the Latin term *succubare* literally means "to lie under," whereas *incubare* means "to lie upon." Lilith would technically be an incubus, not a succubus, since one expression of her supposed "disobedience" was that she would always insist on having sex astride Adam and she also rode the other men that she seduced. But this technicality is especially irrelevant considering the fact that Christian theologians from the time of St. Augustine through to the self-appointed witches' "hammers," who were still reading the *Malleus Maleficarum* (1487) at Salem, Massachusetts in 1692, all claimed that these "demons" could easily change sex.

Sophia drew a comparison between pre-modern accounts of the activities of incubi and succubi on the one hand, and both modern cases of spectral rape and alien sex on the other. While not every case of each type included all of the same elements, as Ludwig Wittgenstein would have put it, the "family resemblances" between these cases were so strong that they pointed to a singular phenomenon that has been interpreted through the lens of different times and places. Even the Christian interpretation of these occurrences as encounters with demonic incubi and succubi was itself an interpretive overlay that redefined what was already a very common experience in pagan Rome and classical Greece. Except that the pagans considered these entities to be titans, gods, demigods, or *daimons*, rather than demons. Alexander the Great was supposedly an offspring of one of these unions, and Zeus is, after all, the most infamous shapeshifting rapist in the whole history of human literature. When committing spectral rape, Zeus seemed to especially enjoy also turning this sex crime into an experience of bestiality for whatever woman had the misfortune of being the momentary focus of his enormous erotic desire.

Sophia wrote that the element of impunity in such cases brought to mind Doctor Mabuse and his Empire of Crime. The most relevant scenes, from the Fritz Lang films based on the novels of Norbert Jacques, come at the close of *The Testament of Doctor Mabuse* by which point it becomes clear that "Mabuse" is not merely a man who can be arrested, confined, or contained like some inmate of an asylum or a particular psychologist who has become obsessively possessed by the insidious idea of "the Empire of Crime." Mabuse is, rather, the very specter of ineradicable criminality itself. Mabuse is a symbol for the life of crime, for crime as an expression of the Life Force, which is beyond human judgments and the reach of civil laws. In the same way that "alien abductors" commit sex crimes worldwide with impunity, remaining beyond the reach of even the world's most powerful governments.

What is the point of all this? Do games have a point? Lang calls Mabuse *Der Spieler*, which is too often translated as "the Gambler" when an at least equally legitimate translation of this German epithet is "the Player." As she pointed this out, Sophia quoted the following passage from Wilson's *Origins of the Sexual Impulse*:

> I am trying to point out that the things human beings normally think of as their 'aims' are superficial, and it does not take a philosopher to discover that most of them are futile. But then, in the same way, all games are futile, since they involve a great deal of effort, but nothing is profoundly changed

by their result. It is the states of consciousness that are achieved *en route* that give them their purpose and meaning.

Sophie even suggested that the compulsively insane child murderer in Fritz Lang's *M*, who is also implied to be a sex fiend, is actually a man under the telepathic control of Mabuse, so that *M* (1931) forms the proper middle volume of a trilogy that includes *Dr. Mabuse, der Spieler* (1922) and *The Testament of Dr. Mabuse* (1933). But this was just a tangent in an argument that used Mabuse's occult criminal empire as a metaphor for a kind of breakaway civilization that increasingly assumed the aspect of an "alien" underworld by using advanced technologies and techniques to predatorily set itself apart from mankind. In this connection, Sophia remarked on how Lang, who had explored the idea of Utopia and Dystopia in his 1927 science-fiction film *Metropolis*, may have been using his *Mabuse* films to critique the aspiration for Utopia. This was a strong connection back to the thesis of her first book, *Making a Messy Future*. One element of any Utopian vision is the eradication of crime. *Mabuse* is about how that is impossible. More than that, the most enduring empire, the State within and beyond the State, is the Empire of Crime.

Returning to the subject of fabricated alienation and noting its similarity to the manner in which Doctor Mabuse uses a plethora of disguises and false fronts for his operations, Sophia suggested that the purpose of this engineered alienation would not simply be predation, but also seduction. Mabuse is also a captivating seducer of female accomplices who aid him like the female vampires of Dracula's harem. Some of those "chosen" would not just be willing alien "abductees" but also participants in something akin to a sacrificial rite that produces an aura of the sacred by projecting a compelling-enough image of alienness. Sophia also offered *Wolfen* and *The Hunger* as examples of this, suggesting that the film adaptations are preferable to the novels by Whitley Strieber because they manage to filter out the Catholic moralistic perspective that eventually came to enmesh and to warp

Strieber's understanding of his own close encounter experiences with entities who clearly do not share his sense of morality. Once freed from this overlay, both the werewolves of *Wolfen* and the vampires of *The Hunger* present striking symbols of "alien" criminality.

Even if there *are* actual aliens, Sophia argued, the sexual aspect of Close Encounters suggests something far more sinister and spectral than a simple hybrid breeding program. The symbol of the "hybrid" must *mean* something, and it is the injection of this seminal meaning into the collective unconscious of the human race that is the real insemination symbolized by the impregnation of female abductees and the gestation of the hybrid fetuses that they carry within their wombs for a brief time.

In search of this hidden meaning, Sophia speculatively suggested that the human race is already dead, but that the mass grave of Man was being violated by others who have taken an interest in what humanity could have become had certain visionaries prevailed in their advocacy for the further evolution of the race. Sophie postulated that at some point in the distant future, another intelligent species evolves from mantids or from octopuses, or both. It has used the kind of technology that Michael Crichton wrote *Jurassic Park* around in order to bring certain specimens of humanity back, not necessarily as a human zoo, but in what Nietzsche called "a hothouse for strange and choice plants." They found evidence of us, not only in the geological record of Earth, which they have inherited *as their planet*, but also in the vastly ancient, ruined structures of Cydonia on Mars, such that they became aware of humanoids having once been a time-traveling solar-system wide species.

They come back from a future after our extinction, as emissaries of the Life Force, by producing an illusion of humanoid "alienness," as Colin Wilson would put it, for the sake of seducing us into the resurrection of at least a worthy part of our species. Never had there been a more "Goth" notion than what Sophie was suggesting. Namely, that future forms of life were feeding upon our memory, and that in the

erotic terror of Close Encounters we were shivering from them danc
ing upon our planetary mass grave. This would be the ultimate form
of the "alienness" that Wilson saw as intrinsic to the experience of *eros*
and that he also identified as being at the core of a religious experience
of the sacred:

> …If the alien-ness is increased by our civilized habit of wearing clothes, of
> cultivating various inhibitions about sex, perhaps even by the belief that
> sex is rather wicked, then the pleasure of breaking down the barriers will
> be greater still.
>
> Religion, in its simplest form, is the belief that nature is not cold, indiffer-
> ent, poker-faced, that a tree is not a tree but a god in disguise. And even
> in its most complex, subjective form, it is still the belief that there is an
> 'otherness' beyond our present boredom and inadequacy, a hidden meaning
> lying in wait, like a tiger behind a bush. And when a mystic has a sudden
> insight into this meaning (or thinks he has), he is also performing an act of
> breakdown of alien-ness, exactly like the sexual breakdown.
>
> De Sade and Baudelaire have in common the need to believe that sex is evil.
> Then there are more barriers to break through in the sexual act, and the
> sense of falling from one level of being to another is more exciting, more
> positive.
>
> …The man who gleefully violates the alien-ness of his newly married wife
> on their honeymoon will continue to feel the same delight for a considerable
> length of time; if he is imaginative, he may still feel it half a century later.
>
> …Some men, like De Sade, not only insist that the biological alien-ness is
> re-created, but also like to re-create the 'artificial,' social taboos that add to
> the joy of violation. This is why Baudelaire liked to feel that sex is basically
> evil.

The religious mystic and the visionary artist both penetrate a meaning behind and beyond things, thereby experiencing the ecstasy of
overcoming their alien aspect. Wilson argued that the intensity of
sexual desire and of its ecstatic fulfillment was proportionate to the
degree of alienness that is being overcome through the transgression
of intimacy:

But the "inner purpose" has constructed a sexual mechanism on the idea of alien-ness. This is why we call the sexual parts our "private parts." All depends upon the idea of violating strangeness. For the most part this mechanism works well enough. But unfortunately the 'inner purpose' failed to place enough checks and guards on the mechanism. When the intensity of sexual response depends on the alien-ness that has been invaded, it follows that men will try to intensify the response still further by going further afield in alien-ness. Since their enjoyment of "normal" sex depends on the sense of violating a taboo, it follows that they will try to increase their satisfaction by including as many taboos as possible in the sexual object. In a simple form, this can be found in German romanticism — in Wagner and Mann, for example — in the preoccupation with incest. If, on the contrary, we lived in a civilization in which you were expected to have sexual intercourse with parents and siblings, the idea of sleeping with one's mother or sister would be incredibly tedious ("but we see them all the time!"), and the thought of "violating" an alien girl correspondingly exciting. All sexual perversions, from mere adultery to necrophily, can be seen as attempts to increase the alien-ness of the act by increasing the number of taboos involved. Sex can never, on any level, be "healthy" or "normal." It always depends on the violating of taboos — or, as Baudelaire would have said, on the sense of sin.

Wilson comes back to the subject of incest a number of times throughout the course of *Origins of the Sexual Impulse*. Consider these reflections on Nabokov's *Lolita*:

> Humbert's passion for Lolita is only the passion of modern man for the forbidden. Humbert seems to contain the seed of most of the sexual perversions, with the exception of sadism.

> …I can think of only two possible ways of treating the subject fictionally: to write about a rapist or sexual killer — or to write about some other form of sexual indulgence that can be treated as wholly forbidden.

> …it is almost impossible to write a novel about… [taboo breaking]… in the mid-twentieth century, since all the symbols have lost their shock value. Nabokov's choice of Lolita as a symbol was perhaps the only one possible — apart, that is, from multiple rape.

It would be even more profoundly shocking if Nabokov had written the novel in a way where Humbert's love affair with Lolita — or at least her precocious experiences with the far more competent, cunning, and excitingly enigmatic Clare Quilty — were to have led to an expansion of consciousness and a power over the world that exceeds normal human limitations, rather than to Dolores' depressing resignation to the life of a poverty-stricken housewife. Even if she were to have met her demise, it ought to have been the death of one martyred by the jealousy of mere mortals who could not suffer her being a living refutation of their pathetic morals.

Humbert is not literally Dolores' father, but his assuming that role renders sex with her a taboo that he sees himself as having a right to violate on account of his being an intellectual and aesthete who is above the moral code that the masses bind themselves with:

> ...Humbert is not arguing about the kind of sexual fulfilment enjoyed by most people; he argues, in effect, that he is a poet, that he has the poet's *supernormal* capacity to "drink of life as lesser men drink wine," and that he therefore deserves to be allowed the means to this supernormal ecstasy. ... Humbert's is already unreasonable and unsocial, since the essence of poetry is non-rational and non-social.
>
> This introduces an interesting problem into the discussion of what is "permissible." Most of our moral judgments are based on the social *status quo* (in the question of banning books, for example).

Wilson points out that, at the time he wrote *Origins of the Sexual Impulse*, the majority of husbands and wives in a number of American states were technically committing sex crimes in their bedrooms, since large parts of the United States still had criminal laws against "sodomy" and oral sex, whether fellatio or cunnilingus, regardless of who was performing it or irrespective of how consensually. This raises the general question of acts that are branded "criminal" even though they are consensual, because these acts involve the violation of a particular culture's sexual taboos.

Consider the following case of incest between a father and his fifteen-year-old daughter. As Wilson points out, to object that she was "under age" is ridiculous, especially considering the fact that for most of human history, most cultures, including Wilson's native Britain prior to the nineteenth century, put the age of sexual consent at around thirteen, when the vast majority of both girls and boys have already become sexually aware beings. Of this incest case, Wilson relates,

> Another case where excessive moral indignation seems to have led to a savage sentence is that of a forty-two-year-old man serving a sentence of twenty years for incest with his fifteen-year-old daughter. The arresting sheriff describes the case as "one of the worst on record." Luke, the offender, was described by the prison psychologist as "slightly antagonistic," but otherwise lacking in "abnormal personality traits." Reinhardt remarks that Luke seems to regard the whole business as an unjustified interference with his personal affairs. From the details he then offers, it would appear that Luke is partly in the right. He was on bad terms with his wife, who had refused him sexual satisfaction for a long period. They had six children, and were extremely poor; Luke remarked: "We didn't go nowhere hardly at all; we were too poor and had too many kids."

> He was aware that his two elder daughters were leading "fast sexual lives," the fifteen-year-old worked in a cheap eating place as a waitress and prostituted herself to the customers for money; the eldest daughter worked in a factory and also had many lovers. Luke decided to approach his daughters sexually; they were willing, and intercourse with them took place frequently. The mother suspected, and reported it to the police, who extorted confessions from the daughters by threats of a reformatory (for their general promiscuity). The upshot was Luke's twenty-year-sentence.

> It could be argued here that the only real offence was having intercourse with a minor. He could not be accused of impairing morals that were already past recovery. ...Under the circumstances, Luke's attitude of "slight antagonism" seems justified, and his comments can hardly be judged as revealing incorrigible moral obliquity: "I can't see what business it was of anyone else's — we weren't hurting nobody... I ain't done no worse than lots of people, and I don't know why people had to make so much of it." He declared his belief that incest was common, only "others is smart enough

not to get caught." Reinhardt remarks that the other prisoners treat him with contemptuous tolerance... and that he is accorded only "minimal social acceptance" by his fellow prisoners. His prison record was good. (He had no previous convictions.) The prison chaplain noted his indifference to religion, and Luke himself commented that, while he is willing to do whatever is expected of him in jail, he does not "want anyone preaching to him about what he should do or what he shouldn't have done."

Poor Luke. He was certainly no Humbert, nor do I imagine that his daughter was anything like Lolita. His case brings us back to the question of the intersection of sexuality with criminality, apparently even in cases where there is consent between the supposedly offending parties. Let alone in cases where transgression involves a violation of some kind. Wilson writes,

> ...What is the permissible limit for human sexual satisfaction? In this form it is possible to carry the analysis a great deal further. For the sentence involves a number of ideas that have been raised in the previous chapter. 'Permissible' immediately leads to the question: "Permitted by whom, or according to what standard of values?" And the idea of a limit to sexual satisfaction — some ultimately satisfying experience — raises again the question of the boundaries of human consciousness, and therefore the question of 'vision.' ...in speaking of the values involved in forms of sexual activity, *the "limitation of consciousness" is the villain of the piece.*

What is entirely permitted, wholesomely "good," wholly familiar, the same, and lacking any occulted depth or hidden dimension, is not conducive to erotic desire. Nor can it become material for the symbolism of great art or of religious mysticism. What is a still darker realization is that art and religion share with transgressive eroticism, or even with sex crimes, the element of sacrifice. The lives of great artists are full of sacrifice, and many of them ultimately sacrificed themselves to their work. Ritual sacrifice, whether of humans or even of a god, such as the sacrifice of Prometheus, Christ, or the Shi'ite Imams, lies at the mystical core of all authentic religious experience. It is also intrinsic to the truly erotic.

The most dangerous forms of so-called sexual "perversion" are sado-masochistic forms of bondage, regardless of whether the bondage involves actual ropes, straps, whips and so forth, or whether, in a more revealing manner, it is the bondage of fear in the face of a knife's edge and the ecstasy of relenting to rape. An inordinately unspeakable number of women excitedly masturbate to rape fantasies. (If the reader is one of these women there is no reason to be embarrassed, she is in good company.) As Wilson quotes from Huxley's *Point Counter Point* in his *Origins of the Sexual Impulse*: "Martyrdom's exciting. Letting oneself be hurt, humiliated, used like a doormat — queer. I like it." It is not just masochism, but the godlike power of the sexual sadist that many people secretly desire. Sophia quoted from Wilson's argument for this on the basis of the response to the 1947 rape, sexual torture, and ritual sacrifice of Elizabeth Short, the "Black Dahlia," whose mutilated corpse some compared to a surrealist work of art. More than the copycat crimes, the tens of false confessions that came in to the Los Angeles police really make the point. Wilson writes,

> [I]t is certain that the Black Dahlia murderer inspired something of a sex-crime wave in Los Angeles in 1947; six more murders of the same type occurred in that year in the same area; in one case, the murderer actually scrawled "B.D." (Black Dahlia?) in lipstick on his victim's breast. Twenty-seven men confessed to the Dahlia killing; all their confessions proved false. The twenty-eighth false confession came nine years after the murder — this time it was a Lesbian. These false confessions might be regarded as a kind of substitute for an imitative crime; they spring from the same envy of the murderer's experience, and a desire to participate in it. Here is a case where one sadistic sex crime triggered off thirty-four parallel reactions — six murders and twenty-eight false confessions — in an area about the size of Greater London. How many other inhabitants of Los Angeles felt the same envy of the murderer's experience, but confined their imitations to the imagination?

Elizabeth Short, an unsuccessful actress, led a rather scandalous life and was known to prowl parts of Hollywood. Who knows how

complicit the already infamous "Black Dahlia" was in her own sur
realistic sacrifice? What states of sexual masochism reveal is that "...
the sexual instinct... works on a deeper level than any other human
impulse — even, perhaps, that of self-preservation." In other words,
eros is what reveals that the Life Force is not actually about preserving
life in the form of any one or another individual. It is certainly not
about preserving decency or any of the culturally divergent human
codes of moral conduct. The ultimate and occulted aim of the erotic
is revealed precisely in states wherein the ecstatic power of life rubs
up against death, not without fear (which intensifies the ecstasy), but
fearlessly enough to court and overcome death. As one of Sophia's
quotes from Wilson put it: "...the basic sexual striving is a striving
for godhead, for the 'god-like' sensation of affirmation in the orgasm,
and that this is true of *all human effort*, from writing symphonies to
committing murders."

Who is to say that this sensation is not what a supposed "nymphomaniac" was striving for in the following case cited by Wilson in his
Origins of the Sexual Impulse:

> It would be a mistake, though, to regard all nymphomaniacs as slow to
> reach orgasm. Mr. Rexroth, the American poet, has related a case that
> disproves the idea. The girl in question was arrested and charged with pros-
> titution; the police were unable to prove their case because the girl never
> took money for her services, and she came before a psychiatric board, of
> which Mr. Rexroth was a member. She told how, on the day she was mar-
> ried, she and her husband spent several hours in bed in a hotel room on
> Park Avenue. Immediately after this, she went out and allowed herself to
> be 'picked up' by a man in Central Park; she accompanied him to a hotel
> room, and intercourse took place. She picked up several more men before
> she returned to her husband. Later, when her husband was at work, she
> made a habit of going to bed with strangers picked up on the streets. Her
> last client was a detective who 'framed' her by putting marked money into
> her handbag and then arresting her.

> The board asked her if her original experience with her husband was so un-
> satisfactory that she felt impelled to seek satisfaction elsewhere. She replied:

"Oh no. I enjoyed it so much that I wanted to do it again immediately." She insisted that she experienced an orgasm with every man, and was completely satisfied, but that the desire would re-form an hour later. The board regarded her as an unusual case of insatiable sexual appetite.

Why a necessarily and narrowly "sexual" appetite rather than a pursuit of the same peak experiences that artistic geniuses and religious mystics are striving for? Sophia suggested that this woman might have sooner found what she was looking for had she let herself be bound and forcibly stimulated through a successive series of almost unbearably intense orgasms. Here bondage was not a fetish, but a necessity. Otherwise, the woman would use her arms and legs to shove or kick her lover away when the pleasure became too intense — or, rather, more intense than she was used to bearing before she gave up.

Sophia's idea was that a woman experiencing continued stimulation throughout the extreme pleasure of successive orgasms, and who has been bound such that she cannot resist receiving more of it, would not at once be subjected to the kind of torturous pain characteristic of excessive tickling. Rather, the *"petit mort"* [little death] that the French so aptly use as a euphemism for orgasm, would cease to be "little" as the woman approached the threshold of no longer being able to bear her mundane flesh. Being almost on the point of death, the peak of a climax would have already opened unto the Devil's Path along a mountain chain of many snowy peaks, but now the climber would throw herself — or be pushed — like Empedocles over the edge and into the volcanic depths of Etna, until her blood coursed like incandescent lava.

During Near Death Experiences (NDEs), whether of someone who has been in a (potentially fatal) car crash or who has (unsuccessfully) attempted suicide by jumping off a ledge that was not high enough, there is a threshold that triggers an Out of Body Experience (OBE). Passing this threshold of traumatic embodiment, the bound woman would *come* right out of her body and look down on it or stand beside it. She would literally be "beside herself" with pleasure, as her spectral eyes watch her mundane flesh swoon into a comatose state for moments that would no doubt seem longer to her than to the man or machine that was relentlessly pleasuring her.

When I first read this part of Sophie's manuscript, I could not resist asking if she knew for a fact that this was true. She confessed to me that she had carried out an "experiment" to verify the claim empirically. Sophie told me that she had some master of Shibari tie her up on a wooden scaffold that had been custom-built to offer the perfect angle of approach for a whole set of virile and well-endowed men she had picked for this purpose. I did not stop her story to ask her how she had managed to recruit such beasts. She had them fuck her, one after another, until every single one of these bulls was finally defeated. Then Zoe, one of Sophie's most ribald-tongued and trustworthy girlfriends, who I had the pleasure of meeting on more than one occasion, was in position to keep giving it to her, albeit mechanically, with a rather large and energetic contraption in hand. Sophie explained that Zoe was, from the start of the thing, armed with a pistol—and wearing little more than the holster holding it—ready to blow the balls off any of the thralls if they got out of line.

Sophie said that she had set up a camera to film the whole thing, so that, in case she lost count (which she did early on), she could try to reconstruct how many orgasms in a row it took to leave her body, and how many she was able to still have once she came back into it. Then she told me that, at the moment she left her body, the camera had registered some kind of distortion or interference that was clearly visible in the footage, and that came and went in waves, until the moment when one could see, from her writhing limbs tugging on the ropes, that she was coming back to the consciousness of her bound body.

I asked Sophie if she still had the video. My daughter gave me that penetrating stare, with an ever so slight but diabolically mischievous smile, which had long since sent me to hell. The rest of that night was rather unforgettable. I have never been able to get those images out of my mind. When the film captured the fluttering of her disembodied soul, I broke out into goosebumps and shivered. What is even more in-delibly branded in my memory is the most overpowering of the many emotions that seized me while seeing the most precious person to me in all the world put herself into such a state. Indelible, because I was shocked by what I felt: a positively Satanic *pride*. Not once, in all her heart-rending and soul-piercing cries, did she ever slip and utter, "Oh God!" Instead, when she could even form words amidst her unending waves of ecstasy, Sophia made of an unmitigated litany of profanity a Satanic hymn so sacred that molten lead would have to be poured into the ears of any Brahmin who chanced to hear it.

That night ended, in the indigo hour, with us drunkenly agree-ing that, in line with properly scientific standards, no single experi-ment — no matter how well-recorded — sufficed to verify a hypothesis. It simply *must* be repeatable to pass muster. Already half asleep, Sophie explained to me how she and Zoe had recruited the "participants." But I digress.

The text of *Sex, Crime, and the Spectral* moved from those insights of Colin Wilson recapitulated above to an augmentation of Wilson's argument with reference to Georges Bataille, and then a comparison of Bataille to Max Stirner on the question of transgression, morality, law, and the essence of the sacred. The conclusion of Sophia's text was that eros as transgression has a unique power to reveal the essence of the sacred that is conventionally occulted by the taboos and norms of any one or another society.

Sophia argued that Georges Bataille's *Erotism* and Colin Wilson's *God of the Labyrinth* both make this point. Bataille explores eroticism as a philosophical concept, ultimately arguing that eros exceeds the rational bounds of philosophia and demands a different relationship to wisdom (*Sophia*). He views the erotic as a fundamental aspect of human existence that confronts and disrupts conventional societal norms and boundaries. Wilson's novel is a murder mystery that in-vestigates the connection between eroticism, creativity, and criminal-ity. In *Erotism*, Bataille explores the idea that eroticism is inherently transgressive. It breaks down the usual barriers and distinctions that structure our daily lives, creating a momentary dissolution of the self. This loss of self, according to Bataille, brings individuals closer to a more fundamental reality that exists beyond the rational and orderly world that we normally inhabit. He also connects eroticism with death, seeing both as experiences that break down the boundaries of the self and challenge the idea of individuality. Taking as his point of departure the French euphemism for an orgasm, namely "the little death" (*le petit mort*), this is one of the many meditations on sex and death that Bataille offers us in the final chapter of his *Erotism*, titled "Mysticism and Sensuality":

> The orgasm is popularly termed "the little death." ...Death is exceptional, the extreme case; each loss of normal energy is indeed only a little death compared with the death of the drone, but whether obscurely or clearly this little death is what is feared. On the other hand it is also desired... No one could deny that one essential element of excitement is the feeling of being swept off one's feet, of falling headlong. If love exists at all it is, like death, a swift movement of loss within us, quickly slipping into tragedy and stopping only with death. For the truth is that between death and the reeling, heady motion of the little death the distance is hardly noticeable.

> The desire to go keeling helplessly over, that assails the innermost depths of every human being is nevertheless different from the desire to die in that it is ambiguous. It may well be a desire to die, but it is at the same time a desire to live to the limits of the possible and the impossible with ever-increasing intensity. It is the desire to live while ceasing to live, or to die without ceasing to live, the desire of an extreme state... the turbulence and disastrousness of sexuality are of the essence of temptation. Temptation is the desire to fall, to fail, to faint and to squander all one's reserves until there is no firm ground beneath one's feet... [That is] a starting point to investigate the way that sexual and mystical experience are linked.

> ...In essence, love raises the feeling of one being for another to such a pitch that the threatened loss of the beloved or the loss of his love is felt no less keenly than the threat of death. Hence love is based on a desire to live in anguish in the presence of an object of such high worth that the heart cannot bear to contemplate losing it. The fever of the senses is not a desire to

die. Nor is love the desire to lose but the desire to live in fear of possible loss, with the beloved holding the lover on the very threshold of a swoon. At that price alone can we feel the violence of rapture before the beloved.

In *God of the Labyrinth*, Wilson gives us an example of how this basic erotic desire to become a potential sacrificial object at the mercy of a beloved that one could lose can be transformed into the core of a ritual practice in the service of a beloved with the anonymity and alienness of a god or goddess. Witness this description of the rites of a secret society studied by Wilson's protagonist in passages that Sophia quoted at length:

But what exactly did the Sect of the Phoenix *do*? Esmond expresses its basic aim in one sentence: 'Our purpose is not to degrade and pollute religious feelings with venery, but to raise venery to the level of a religious feeling.' But how was this to be done?

...The Sect believed that man approaches the sense of the world as a 'magical mystery' more frequently through the sexual act than through religion or art.

...The tradition of the Sect — dating back four centuries — insisted that women should be treated as vessels of a religious mystery. ...[Their] first leader... chose a beautiful young girl as a kind of pythoness, and another dozen girls as her handmaidens; these latter were also priestesses. The women were worshipped as divinities; but the males of the sect were allowed a certain amount of contact with the divinities, which could even culminate in sexual intercourse. In order to qualify for this, the male had to fast for three days out of every week for many months beforehand, and go through a number of well-defined stages of approach to the mystery. If he could lie on the steps of the 'temple' naked on a winter night — from dusk until dawn — he was allowed to act as a servant to three of the priestesses for an hour every day, bringing their food and cleaning their rooms. He was allowed to eat the left-over scraps of food. After more tests... he was allowed to become a 'body servant' to another three, laundering and sewing their clothes and washing their hair. Their physical waste products were regarded as sacred, and it was his job to take them into the depth of the forest and bury them in a place where no other males of the tribe could find them. He was allowed to smear himself with excrement and wash it off with their urine — a privilege envied by all the other males of the tribe. The mingling of the worshipper's semen with the waste products of the 'holy ones' was regarded as the first degree of union with the divinity. If he could pass increasingly difficult and painful tasks, he was allowed an increasing number of privileges, until he might be one of the eight men who were the body servants of the Holy One herself.

...If he lost his erection at any time in the presence of the priestesses, he would be flogged and sent back to the tribe in disgrace. It will also be noted that his position was really that of a maidservant; he was treated as a woman, so that he would feel humiliated...

Throughout *God of the Labyrinth*, Wilson uses the character of Gerard Sorme to explore the connection between eroticism and creativity, and ultimately criminality. Through Sorme's exploration of the erotic, Wilson portrays eroticism as a pathway towards self-transcendence and heightened awareness — an idea that resonates with Bataille's conception of eroticism as a transgressive force that breaks down the boundaries that define the persona. As Wilson put it in *God of the Labyrinth* when writing of "the relation between sex and the mystical experience... sex gives us a glimpse of a concentration of the mind that would make us god-like if we could command it in other spheres." A little later in his narrative, Wilson's protagonist elaborates in these passages quoted by Sophie:

And in a flash I understood the meaning of sex. It is a craving for the mingling of consciousness, whose symbol is the mingling of bodies...

...Human beings are so mediocre that they can scarcely be said to possess minds in any real sense. In a flash, I understood the absurd and obvious truth: nothing is worth possessing except intensity of consciousness. This is the truth we glimpse in the orgasm. If human beings understood it — if their minds were not so incapable of understanding even the simplest things — they would abandon all other pursuits for this one. What does it matter where you are, what you are doing, how much you possess, if your mind is limp and feeble? — just as the most beautiful surroundings mean nothing to a man suffering from a fever.

Sophia made the case that given Bataille's emphasis on the transgressive nature of eroticism, he would view Wilson's *God of the Labyrinth*
as a dramatization of the idea that criminality is an extreme manifestation of the disruptive power of erotic desire. Sex crimes only serve
to highlight this broader and deeper connection. As Bataille puts it,
"Beneficent sexuality is close to animal sexuality, unlike eroticism
which is man's own... Eroticism is a principle representing Evil and
the diabolic." Taboos that structure our relationship with the sacred
as defined against not just the profane but also the obscene are as intrinsic to the power of the erotic as they are to the pleasure of ecstatic
sacrilege. In *Erotism*, Bataille uses the taboo on incest as a particularly
powerful example of this. The passages, which I will truncate somewhat as compared to the length at which they are quoted in Sophia's
book, begin with Bataille's observation that humans typically do not
eat each other's shit, which dogs *are* known to occasionally do, even
when actual food is available:

> Man flatly denies the existence of his animal needs; most of his taboos
> relate to them and these taboos are so strikingly universal and apparently
> so unquestioned that they are never discussed. Ethnography does deal with
> the menstruation taboo, it is true, but only the Bible can really be said to
> specify a particular form of the general taboo on obscenity... But nobody
> mentions the horror of excremental matter which belongs to man alone.
> The conventions regarding our bodily waste products are not given any
> conscious consideration by adults and are not even entered on the list of
> taboos. There is therefore an aspect of the transition from animal to human
> so radically negative that no one talks about it. ...But if incest in particular
> is the subject under discussion... How indeed could we not define incest
> with that as a starting point? We cannot say that such and such a thing
> is obscene. Obscenity is relative. There is no "obscenity" in the sense that
> there is "fire" or "blood," but only in the way that an "outrage to modesty"
> exists. Such and such a thing is obscene if this or that person thinks it is and
> says so; it is not exactly an object, but a relationship between an object and
> the mind of a person [projecting his own intentionality onto that object].
> In this sense we can define situations of which given aspects are or at least
> seem to be obscene. Moreover, these situations are unstable and always

presuppose certain ill-defined elements; or else what instability they have has an arbitrary character. Similarly they often have to be adapted to fit the necessities of life. Incest is a situation of this kind which has its arbitrary existence only within the mind of man.

This way of seeing it is so necessary and unavoidable that if we were unable to affirm the universality of incest we should hardly be able to demonstrate the universal character of the taboo on obscenity [in general]. Incest is the first proof of the fundamental connection between man and the denial of sensuality, of the carnal and animal.

...This symbol does not only indicate the boundaries that make the mother sacrosanct to the son, the daughter to the father. It is in a general way the image — or the sanctuary — of humanity unsexed, holding its values aloft safe from violence and sullying passion. *The essence of humanity is to be found in the taboo on incest and the gift of women resulting from it...*

The gift itself is a renunciation, the refusal of an immediate animal satisfaction with no strings attached. Marriage is a matter less for the partners than for the man who gives the woman away, the man whether father or brother who might have freely enjoyed the woman, daughter or sister, yet who bestows her on someone else. This gift is perhaps a substitute for the sexual act... For a close relation to renounce his right, to forego the enjoyment of his own property: this is what defines human beings in complete contrast to the greedy animals. ...Without the counterbalance of the respect for forbidden objects of value there would be no eroticism.

...The taboo does not alter the violence of sexual activity, but for disciplined mankind it opens a door closed to animal nature, namely, the transgression of the law... moments of transgression when eroticism is a complete upheaval.

She knew what she was writing about. It is at this point that Sophia brought Max Stirner into *Sex, Crime, and the Spectral*. She argued that although, on the surface, it seems like Bataille's conception of the erotic challenges individuality, whereas Stirner's *Ego and Its Own* argues for individualism to the point of egotism, there is a deeper critique of a fixed conception of the ego with its "spooks" in Stirner, and this ultimately converges with Bataille's view that transgressive eros offers the potential of an unmediated encounter with the sacred — for example, in a sacred incest that is godlike rather than sub-humanly animal. According to Sophia, although Stirner is often labeled as an egoist or individualist, he does not simply advocate rampant self-interest. Instead, Stirner deconstructs the notion of a fixed ego and critiques the "spooks" or fixed ideas that people often become beholden to, including the very idea of a rigid self or ego. In this sense, Stirner's egoism is more about freeing oneself from these "spooks" and recognizing the fluid, dynamic nature of the self. For Stirner, the individual is a "creative nothing" or a process of continual self-creation and self-overcoming, unrestricted by any pre-existing norms, identities, or ideologies.

Stirner's conception of the ego is self-deconstructing, and not at all a concept of a substantial self: "But it is not that the ego *is* all, but the ego *destroys* all, and only the self-dissolving ego, the never-being ego, the — *finite* ego is really I." Stirner is not a nihilist in the conventional sense, but beyond the superficial impression that he is affirming some substantive ego one can discern an attempt on his part to actually deconstruct this as the final illusion as compared to a kind of creative nothingness. This requires making a nullity out of everything that one has formerly projected onto things as a spirit of substantiality from out of one's fixed ideas. "But who, then, will dissolve the spirit into its *nothing*?" Stirner asks. "He who by means of the spirit set forth nature as the *null*, finite, transitory, he alone can bring down the spirit too to like nullity. *I can*; each one among you can, who does his will as an absolute I; in a word, the *egoist* can." But to this apparent affirmation of the self over the world, he ironically adds, "Nothing is more to me than myself!" This is a double entendre. No thing is more important than the self, and the Nothing is more important than the ego because it is the matrix for any conception of self.

Another powerful double entendre involving Nothingness, which moves from the realm of psychology to the even deeper dimension of ontology, is this gem: "Nothing at all is justified by *being*." In other words, just because a thing is does not mean that it ought to be. This aspect of the meaning of this statement is, by itself, a huge slap in the face of anyone deluded enough to believe that the world as a whole and as such is an expression of God's will. But the phrase also means that all the "Nothing" lies behind all beings — not any "God."

Here is a lengthy passage from *The Ego and Its Own* that makes the same point, namely that Stirner is not actually an "egoist" in anything like the sense that most people would misunderstand that:

> They say of God, "Names name thee not." That holds good of me: no *concept* expresses me, nothing that is designated as my essence exhausts me; they are only names. Likewise they say of God that he is perfect and has no calling to strive after perfection. That too holds good of me alone.
>
> I am *owner* of my might, and I am so when I know myself as *unique*. In the *unique one* the owner himself returns into his creative nothing, out of which he is born. Every higher essence above me, be it God, be it man, weakens the feeling of my uniqueness, and pales only before the sun of this consciousness. If I concern myself for myself, the unique one, then my concern rests on its transitory, mortal creator, who consumes himself, and I may say: All things are nothing to me.

Sophie pointed out that Bataille, in his exploration of eroticism, similarly breaks down the conventional boundaries of the self. Erotic experiences, according to Bataille, shatter the orderly, rational self and bring individuals into contact with a deeper, more fundamental aspect of existence that is often hidden or repressed by societal norms. Bataille sees in eroticism a transgression of the normal boundaries of the self and an encounter with the limit of individuality. Sophia showed how this aligns in an interesting and unexpected way with Stirner's conception of the self as a "creative nothing," a process rather than a fixed entity.

Sophia forwarded the thesis that, despite the superficial differences in their conceptions of the sacred, the seemingly secular Stirner is actually engaging in something like a battle against idolatry, exorcising "spooks" that condition our conception of the sacred, thereby freeing us for an encounter with the sacred in its essence, as understood by

Bataille. But how could Stirner who exposes all "essences" as "spooks" be concerned with an "essence of the sacred"? Sophia conceded that perhaps "essence" is the wrong word here. Instead, she volunteered, "the defining function of the sacred." In his own way Stirner agrees with Bataille and Colin Wilson that this involves alien-ness or alienation and the overcoming of the alien.

One of the most powerfully evocative lines in *The Ego and Its Own* is: "If you *devour the sacred*, you have made it your *own!*" Elsewhere Stirner also implicitly references alienation when he writes, "It must therefore become our *own*, instead of, as hitherto, serving a spook." In this line, with its reference to the alien, this is even clearer: "We must first come down to the most ragamuffin-like, most poverty-stricken condition if we want to arrive at *ownness*, for we must strip off everything alien. …This is no longer mere ragamuffinhood: because even the last rag has fallen off, here stands real nakedness, denudation of everything alien."

That devouring the sacred is an overcoming of an unnatural and acculturated alienation is clear from Stirner's explanation of why children have no conception of "the sacred" before their minds are conditioned by all kinds of binary concepts that inculcate them with the sense of reverence:

> For little children, just as for animals, nothing sacred exists, because, in order to make room for this conception, one must already have progressed so far in understanding that he can make distinctions like "good and bad," "warranted and unwarranted," etc.; only at such a level of reflection or intelligence — the proper standpoint of religion — can unnatural (*i.e.* brought into existence by thinking) *reverence*, "sacred dread," step into the place of natural *fear*.

Children can no more be criminals than they can appreciate the sacred, because "only against a sacred thing are there criminals." The sacred, in a negative sense, is conditioned by thoughts, and this conditioning of thought produces a *heiros arche* ("Holy Order") that neither children nor the really uncultured can comprehend, let alone respect:

> But the uncultured are really nothing but children, and he who attends only to the necessities of his life is indifferent to those spirits; but, because he is also weak before them, he succumbs to their power, and is ruled by — thoughts. This is the meaning of hierarchy.
>
> *Hierarchy is the dominion of thoughts, dominion of mind!*
>
> We are hierarchic to this day, kept down by those who are supported by thoughts. Thoughts are the sacred.

Stirner rejects any higher power that would demand dutiful self-abasement because it forms the pinnacle of one or another hierarchy:

> I no longer *humble* myself before any power, and I recognize that all powers are only my power, which I have to subject at once when they threaten to become a power *against* or *above* me.

Stirner compares being haunted and moved by "spooks" to being possessed, and not just by the Devil, but more likely by God and associated "ideas" of virtue, morality, and law:

> Is it perchance only people possessed by the devil that meet us, or do we as often come upon people *possessed* in the contrary way, possessed by "the good," by virtue, morality, the law, or some "principle" or other? Possessions of the devil are not the only ones. God works on us, and the devil does; the former "workings of grace," the latter "workings of the devil." Possessed people are *set* in their opinions.

These opinions and fixed ideas veil or occult the "essence" of the sacred in the sense of its most fundamental function. Both Stirner and Bataille ultimately aim to strip away illusory conceptions of the sacred to arrive at a more profound and essential understanding. Stirner's deconstruction of the taboos and archetypes that mediate our relationship with the sacred through the "spooks" or fixed ideas that haunt our minds and move us to act and react, largely unconsciously, is a deconstruction that seeks to liberate the individual from psycho-social constructs that limit our perception and experience of the sacred. Once these idolatrous "spooks" have been dismissed, the individual might be more open to an authentic encounter with the sacred. Bataille also advocates experiences that breach societal and individual norms — especially in eroticism — that decondition us in ways that allow us to touch the sacred in its raw, unfiltered essence. This is akin to overcoming "the robot" of Wilson through peak experiences that herald the evolution of a kind of Superconsciousness.

Sophia showed how, throughout his vast body of work, Colin Wilson focuses on the human potential to achieve states of consciousness beyond the everyday. Like Stirner, Wilson challenges societal constructs or limitations that prevent us from realizing our full potential. For Wilson, everyday consciousness is often conditioned by what he calls "the robot," an automated pattern of behavior that narrows our perceptions and experiences. By engaging in certain occult practices, or otherwise bringing about the extreme states of consciousness found in criminal acts and in intense erotic experiences, as well as in the expression of creative genius by an artist or writer, Wilson suggests that we can break free from this "robotic" condition and reach "peak" experiences of exceptional consciousness.

For Wilson, our reliance on "the robot" keeps us tethered to a mundane reality. Bataille, similarly, sees social norms and ordinary consciousness as a kind of cage, limiting our experiences and understanding of the world. The erotic, in Bataille's view, serves as a powerful antidote to this limited consciousness. It is a poison that is a cure, a *pharmakon*. The intensity and transgression inherent in eroticism shake us from our usual state, dissolving the barriers of the self, much like Wilson's methods to jolt one out of the robotic state. The peak experiences that Wilson describes are, in Sophie's view, of a piece with the kind of direct encounter with the sacred that Bataille explores. Bataille suggests that we can touch the sacred in moments of transgression and intensity that challenge our normal sense of self.

Wilson's study of the erotic, the occult, and even criminality, can be seen as staking out the same territory.

Sex, Crime, and the Spectral was published in 2045, when Sophie was 29 years old. I don't know about crime, but as far as sex was concerned, she certainly had a lot of experience to draw from. I personally met at least a dozen of Sophie's girlfriends over the years, and those were only the most serious ones. Zoe was my favorite of them. No surprise there, since she was the only one who had studied Philosophy. My encounters with a handful of the men, and a couple of boy toys, that she kept around were a bit more awkward. She wasn't a nymphomaniac, but I know of more than one occasion when Sophie slept with — I mean had sex with — several people on the same day and night (there was no sleeping involved). I am not talking about the orgies, although there were plenty of those as well.

One of the reasons why Sophie was so promiscuous is that she liked to fuck people just to satisfy her curiosity about them. She wouldn't care all that much whether a guy, or for that matter a girl, was physically attractive in a conventional sense. If she found someone mysteriously interesting, uniquely engaging, or enigmatically intriguing, she would go out of her way to lure that person into bed with her for the sake of figuring him or her out. She had explained to me that with some of them she had to employ all the lures of a huntress stalking her prey, whereas with others, it was as simple as looking them dead in the eyes and asking, rather rhetorically, "Don't you want to fuck me?"

When she was with those who *were* attractive, but not all that compelling in terms of their character or inner life, she would treat sex with them as an ecstatic sport, seeing how many times in a row each of them could make her come. But what was most fun for her was finding out whether she could reduce such well-kept specimens of beauty to a writhing mass of subhuman pleasure so intense that they would cry and make her beg to stop revealing the animal, or the feral child, within them.

Once, when she was 27, shortly after I had become Director General of UNESCO, we were sipping cognac together late on a snowy winter night in our Paris apartment, after having spent the evening watching a couple of Dusan Makavejev's films together, *WR: Mysteries of the Organism* and *Sweet Movie*. I paused *Sweet Movie* after the scene of the orgy in the Actionist commune, which never ceased to make us laugh our hearts out together, and I asked Sophie how many different people she had fucked. She had to think hard, with those beautiful long fingers of hers pressing into that tall and broad forehead, before she finally shook her head with a bit of a smirk and chuckle, winced at me, and replied, "I don't know. I lost count at around a hundred." I wondered how much I had been responsible for thoroughly corrupting her. But I didn't say that. Instead, I asked, "How many of them were any good?" "Less than half," she answered. "Maybe a third of them."

Then I had the audacity to look her dead in the eyes and ask, "How many of them made you cum so hard that you cried?" Sophie only balked for a moment, staring at me a bit wide-eyed before her expression broke into a mixture of a mischievous grin and a reproachful gaze. "Maybe half a dozen." Then, after a brief silence she came back with, "Aren't you going to ask how many of them *I* made cry?" "Many of your girlfriends, I imagine. But did you make any of the guys cry?"

"Oh, I can make *all* of them cry, Papa, if I'm in the *mood* to. I don't even have to pull out my whip. I still have it though. You know, the one you gave me. My little Lasso of Truth. But with men it's different, even with the boys. You need more than unbearable pleasure to make them cry. There's something inside every man that will break him and bring him to weep like an inconsolable child. I know how to find what that is. If and when I care to. In every man there are desires buried so deeply that you will make him cry before he can bear to see them reflected in your eyes."

The snow was falling so hard that we could barely see the Eiffel Tower out the window, and with the light of the fireplace glowing in our cognac glasses, I toasted my daughter. "*Ya haq*, Sophie!" "*Ya haq*, Papa!" Far be it from us to cheers with "*Santé!*" We were both hopelessly sick. But it was the morning sickness, before sunrise, of a pregnancy destined to give birth to a star. Lucifera was rising.

If we are going to speak the truth now as straightly as the Amazons shot their arrows, then why hold back what must have already dawned on any discerning reader? Namely, that in the years after the untimely murder of my wife in that effaced life, Sophia became far more than just my daughter. Now I know why the theme of sacred incest runs throughout my philosophical corpus. It has hounded me like the black bitch of the Huntress, until finally, I remember, even if only through a glass darkly. A glass full of wine that is actually blood from between her strong thighs.

It would be wrong to say that I initiated my daughter because Sophia was Lucifera, who graced me with her becoming flesh. In truth, I was the initiate. "Sophia Grace Jorjani," her very name is an imperative mantra. A serpentine prayer. This mantra unlocks the esoteric chambers of that Frankenstein's castle called "Prometheism." It leads down the dark spiral of stone staircases into the dungeon, a dungeon with a platform ready to raise the corpse of a monstrous woman into the night sky so that she can be resurrected by the strikes of thunder. This prayer takes us beyond the horizon of *philosophia* into what cannot be encompassed by it: *Erosophia*. The morning star and bringer of the dawn beyond the darkness of the terminator. The white Venus of the Black Lodge riding lightning bolts.

OTHER BOOKS PUBLISHED BY ARKTOS

VIRGINIA ABERNETHY   *Born Abroad*

SRI DHARMA PRAVARTAKA ACHARYA   *The Dharma Manifesto*

JOAKIM ANDERSEN   *Rising from the Ruins*

WINSTON C. BANKS   *Excessive Immigration*

ALAIN DE BENOIST   *Beyond Human Rights*
                                        Carl Schmitt Today
                                        The Ideology of Sameness
                                        The Indo-Europeans
                                        Manifesto for a European Renaissance
                                        On the Brink of the Abyss
                                        The Problem of Democracy
                                        Runes and the Origins of Writing
                                        View from the Right (vol. 1–3)

ARMAND BERGER   *Tolkien, Europe, and Tradition*

ARTHUR MOELLER VAN DEN BRUCK   *Germany's Third Empire*

MATT BATTAGLIOLI   *The Consequences of Equality*

KERRY BOLTON   *The Perversion of Normality*
                                        Revolution from Above
                                        Yockey: A Fascist Odyssey

ISAC BOMAN   *Money Power*

CHARLES WILLIAM DAILEY   *The Serpent Symbol in Tradition*

RICARDO DUCHESNE   *Faustian Man in a Multicultural Age*

ALEXANDER DUGIN   *Ethnos and Society*
                                        Ethnosociology
                                        Eurasian Mission
                                        The Fourth Political Theory
                                        The Great Awakening vs the Great Reset
                                        Last War of the World-Island
                                        Political Platonism
                                        Putin vs Putin
                                        The Rise of the Fourth Political Theory
                                        The Theory of a Multipolar World

EDWARD DUTTON   *Race Differences in Ethnocentrism*

MARK DYAL   *Hated and Proud*

CLARE ELLIS   *The Blackening of Europe*

KOENRAAD ELST   *Return of the Swastika*

JULIUS EVOLA   *The Bow and the Club*
                                        Fascism Viewed from the Right
                                        A Handbook for Right-Wing Youth
                                        Metaphysics of Power
                                        Metaphysics of War
                                        The Myth of the Blood
                                        Notes on the Third Reich
                                        The Path of Cinnabar
                                        Recognitions
                                        A Traditionalist Confronts Fascism

OTHER BOOKS PUBLISHED BY ARKTOS

GUILLAUME FAYE	*Archeofuturism*
	Archeofuturism 2.0
	The Colonisation of Europe
	Convergence of Catastrophes
	Ethnic Apocalypse
	A Global Coup
	Prelude to War
	Sex and Deviance
	Understanding Islam
	Why We Fight
DANIEL S. FORREST	*Suprahumanism*
ANDREW FRASER	*Dissident Dispatches*
	Reinventing Aristocracy in the Age of Woke Capital
	The WASP Question
GÉNÉRATION IDENTITAIRE	*We are Generation Identity*
PETER GOODCHILD	*The Taxi Driver from Baghdad*
	The Western Path
PAUL GOTTFRIED	*War and Democracy*
PETR HAMPL	*Breached Enclosure*
PORUS HOMI HAVEWALA	*The Saga of the Aryan Race*
LARS HOLGER HOLM	*Hiding in Broad Daylight*
	Homo Maximus
	Incidents of Travel in Latin America
	The Owls of Afrasiab
RICHARD HOUCK	*Liberalism Unmasked*
INSTITUT ILIADE	*For a European Awakening*
A. J. ILLINGWORTH	*Political Justice*
ALEXANDER JACOB	*De Naturae Natura*
JASON REZA JORJANI	*Artemis Unveiled*
	Closer Encounters
	Faustian Futurist
	Iranian Leviathan
	Lovers of Sophia
	Novel Folklore
	Prometheism
	Promethean Pirate
	Prometheus and Atlas
	Psychotron
	Uber Man
	World State of Emergency
HENRIK JONASSON	*Sigmund*
EDGAR JULIUS JUNG	*The Significance of the German Revolution*
RUUBEN KAALEP & AUGUST MEISTER	*Rebirth of Europe*
RODERICK KAINE	*Smart and SeXy*

OTHER BOOKS PUBLISHED BY ARKTOS

PETER KING	*Here and Now*
	Keeping Things Close
	On Modern Manners
JAMES KIRKPATRICK	*Conservatism Inc.*
LUDWIG KLAGES	*The Biocentric Worldview*
	Cosmogonic Reflections
	The Science of Character
ANDREW KORYBKO	*Hybrid Wars*
PIERRE KREBS	*Guillaume Faye: Truths & Tributes*
	Fighting for the Essence
JULIEN LANGELLA	*Catholic and Identitarian*
JOHN BRUCE LEONARD	*The New Prometheans*
STEPHEN PAX LEONARD	*The Ideology of Failure*
	Travels in Cultural Nihilism
WILLIAM S. LIND	*Reforging Excalibur*
	Retroculture
PENTTI LINKOLA	*Can Life Prevail?*
H. P. LOVECRAFT	*The Conservative*
NORMAN LOWELL	*Imperium Europa*
RICHARD LYNN	*Sex Differences in Intelligence*
JOHN MACLUGASH	*The Return of the Solar King*
CHARLES MAURRAS	*The Future of the Intelligentsia &*
	For a French Awakening
JOHN HARMON MCELROY	*Agitprop in America*
MICHAEL O'MEARA	*Guillaume Faye and the Battle of Europe*
	New Culture, New Right
MICHAEL MILLERMAN	*Beginning with Heidegger*
MAURICE MURET	*The Greatness of Elites*
BRIAN ANSE PATRICK	*The NRA and the Media*
	Rise of the Anti-Media
	The Ten Commandments of Propaganda
	Zombology
TITO PERDUE	*The Bent Pyramid*
	Journey to a Location
	Lee
	Morning Crafts
	Philip
	The Sweet-Scented Manuscript
	William's House (vol. 1–4)
JOHN K. PRESS	*The True West vs the Zombie Apocalypse*
RAIDO	*A Handbook of Traditional Living* (vol. 1–2)
CLAIRE RAE RANDALL	*The War on Gender*
P R REDDALL	*Towards Awakening*
STEVEN J. ROSEN	*The Agni and the Ecstasy*
	The Jedi in the Lotus

OTHER BOOKS PUBLISHED BY ARKTOS

NICHOLAS ROONEY	*Talking to the Wolf*
RICHARD RUDGLEY	*Barbarians*
	Essential Substances
	Wildest Dreams
ERNST VON SALOMON	*It Cannot Be Stormed*
	The Outlaws
WERNER SOMBART	*Traders and Heroes*
PIERO SAN GIORGIO	*CBRN*
	Giuseppe
	Survive the Economic Collapse
SRI SRI RAVI SHANKAR	*Celebrating Silence*
	Know Your Child
	Management Mantras
	Patanjali Yoga Sutras
	Secrets of Relationships
GEORGE T. SHAW (ED.)	*A Fair Hearing*
FENEK SOLÈRE	*Kraal*
	Reconquista
OSWALD SPENGLER	*The Decline of the West*
	Man and Technics
RICHARD STOREY	*The Uniqueness of Western Law*
TOMISLAV SUNIC	*Against Democracy and Equality*
	Homo Americanus
	Postmortem Report
	Titans are in Town
ASKR SVARTE	*Gods in the Abyss*
HANS-JÜRGEN SYBERBERG	*On the Fortunes and Misfortunes of Art in Post-War Germany*
ABIR TAHA	*Defining Terrorism*
	The Epic of Arya (2nd ed.)
	Nietzsche's Coming God, or the Redemption of the Divine
	Verses of Light
JEAN THIRIART	*Europe: An Empire of 400 Million*
BAL GANGADHAR TILAK	*The Arctic Home in the Vedas*
DOMINIQUE VENNER	*For a Positive Critique*
	The Shock of History
HANS VOGEL	*How Europe Became American*
MARKUS WILLINGER	*A Europe of Nations*
	Generation Identity
ALEXANDER WOLFHEZE	*Alba Rosa*
	Rupes Nigra

www.ingramcontent.com/pod-product-compliance
Lightning Source LLC
Chambersburg PA
CBHW031234260626
47169CB00007B/2295